Selected
Famous Erotic
Short Stories

21
EROTIC
STORIES

JAICO PUBLISHING HOUSE

Mumbai • Delhi • Bangalore • Kolkata
Hyderabad • Chennai • Ahmedabad • Bhopal

Published by Jaico Publishing House
121 Mahatma Gandhi Road
Mumbai - 400 023
jaicopub@vsnl.com
www.jaicobooks.com

© Jaico Publishing House

21 EROTIC STORIES
ISBN 81-7224-354-5

First Jaico Impression: 1994
Seventh Jaico Impression : 2006

Printed by :
Anubha Printers
B-48, Sector-7, Noida - 201301

Contents

Selected Famous Erotic Short Stories

from THE KAMA SUTRA
Vatsayanana

The Kama Sutra *remains the greatest of all the classical Indian texts on love and love-making. Written some seventeen . centuries ago, the techniques mentioned are translated for the modern aficionado of erotica.*

Of the way how to begin and how to end the congress Different kinds of congress and love quarrels

In the pleasure-room, decorated with flowers, and fragrant with perfumes, attended by his friends and servants, the citizen should receive the woman, who will come bathed and dressed, and will invite her to take refreshment and to drink freely. He should then seat her on his left side, and holding her hair, and touching also the end and knot of her garment, he should gently embrace her with his right arm. They should then carry on an amusing conversation on various subjects, and may also talk suggestively of things which would be considered as coarse, or not to be mentioned generally in society. They may then sing, either with or without gesticulations, and play on musical instruments, talk about the arts, and persuade each other to drink. At last when the woman is overcome with love and desire, the citizen should dismiss the people that may be with him, giving them flowers, ointments, and betel leaves, and then when the two are left alone, they should proceed as has been already described in the previous chapters.

Such is the beginning of sexual union. At the end of the congress, the lovers with modesty, and not looking at each other, should go separately to the washing-room. After this, sitting in their own places, they should eat some betel leaves, and the citizen should apply with his own hand to the body of the woman some pure sandal wood ointment, or ointment of some other kind. He should then embrace her with his left arm, and with agreeable words should cause her to drink from a cup held in his own hand, or he may give her water to drink. They can then eat sweetmeats, or anything else, according to their likings, and may drink fresh juice, soup, gruel, extracts of meat, sherbet, the juice of mangoe fruits, the extract of the juice of the citron tree mixed with sugar, or anything that may be liked in different countries, and known to be sweet, soft, and pure. The lovers may also sit on the terrace of the palace or house, and enjoy the moonlight, and carry on an agreeable conversation. At this time, too, while the woman lies in his lap, with her face towards the moon, the citizen should show her the different planets, the morning star, the polar star, and the seven Rishis, or Great Bear.

This is the end of sexual union.

Congress is of the following kinds, viz.:

> Loving congress.
> Congress of subsequent love.
> Congress of artificial love.
> Congress of transferred love.
> Congress like that of eunuchs.
> Deceitful congress.
> Congress of spontaneous love.

(1) When a man and a woman, who have been in love with each other for some time, come together with great difficulty, or when one of the two returns from a journey, or is reconciled after having been separated on account of a quarrel, then congress is called the 'loving congress.' It is carried on according to the liking of the lovers, and as long as they choose.

(2) When two persons come together, while their love for each other is still in its infancy, their congress is called the 'congress of subsequent love.'

(3) When a man carries on the congress by exciting himself by means of the sixty-four ways, such as kissing, etc., etc., or when a man and a woman come together, though in reality they are both attached to different persons, their congress is then called 'congress of artificial love.' At this time all the ways and means mentioned in the Kama Shastra should be used.

(4) When a man, from the beginning to the end of the congress, though having connection with the woman, thinks all the time that he is enjoying another one whom he loves, it is called the 'congress of transferred love.'

(5) Congress between a man and a female water carrier, or a female servant of a caste lower than his own, lasting only until the desire is satisfied, is called 'congress like that of eunuchs.' Here external touches, kisses, and manipulations are not to be employed.

(6) The congress between a courtezan and a rustic, and that between citizens and the women of villages, and bordering countries, is called 'deceitful congress.'

(7) The congress that takes place between two persons who are attached to one another, and which is done according to their own liking is called 'spontaneous congress.'

Thus ends the kinds of congress.

We shall now speak of love quarrels.

A woman who is very much in love with a man cannot bear to hear the name of her rival mentioned, or to have any

3

conversation regarding her, or to be addressed by her name through mistake. If such takes place, a great quarrel arises, and the woman cries, becomes angry, tosses her hair about, strikes her loveer, falls from her bed or seat, and, casting aside her garlands and ornaments, throws herself down on the ground.

At this time, the lover should attempt to reconcile her with conciliatory words, and should take her up carefully and place her on her bed. But she, not replying to his questions, and with increased anger, should bend down his head by pulling his hair, and having kicked him once, twice, or thrice on his arms, head, bosom or back, should then proceed to the door of the room. Dattaka says that she should then sit angrily near the door and shed tears, but should not go out, because she would be found fault with for going away. After a time, when she thinks that the conciliatory words and actions of her lover have reached their utmost, she should then embrace him, talking to him with harsh and reproachful words, but at the same time showing a loving desire for congress.

When the woman is in her own house, and has quarrelled with her lover, she should go to him and show how angry she is, and leave him. Afterwards the citizen having sent the Vita, the Vidushaka or the Pithamurda to pacify her, she should accompany them back to the house, and spend the night with her lover.

Thus ends the love quarrels.

In conclusion.

A man, employing the sixty-four means mentioned by Babhravya, obtains his object, and enjoys the woman of the first quality. Though he may speak well on other subjects, if he does not know the sixty-four divisions, no great respect is paid to him in the assembly of the learned. A man, devoid of other knowledge, but well acquainted with the sixty-four divisions, becomes a leader in any society of men and women. What man will not respect the sixty-four

4

parts, considering they are respected by the learned, by the cunning, and by the courtezans. As the sixty-four parts are respected, are charming, and add to the talent of women, they are called by the Acharyas dear to women. A man skilled in the sixty-four parts is looked upon with love by his own wife, by the wives of others, and by courtezans.

On kissing

It is said by some that there is no fixed time or order between the embrace, the kiss, and the pressing or scratching with the nails or fingers, but that all these things should be done generally before sexual union takes place, while striking and making the various sounds generally takes place at the time of the union. Vatsyayana however, thinks that anything may take place at any time, for love does not care for time or order.

On the occasion of the first congress, kissing and the other things mentioned above should be done moderately, they should not be continued for a long time, and should be done alternately. On subsequent occasions however the reverse of all this may take place, and moderation will not be necessary, they may continue for a long time, and for the purpose of kindling love, they may be all done at the same time.

The following are the places for kissing, viz., the forehead, the eyes, the cheeks, the throat, the bosom, the breasts, the lips, and the interior of the mouth. Moreover the people of the Lat country kiss also on the following places, viz, the joints of the thighs, the arms and the navel. But Vatsyayana thinks that though kissing is practised by these people in the above places on account of the intensity of their love, and the customs of their country, it is not fit to be practised by all.

Now in a case of a young girl there are three sorts of kisses, viz.:

The nominal kiss.
The throbbing kiss.
The touching kiss.

(1) When a girl only touches the mouth of her lover with her own, but does not herself do anything, it is called the 'nominal kiss.'

(2) When a girl, setting aside her bashfulness a little, wishes to touch the lip that is pressed into her mouth, and with that object moves her lower lip, but not the upper one, it is called the 'throbbing kiss.'

(3) When a girl touches her lover's lip with her tongue, and having shut her eyes, places her hands on those of her lover, it is called the 'touching kiss.'

Other authors describe four other kinds of kisses, viz.:

The straight kiss.
The bent kiss.
The turned kiss.
The pressed kiss.

(1) When the lips of two lovers are brought into direct contact with each other, it is called a 'straight kiss.'

(2) When the heads of two lovers are bent towards each other, and when so bent, kissing takes place, it is called a 'bent kiss.'

(3) When one of them turns up the face of the other by holding the head and chin, and then kissing, it is called a 'turned kiss.'

(4) Lastly when the lower lip is pressed with much force, it is called a 'pressed kiss.'

There is also a fifth kind of kiss called the 'greatly pressed kiss,' which is effected by taking hold of the lower lip between two fingers, and then after touching it with the tongue, pressing it with great force with the lip.

As regards kissing, a wager may be laid as to which will get hold of the lips of the other first. If the woman loses, she should pretend to cry, should keep her lover off by shaking her hands, and turn away from him and dispute with him saying, 'let another wager be laid.' If she loses this a second time, she should appear doubly distressed, and when her lover is off his guard or asleep, she should get hold of his lower lip, and hold it in her teeth, so that it should not slip away, and then she should laugh, make a loud noise, deride him, dance about, and say whatever she likes in a joking way, moving her eyebrows, and rolling her eyes. Such are the wagers and quarrels as far as kissing is concerned, but the same may be applied with regard to the pressing or scratching with the nails and fingers, biting and striking. All these however are only peculiar to men and women of intense passion.

When a man kisses the upper lip of a woman, while she in return kisses his lower lip, it is called the 'kiss of the upper lip.'

When one of them takes both the lips of the other between his or her own, it is called a 'clasping kiss.' A woman, however, only takes this kind of kiss from a man who has no moustache. And on the occasion of this kiss, if one of them touches the teeth, the tongue, and the palate of the other, with his or her tongue, it is called the 'fighting of the tongue.' In the same way, the pressing of the teeth of the one against the mouth of the other is to be practised.

Kissing is of four kinds, viz., moderate, contracted, pressed, and soft, according to the different parts of the body which are kissed, for different kinds of kisses are appropriate for different parts of the body.

When a woman looks at the face of her lover while he is asleep, and kisses it to show her intention or desire, it is called a 'kiss that kindles love.'

When a woman kisses her lover while he is engaged in business, or while he is quarrelling with her, or while he is looking at something else, so that his mind may be turned away, it is called a 'kiss that turns away.'

When a lover coming home late at night kisses his beloved, who is asleep on her bed, in order to show her his desire, it is called a 'kiss that awakens.' On such an occasion the woman may pretend to be asleep at the time of her lover's arrival, so that she may know his intention and obtain respect from him.

When a person kisses the reflection of the person he loves in a mirror, in water, or on a wall, it is called a 'kiss showing the intention.'

When a person kisses a child sitting on his lap, or a picture, or an image, or figure, in the presence of the person beloved by him, it is called a 'transferred kiss.'

When at night at a theatre, or in an assembly of caste men, a man coming up to a woman kisses a finger of her hand if she be standing, or a toe of her foot if she be sitting, or when a woman is shampooing her lover's body, places her face on his thigh (as if she was sleepy) so as to inflame his passion, and kisses his thigh or great toe, it is called a 'demonstrative kiss.'

On pressing, or marking, or scratching with the nails

When love becomes intense, pressing with the nails or scratching the body with them is practised, and it is done on the following occasions: On the first visit; at the time of setting out on a journey; on the return from a journey; at the time when an angry lover is reconciled; and lastly when a woman is intoxicated.

But pressing with the nails is not an usual thing except with those who are intensely passionate, i.e., full of passion. It is employed together with biting, by those to whom the practice is agreeable.

Pressing with the nails is of the eight following kinds, according to the forms of the marks which are produced, viz.:

1. Sounding.
2. Half moon.
3. A circle.

8

4. A line.
5. A tiger's nail or claw.
6. A peacock's foot.
7. The jump of a hare.
8. The leaf of a blue lotus.

The places that are to be pressed with the nails are as follows: the arm pit, the throat, the breasts, the lips, the jaghana, or middle parts of the body, and the thighs. But Suvarnanabha is of opinion that when the impetuosity of passion is excessive, then the places need not be considered.

The qualities of good nails are that they should be bright, well set, clean, entire, convex, soft, and glossy in appearance. Nails are of three kinds according to their size, viz.:

> Small.
> Middling.
> Large.

Large nails, which give grace to the hands, and attract the hearts of women from their appearance, are possessed by the Bengalees.

Small nails, which can be used in various ways, and are to be applied only with the object of giving pleasure, are possessed by the people of the southern districts.

Middling nails, which contain the properties of both the above kinds, belong to the people of the Maharashtra.

(1) When a person presses the chin, the breasts, the lower lip, or the jaghana of another so softly that no scratch or mark is left, but only the hair on the body becomes erect from the touch of the nails, and the nails themselves make a sound, it is called a 'sounding or pressing with the nails.'

This pressing is used in the case of a young girl when her lover shampoos her, scratches her head, and wants to trouble or frighten her.

(2) The curved mark with the nails, which is impressed on the neck and the breasts, is called 'the half moon.'

9

(3) When the half moons are impressed opposite to each other, it is called a 'circle.' This mark with the nails is generally made on the navel, the small cavities about the buttocks, and on the joints of the thigh.

(4) A mark in the form of a small line, and which can be made on any part of the body, is called a 'line.'

(5) This same line, when it is curved, and made on the breast, is called a 'tiger's nail.'

(6) When a curved mark is made on the breast by means of the five nails, it is called a 'peacock's foot.' This mark is made with the object of being praised, for it requires a great deal of skill to make it properly.

(7) When five marks with the nails are made close to one another near the nipple of the breast, it is called 'the jump of a hare.'

(8) A mark made on the breast or on the hips in the form of a leaf of the blue lotus, is called the 'leaf of a blue lotus.'

When a person is going on a journey, and makes a mark on the thighs, or on the breast, it is called a 'token of remembrance.' On such an occasion three or four lines are impressed close to one another with the nails.

Here ends the marking with the nails. Marks of other kinds than the above may also be made with the nails, for the ancient authors say, that as there are innumerable degrees of skill among men (the practice of this art being known to all), so there are innumerable ways of making these marks. And as pressing or marking with the nails is independent of love, no one can say with certainty how many different kinds of marks with the nails do actually exist. The reason of this is, Vatsyayana says, that as variety is necessary in love, so love is to be produced by means of variety. It is on this account that courtezans, who are well acquainted with various ways and means, become so desirable, for if variety is sought in all the arts and amusements, such as archery and others, how much more should it be sought after in the present case.

The marks of the nails should not be made on married women, but particular kinds of marks may be made on their private parts for the remembrance and increase of love.

There are also some verses on the subject, as follows:

'The love of a woman who sees the marks of nails on the private parts of her body, even though they are old and almost worn out, becomes again fresh and new. If there be no marks of nails to remind a person of the passages of love, then love is lessened in the same way as when no union takes place for a long time.'

Even when a stranger sees at a distance a young woman with the marks of nails on her breast, he is filled with love and respect for her.

A man, also, who carries the marks of nails and teeth on some parts of his body, influences the mind of a woman, even though it be ever so firm. In short, nothing tends to increase love so much as the effects of marking with the nails, and biting.

Of the different ways of lying down, and various kinds of congress

On the occasion of a 'high congress' the Mrigi (Deer) woman should lie down in such a way as to widen her yoni, while in a 'low congress' the Hastini (Elephant) woman should lie down so as to contract hers. But in an 'equal congress' they should lie down in the natural position. What is said above concerning the Mrigi and the Hatini applies also to the Vadawa (Mare) woman. In a 'low congress' the woman should particularly make use of medicine, to cause her desires to be satisfied quickly.

The Deer-woman has the following three ways of lying down.

The widely opened position.
The yawning position.
The position of the wife of Indra.

11

(1) When she lowers her head and raises her middle parts, it is called the 'widely opened position.' At such a time the man should apply some unguent, so as to make the entrance easy.

(2) When she raises her thighs and keeps them wide apart and engages in congress, it is called the 'yawning position.'

(3) When she places her thighs with her legs doubled on them upon her sides, and thus engages in congress, it it called the position of Indrani, and this is learnt only by practice. The position is also useful in the case of the 'highest congress.'

The 'clasping position' is used in 'low congress,' and in the 'lowest congress,' together with the 'pressing position,' the 'twining position,' and the 'mare's position.'

When the legs of both the male and the female are stretched straight out over each other, it is called the 'clasping position.' It is of two kinds, the side position and the supine position, according to the way in which they lie down. In the side position the male should invariably lie on his left side, and cause the woman to lie on her right side, and this rule is to be observed in lying down with all kinds of women.

When, after congress has begun in the clasping position, the woman presses her lover with her thighs, it is called the 'pressing position.'

When the woman places one of her thighs across the thigh of her lover, it is called the 'twining position.'

When a woman forcibly holds in her yoni the lingam after it is in, it is called the 'mare's position.' This is learnt by practice only, and is chiefly found among the women of the Andra country.

The above are the different ways of lying down, mentioned by Babhravya; Survarnanabha, however, gives the following in addition.

When the female raises both of her thighs straight up, it is called the 'rising position.'

When she raises both of her legs, and places them on her lover's shoulders, it is called the 'yawning position.'

When the legs are contracted, and thus held by the lover before his bosom, it is called the 'pressed position.'

When only one of her legs is stretched out, it is called the 'half pressed position.'

When the woman places one of her legs on her lover's shoulder, and stretches the other out, and then places the latter on his shoulder, and stretches out the other and continues to do so alternately, it is called the 'splitting of a bamboo.'

When one of her legs is placed on the head, and the other is stretched out, it is called the 'fixing of a nail.' This is learnt by practice only.

When both the legs of the woman are contracted, and placed on her stomach, it is called the 'crab's position.'

When the thighs are raised and placed one upon the other, it is called the 'packed position.'

When the shanks are placed one upon the other, it is called the 'lotus-like position.'

When a man, during congress, turns round, and enjoys the woman without leaving her, while she embraces him round the back all the time, it is called the 'turning position,' and is learnt only by practice.

Thus says Suvarnanabha, these different ways of lying down, sitting, and standing should be practised in water, because it is easy to do so therein. But Vatsyayana is of opinion that congress in water is improper, because it is prohibited by the religious law.

When a man and a woman support themselves on each other's bodies, or on a wall, or pillar, and thus while standing engage in congress, it is called the 'supported congress.'

When a man supports himself against a wall, and the

13

woman, sitting on his hands joined together and held underneath her, throws her arms round his neck, and putting her thighs alongside his waist, moves herself by her feet, which are touching the wall against which the man is leaning, it is called the 'suspended congress.'

When a woman stands on her hands and feet like a quadruped, and her lover mounts her like a bull, it is called the 'congress of a cow.' At this time everything that is ordinarily done on the bosom should be done on the back.

In the same way can be carried on the congress of a dog, the congress of a goat, the congress of a deer, the forcible mounting of an ass, the congress of a cat, the jump of a tiger, the pressing of an elephant, the rubbing of a boar, and the mounting of a horse. And in all these cases the characteristics of these different animals should be manifested by acting like them.

When a man enjoys two women at the same time, both of whom love him equally, it is called the 'united congress.'

When a man enjoys many women altogether, it is called the 'congress of a herd of cows.'

The following kinds of congress, viz., sporting in water, or the congress of an elephant with many female elephants which is said to take place only in the water, the congress of a collection of goats, the congress of a collection of deer, take place in imitation of these animals.

In Gramaneri many young men enjoy a woman that may be married to one of them, either one after the other, or at the same time. Thus one of them holds her, another enjoys her, a third uses her mouth, a fourth holds her middle part, and in this way they go on enjoying her several parts alternately.

The same things can be done when several men are sitting in company with one courtezan, or when one courtezan is alone with many men. In the same way this can be done by

14

the women of the King's harem when they accidentally get hold of a man.

The people in the Southern countries have also a congress in the anus, that is called the 'lower congress.'

Thus ends the various kinds of congress. There are also two verses on the subject as follows.

'An ingenious person should multiply the kinds of congress after the fashion of the different kinds of beasts and of birds. For these different kinds of congress, performed according to the usage of each country, and the liking of each individual, generate love, friendship, and respect in the hearts of women.'

Of the auparishtaka or mouth congress

There are two kinds of eunuchs, those that are disguised as males, and those that are disguised as females. Eunuchs disguised as females imitate their dress, speech, gestures, tenderness, timidity, simplicity, softness and bashfulness. The acts that are done on the jaghana or middle parts of women, are done in the mouths of these eunuchs, and this is called Auparishtaka. These eunuchs derive their imaginable pleasure, and their livelihood from this kind of congress, and they lead the life of courtezans. So much concerning eunuchs disguised as females.

Eunuchs disguised as males keep their desires secret, and when they wish to do anything they lead the life of shampooers. Under the pretence of shampooing, an eunuch of this kind embraces and draws towards himself the thighs of the man whom he is shampooing, and after this he touches the joints of his thighs and his jaghana, or central portions of his body. Then, if he finds the lingam of the man erect, he presses it with his hands, and chaffs him for getting into that state. If after this, and after knowing his intention, the man does not tell the eunuch to proceed, then the latter does it of his own accord and begins the congress.

15

If however he is ordered by the man to do it, then he disputes with him, and only consents at last with difficulty.

The following eight things are then done by the eunuch one after the other, viz.

> The nominal congress.
> Biting the sides.
> Pressing outside.
> Pressing inside.
> Kissing.
> Rubbing.
> Sucking a mangoe fruit.
> Swallowing up.

At the end of each of these, the eunuch expresses his wish to stop, but when one of them is finished, the man desires him to do another, and after that is done, then the one that follows it, and so on.

(1) When, holding the man's lingam with his hand, and placing it between his lips, the eunuch moves about his mouth, it is called the 'nominal congress.'

(2) When, covering the end of the lingam with his fingers collected together like the bud of a plant or flower, the eunuch presses the sides of it with his lips, using his teeth also, it is called 'biting the sides.'

(3) When, being desired to proceed, the eunuch presses the end of the lingam with his lips closed together, and kisses it as if he were drawing it out, it is called the 'outside pressing.'

(4) When, being asked to go on, he puts the lingam further into his mouth, and presses it with his lips and then takes it out, it is called the 'inside pressing.'

(5) When, holding the lingam in his hand, the eunuch kisses it as if he were kissing the lower lip, it is called 'kissing.'

(6) When, after kissing it, he touches it with his tongue everywhere, and passes the tongue over the end of it, it is called 'rubbing.'

16

(7) When, in the same way, he puts the half of it into his mouth, and forcibly kisses and sucks it, this is called 'sucking a mangoe fruit.'

(8) And lastly, when, with the consent of the man, the eunuch puts the whole lingam into his mouth, and presses it to the very end, as if he were going to swallow it up, it is called 'swallowing up.'

Striking, scratching, and other things may also be done during this kind of congress.

The Auparishtaka is practised also by unchaste and wanton women, female attendants and serving maids, *i.e.*, those who are not married to anybody, but who live by shampooing.

The Acharyas (*i.e.*, ancient and venerable authors) are of opinion that this Auparishtaka is the work of a dog and not of a man, because it is a low practice, and opposed to the orders of the Holy Writ, and because the man himself suffers by bringing his lingam into contact with the mouths of eunuchs and women. But Vastsyayana says that the orders of the Holy Writ do not affect those who resort to courtezans, and the law prohibits the practice of the Auparishtaka with married women only. As regards the injury to the male, that can be easily remedied.

The people of Eastern India do not resort to women who practice the Auparishtaka.

The people of Ahichhatra resort to such women, but do nothing with them, so far as the mouth is concerned.

The people of Saketa do with these women every kind of mouth congress, while the people of Nagara do not practice this, but do every other thing.

The people of the Shurasena country, on the southern bank of the Jumna, do everything without any hesitation, for they say that women being naturally unclean, no one can be certain about their character, their purity, their conduct, their practices, their confidences, or their speech. They are not however on this account to be abandoned, because

17

religious law, on the authority of which they are reckoned pure, lays down that the udder of a cow is clean at the time of milking, though the mouth of a cow, and also the mouth of her calf, are considered unclean by the Hindoos. Again a dog is clean when he seizes a deer in hunting, though food touched by a dog is otherwise considered very unclean. A bird is clean when it causes a fruit to fall from a tree by pecking at it, though things eaten by crows and other birds are considered unclean. And the mouth of a woman is clean for kissing and such like things at the time of sexual intercourse. Vatsyayana moreover thinks that in all these things connected with love, everybody should act according to the custom of his country, and his own inclination.

There are also the following verses on the subject.

'The male servants of some men carry on the mouth congress with their masters. It is also practised by some citizens who know each other well, among themselves. Some women of the harem, when they are amorous, do the acts of the mouth on the yonis of one another, and some men do the same thing with women. The way of doing this (*i.e.*, of kissing the yoni) should be known from kissing the mouth. When a man and woman lie down in an inverted order, *i.e.*, with the head of the one towards the feet of the other and carry on this congress, it is called the 'congress of a crow.'

For the sake of such things courtezans abandon men possessed of good qualities, liberal and clever, and become attached to low persons, such as slaves and elephant drivers. The Auparishtaka, or mouth congress, should never be done by a learned Brahman, by a minister that carries on the business of a state, or by a man of good reputation, because though the practice is allowed by the Shastras, there is no reason why it should be carried on, and need only be practised in particular cases. As for instance, the taste, and the strength, and digestive qualities of the flesh of dogs are mentioned in works on medicine, but it does not

18

therefore follow that it should be eaten by the wise. In the same way there are some men, some places and some times, with respect to which these practices can be made use of. A man should therefore pay regard to the place, to the time, and to the practice which is to be carried out, as also as to whether it is agreeable to his nature and to himself, and then he may or may not practise these things according to circumstances. But after all, these things being done secretly, and the mind of the man being fickle, how can it be known what any person will do at any particular time and for any particular purpose.

from THE PERFUMED GARDEN

Shaykh Umar ibn Muhammed al *Nefzawi*

Candid and quaint in parts, the sixteenth century manual of sexual practice in India, The Perfumed Garden, *delights and educates.*

Relating to the act of generation

K now, o Vizir (and God protect you!), that if you wish for coition, in joining the woman you should not have your stomach loaded with food and drink, only in that condition will your cohabitation be wholesome and good. If your stomach is full, only harm can come of it to both of you; you will have threatening symptoms of apoplexy and gout, and the least evil that may result from it will be the inability of passing your urine, or weakness of sight.

Let your stomach then be free from excessive food and drink, and you need not apprehend any illness.

Before setting to work with your wife excite her with toying, so that the copulation will finish to your mutual satisfaction.

Thus it will be well to play with her before you introduce your verge and accomplish the cohabitation. You will excite her by kissing her cheeks, sucking her lips and nibbling at

20

her breasts. You will lavish kisses on her navel and thighs, and titillate the lower parts. Bite at her arms, and neglect no part of her body; cling close to her bosom, and show her your love and submission. Interlace your legs with hers, and press her in your arms, for, as the poet has said:

Under her neck my right hand has served her for a
    cushion,
And to draw her to me
I have sent out my left hand,
Which bore her up as a bed.

When you are close to a woman, and you see her eyes getting dim, and hear her, yearning for coition, heave deep sighs, then let your and her yearning be joined into one, and let your lubricity rise to the highest point; for this will be the moment most favourable to the game of love. The pleasure which the woman then feels will be extreme; as for yourself, you will cherish her all the more, and she will continue her affection for you, for it has been said:

If you see a woman heaving deep sighs, with her lips getting red and her eyes languishing, when her mouth half opens and her movements grow heedless; when she appears to be disposed to go to sleep, vacillating in her steps and prone to yawn, know that this is the moment for coition; and if you there and then make your way into her you will procure for her an unquestionable treat. You yourself will find the mouth of her womb clasping your article, which is undoubtedly the crowning pleasure for both, for this before everything begets affection and love.

The following precepts, coming from a profound connoisseur in love affairs, are well known:

Woman is like a fruit, which will not yield its sweetness until you rub it between your hands. Look at the basil plant; if you do not rub it warm with your fingers it will not emit any scent. Do you not know that the amber,

21

unless it be handled and warmed, keeps hidden within its pores the aroma contained in it. It is the same with woman. If you do not animate her with your toying, intermixed with kissing, nibbling and touching, you will not obtain from her what you are wishing; you will feel no enjoyment when you share her couch, and you will waken in her heart neither inclination nor affection, nor love for you; all her qualities will remain hidden.

It is reported that a man, having asked a woman what means were the most likely to create affection in the female heart, with respect to the pleasures of coition, received the following answer:

O you who question me, those things which develop the taste for coition are the toyings and touches which precede it, and then the close embrace at the moment of ejaculation!

Believe me, the kisses, nibblings, suction of the lips, the close embrace, the visits of the mouth to the nipples of the bosom, and the sipping of the fresh saliva, these are the things to render affection lasting.

In acting thus, the two orgasms take place simultaneously, and enjoyment comes to the man and woman at the same moment. Then the man feels the womb grasping his member, which gives to each of them the most exquisite pleasure.

This it is which gives birth to love, and if matters have not been managed this way the woman has not had her full share of pleasure, and the delights of the womb are wanting. Know that the woman will not feel her desires satisfied, and will not love her rider unless he is able to act up to her womb; but when the womb is made to enter into action she will feel the most violent love for her cavalier, even if he be unsightly in appearance.

Then do all you can to provoke a simultaneous discharge of the two spermal fluids; herein lies the secret of love.

One of the savants who have occupied themselves with

this subject has thus related the confidences which one of them made to him:

O you men, one and all, who are soliciting the love of woman and her affection, and who wish that sentiment in her heart to be of an enduring nature, toy with her previous to coition; prepare her for enjoyment, and neglect nothing to attain that end. Explore her with the greater assiduity, and, entirely occupied with her, let nothing else engage your thoughts. Do not let the moment propitious for pleasure pass away; that moment will be when you see her eyes humid, half open. Then go to work, but, remember, not till your kisses and toyings have taken effect.

After you have got the woman into a proper state of excitement, O men! put your member into her, and, if you then observe the proper movements, she will experience a pleasure which will satisfy all her desires.

Lie on her breast, rain kisses on her cheeks, and let not your member quit her vagina. Push for the mouth of her womb. This will crown your labour.

If, by God's favour, you have found this delight, take good care not to withdraw your member, but let it remain there, and imbibe an endless pleasure! Listen to the sighs and heavy breathing of the woman. They witness the violence of the bliss you have given her.

And after the enjoyment is over, and your amorous struggle has come to an end, be careful not to get up at once, but withdraw your member cautiously. Remain close to the woman, and lie down on the right side of the bed that witnessed your enjoyment. You will find this pleasant, and you will not be like a fellow who mounts the woman after the fashion of a mule, without any regard to refinement, and who, after the emission, hastens to get his member out and to rise. Avoid such manners, for they rob the woman of all her lasting delight.

In short, the true lover of coition will not fail to observe all that I have recommended; for, from the observance

23

of my recommendations will result the pleasure of the woman, and these rules comprise everything essential in that respect.

God has made everything for the best!

Concerning everything that is favourable to the act of coition

Know, o Vizir (God be good to you!), if you would have pleasant coition, which ought to give an equal share of happiness to the two combatants and be satisfactory to both, you must first of all toy with the woman, excite her with kisses, by nibbling and sucking her lips, by caressing her neck and cheeks. Turn her over in the bed, now on her back, now on her stomach, till you see by her eyes that the time for pleasure is near, as I have mentioned in the preceding chapter, and certainly I have not been sparing with my observations thereupon.

Then when you observe the lips of a woman to tremble and get red, and her eyes to become languishing, and her sighs to become quicker, know that she is hot for coition; then get between her thighs, so that your member can enter into her vagina. If you follow my advice, you will enjoy a pleasant embrace, which will give you the greatest satisfaction, and leave with you a delicious remembrance.

Someone has said:

If you desire coition, place the woman on the ground, cling closely to her bosom, with her lips close to yours; then clasp her to you, suck her breath, bite her; kiss her breasts, her stomach, her flanks, press her close in your arms, so as to make her faint with pleasure; when you see her so far gone, then push your member into her. If you have done as I said, the enjoyment will come to both of you simultaneously. This it is which makes the pleasure of the woman so sweet. But if you neglect my

24

advice the woman will not be satisfied and you will not have procured her any pleasure.

The coition being finished, do not get up at once, but come down softly on her right side, and if she has conceived, she will bear a male child, if it please God on high!

Sages and Savants (may God grant to all his forgiveness!) have said:

If anyone placing his hand upon the vulva of a woman that is with child pronounces the following words: 'In the name of God! may he grant salutation and mercy to his Prophet (salutation and mercy be with him). Oh! my God! I pray to thee in the name of the Prophet to let a boy issue from this conception,' it will come to pass by the will of God, and in consideration for our lord Mohammed (the salutation and grace of God be with him), the woman will be delivered of a boy.

Do not drink rain-water directly after copulation, because this beverage weakens the kidneys.

If you want to repeat the coition, perfume yourself with sweet scents, then close with the woman, and you will arrive at a happy result.

Do not let the woman perform the act of coition mounted upon you, for fear that in that position some drops of her seminal fluid might enter the canal of your verge and cause a sharp urethritis.

Do not work hard directly after coition as this might affect your health adversely, but go to rest for some time.

Do not wash your verge directly after having with-drawn it from the vagina of the woman, until the irritation has gone down somewhat; then wash it and its opening carefully. Otherwise, do not wash your member frequently. Do not leave the vulva directly after the emission, as this may cause canker.

25

Sundry positions for the coitus

The ways of doing it to women are numerous and variable. And now is the time to make known to you the different positions which are usual.

God, the magnificent, has said:

'Women are your field. Go upon your field as you like.' According to your wish you can choose the position you like best, provided, of course, that coition takes place in the spot destined for it, that is, in the vulva.

Manner the first – Make the woman lie upon her back, with her thighs raised, then, getting between her legs, introduce your member into her. Pressing your toes to the ground, you can rummage her in a convenient, measured way. This is a good position for a man with a long verge.

Manner the second – If your member is a short one, let the woman lie on her back, lift her legs into the air, so that her right leg be near her right ear, and the left one near her left ear, and in this posture, with her buttocks lifted up, her vulva will project forward. Then put in your member.

Manner the third – Let the woman stretch herself upon the ground, and place yourself between her thighs; then putting one of her legs upon your shoulder, and the other under your arm, near the armpit, get into her.

Manner the fourth – Let her lie down, and put her legs on your shoulders; in this position your member will just face her vulva, which must not touch the ground. And then introduce your member.

Manner the fifth – Let her lie down on her side, then lie yourself down by her on your side, and getting between her thighs, put your member into her vagina. But side-long coition predisposes for rheumatic pains and sciatica.

Manner the sixth – Make her get down on her knees and elbows, as if kneeling in prayer. In this position the vulva

26

is projected backwards; you then attack her from that side, and put your member into her.

Manner the seventh – Place the woman on her side, and squat between her thighs, with one of her legs on your shoulder and the other between your thighs, while she remains lying on her side. Then you enter her vagina, and make her move by drawing her towards your chest by means of your hands, with which you hold her embraced.

Manner the eighth – Let her stretch herself upon the ground, on her back, with her legs crossed; then mount her like a cavalier on horseback, being on your knees, while her legs are placed under her thighs, and put your member into her vagina.

Manner the ninth – Place the woman so that she leans with her front, or, if you prefer it, her back upon a moderate elevation, with her feet set upon the ground. She thus offers her vulva to the introduction of your member.

Manner the tenth – Place the woman near to a low divan, the back of which she can take hold of with her hands; then, getting under her, lift her legs to the height of your navel, and let her clasp you with her legs on each side of your body; in this position plant your verge into her, seizing with your hands the back of the divan. When you begin the action your movements must respond to those of the woman.

Manner the eleventh – Let her lie upon her back on the ground with a cushion under her posterior; then getting between her legs, and letting her place the sole of her right foot against the sole of her left foot, introduce your member.

There are other positions besides the above named in use among the peoples of India. It is well for you to know that the inhabitants of those parts have multiplied the different ways to enjoy women, and they have advanced farther than we in the knowledge and investigation of coitus.

Amongst those manners are the following, called:

1. *El asemeud*, the stopperage.
2. *El modefedâ*, frog fashion.
3. *El mokefâ*, with the toes cramped.
4. *El mokeurmeutt*, with legs in the air.
5. *El setouri*, he-goat fashion.
6. *El loulabi*, the screw of Archimedes.
7. *El kelouci*, the summersault.
8. *Hachou en nekanok*, the tail of the ostrich.
9. *Lebeuss el djoureb*, fitting on of the sock.
10. *Kechef el astine*, reciprocal sight of the posteriors.
11. *Nezâ el kouss*, the rainbow arch.
12. *Nesedj el kheuzz*, alternative piercing.
13. *Dok el arz*, pounding on the spot.
14. *Nik el kohoul*, coition from the back.
15. *El keurchi*, belly to belly.
16. *El kebachi*, ram-fashion.
17. *Dok el outed*, driving the peg home.
18. *Sebek el heub*, love's fusion.
19. *Tred ech chate*, sheep-fashion.
20. *Kalen el miche*, interchange in coition.
21. *Rekeud el aïr*, the race of the member.
22. *El modakheli*, the fitter-in.
23. *El khouariki*, the one who stops in the house.
24. *Nik el haddadi*, the smith's coition.
25. *El moheundi*, the seducer.

FIRST MANNER – *El asemeud* (the stopperage). Place the woman on her back, with a cushion under her buttocks, then get between her legs, resting the points of your feet against the ground; bend her two thighs against her chest as far as you can; place your hands under her arms so as to enfold her or cramp her shoulders. Then introduce your member, and at the moment of ejaculation draw her towards you. This position is painful for the woman, for her thighs being bent upwards and her buttocks raised by the cushion, the walls of her vagina tighten, and the uterus tending forward there is not much room for movement, and scarcely space enough for the intruder; consequently the latter enters with

28

difficulty and strikes against the uterus. This position should therefore not be adopted, unless the man's member is short or soft.

SECOND MANNER – *El modefedâ* (frog fashion). Place the woman on her back, and arrange her thighs so that they touch the heels, which latter are thus coming close to the buttocks; then down you sit in this kind of merry thought, facing the vulva, in which you insert your member; you then place her knees under your arm-pits; and taking firm hold of the upper part of her arms, you draw her towards you at the crisis.

THIRD MANNER – *El mokefâ* (with the toes cramped). Place the woman on her back, and squat on your knees, between her thighs, gripping the ground with your toes; raise her knees as high as your sides, in order that she may cross her legs over your back, and then pass her arms round your neck.

FOURTH MANNER – *El mokeurmeutt* (with legs in the air). The woman lying on her back, you put her thighs together and raise her legs up until the soles of her feet look at the ceiling; then enfolding her within your thighs you insert your member, holding her legs up with your hands.

FIFTH MANNER – *El setouri* (he-goat fashion). The woman being crouched on her side, you let her stretch out the leg on which she is resting, and squat down between her thighs with your calves bent under you. Then you lift her uppermost leg so that it rests on your back, and introduce your member. During the action you take hold of her shoulders, or, if you prefer it, by the arms.

SIXTH MANNER – *El loulabi* (the screw of Archimedes). The man being stretched on his back the woman sits on his member, facing him; she then places her hands upon the bed so that she can keep her stomach from touching the man's, and moves up and downwards, and if the man is supple he assists her from below. If in this position she wants to kiss him, she need only stretch her arms along the bed.

SEVENTH MANNER – *El kelouci* (the summersault). The woman must wear a pair of pantaloons, which she lets drop upon her heels; then she stoops, placing her head between her feet, so that her neck is in the opening of her pantaloons. At that moment, the man, seizing her legs, turns her upon her back, making her perform a summersault; then with his legs curved under him he brings his member right against her vulva, and, slipping it between her legs, inserts it.

It is alleged that there are women who, while lying on their back, can place their feet behind their head without the help of pantaloons or hands.

EIGHTH MANNER – *Hachou en nekanok* (the tail of the ostrich). The woman lying on her back along the bed, the man kneels in front of her, lifting up her legs until her head and shoulders only are resting on the bed; his member having penetrated into her vagina, he seizes and sets into motion the buttocks of the woman who, on her part, twines her legs around his neck.

NINTH MANNER – *Lebeuss el djoureb* (fitting on of the sock). The woman lies on her back. You sit down between her legs and place your member between the lips of her vulva, which you fit over it with your thumb and first finger; then you move so as to procure for your member, as far as it is in contact with the woman, a lively rubbing, which action you continue until her vulva gets moistened with the liquid emitted from your verge. When she is thus amply prepared for enjoyment by the alternate coming and going of your weapon in her scabbard, put it into her in full length.

TENTH MANNER – *Kechef el astine* (reciprocal sight of the posteriors). The man lying stretched out on his back, the woman sits down upon his member with her back to the man's face, who presses her sides between his thighs and legs, whilst she places her hands upon the bed as a support for her movements, and lowering her head, her eyes are turned towards the buttocks of the man.

ELEVENTH MANNER – *Nezâ el kouss* (the rainbow arch). The

30

woman is lying on her side; the man also on his side, with his face towards her back, pushes in between her legs and introduces his member, with his hands lying on the upper part of her back. As to the woman, she then gets hold of the man's feet, which she lifts up as far as she can, drawing him close to her; thus she forms with the body of the man an arch, of which she is the rise.

TWELFTH MANNER – *Nesedj el kheuzz* (the alternate movement of piercing). The man in sitting attitude places the soles of his feet together, and lowering his thighs, draws his feet nearer to his member; the woman sits down upon his feet, which he takes care to keep firm together. In this position the two thighs of the woman are pressed against the man's flanks, and she puts her arms round his neck. Then the man clasps the woman's ankles, and drawing his feet nearer to his body, brings the woman, who is sitting on them, within range of his member, which then enters her vagina. By moving his feet he sends her back and brings her forward again, without ever with-drawing his member entirely.

The woman makes herself as light as possible, and assists as well as she can in this come-and-go movement; her co-operation is, in fact, indispensable for it. If the man apprehends that his member may come out entirely, he takes her round the waist, and she receives no other impulse than that which is imparted to her by the feet of the man upon which she is sitting.

THIRTEENTH MANNER – *Dok el arz* (pounding on the spot). The man sits down with his legs stretched out; the woman then places herself astride on his thighs, crossing her legs behind the back of the man, and places her vulva opposite his member, which latter she guides into her vagina; she then places her arms round his neck, and he embraces her sides and waist, and helps her to rise and descend upon his verge. She must assist in his work.

FOURTEENTH MANNER – *Nik el kohoul* (coitus from the

back). The woman lies down on her stomach and raises her buttocks by help of a cushion; the man approaches from behind, stretches himself on her back and inserts his tool, while the woman twines her arms round the man's elbows. This is the easiest of all methods.

FIFTEENTH MANNER – *El keurchi* (belly to belly). The man and the woman are standing upright, face to face; she opens her thighs; the man then brings his feet forward between those of the woman, who also advances hers a little. In this position the man must have one of his feet somewhat in advance of the other. Each of the two has the arms round the other's hips; the man introduces his verge, and the two move thus intertwined after a manner called *neza' el dela*, which I shall explain later, if it please God the Almighty. (See FIRST MANNER.)

SIXTEENTH MANNER – *El kebachi* (after the fashion of the ram). The woman is on her knees, with her forearms on the ground; the man approaches from behind, kneels down, and lets his member penetrate into her vagina, which she presses out as much as possible; he will do well in placing his hands on the woman's shoulders.

SEVENTEENTH MANNER – *Dok el outed* (driving the peg home). The woman enlaces with her legs the waist of the man, who is standing, with her arms passed round his neck, steadying herself by leaning against the wall. Whilst she is thus suspended the man insinuates his pin into her vulva.

EIGHTEENTH MANNER – *Sebek el heub* (love's fusion). While the woman is lying on her right side, extend yourself on your left side; your left leg remains extended, and you raise your right one till it is up to her flank, when you lay her upper leg upon your side. Thus her uppermost leg serves the woman as a support for her back. After having introduced your member you move as you please, and she responds to your action as she pleases.

NINETEENTH MANNER – *Tred ech chate* (coitus of the sheep). The woman is on her hands and knees; the man, behind her, lifts her thighs till her vulva is on a level with his member, which he then inserts. In this position she ought to place her head between her arms.

TWENTIETH MANNER – *Kaleb el miche* (interchange in coition). The man lies on his back. The woman, gliding in between his legs, places herself upon him with her toe-nails against the ground; she lifts up the man's thighs, turning them against his own body, so that his virile member faces her vulva, into which she guides it; she then places her hands upon the bed by the sides of the man. It is, however, indispensable that the woman's feet rest upon a cushion to enable her to keep her vulva in concordance with his member.

In this position the parts are exchanged, the woman fulfilling that of the man, and vice-versa.

There is a variation to this manner. The man stretches himself out upon his back, while the woman kneels with her legs under her, but between his legs. The remainder conforms exactly to what has been said above.

TWENTY-FIRST MANNER – *Rekeud el aïr* (the race of the member). The man, on his back, supports himself with a cushion under his shoulders, but his posterior must retain contact with the bed. Thus placed, he draws up his thighs until his knees are on a level with his face; then the woman sits down, impaling herself on his member; she must not lie down, but keep seated as if on horseback, the saddle being represented by the knees and the stomach of the man. In that position she can, by the play of her knees, work up and down and down and up. She can also place her knees on the bed, in which case the man accentuates the movement by plying his thighs, whilst she holds with her left hand on to his right shoulder.

TWENTY-SECOND MANNER – *El modakheli* (the fitter-in). The woman is seated on her coccyx, with only the points of her buttocks touching the ground; the man takes the same position, her vulva facing his member. Then the woman puts her right thigh over the left thigh of the man, whilst he on his part puts his right thigh over her left one.

The woman, seizing with her hands her partner's arms, gets his member into her vulva; and each of them leaning alternately a little back, and holding each other by the upper part of the arms, they initiate a swaying movement, moving with little concussions, and keeping their movements in exact rhythm by the assistance of their heels, which are resting on the ground.

TWENTY-THIRD MANNER — *El khouariki* (the one who stops at home). The woman being couched on her back, the man lies down upon her, with cushions held in his hands.

After his member is in, the woman raises her buttocks as high as she can off the bed, the man following her up with his member well inside; then the woman lowers herself again upon the bed, giving some short shocks, and although they do not embrace, the man must stick like glue to her. This movement they continue, but the man must make himself light and must not be ponderous, and the bed must be soft; in default of which the exercise cannot be kept up without break.

TWENTY-FOURTH MANNER — *Nik el haddadi* (the coition of the blacksmith). The woman lies on her back with a cushion under her buttocks, and her knees raised as far as possible towards her chest, so that her vulva stands out as a target; she then guides her partner's member in.

The man executes for some time the usual action of coition, then draws his tool out of the vulva, and glides it for a moment between the thighs of the woman, as the smith withdraws the glowing iron from the furnace in order to plunge it into cold water. This manner is called *sferdgeli*, position of the quince.

TWENTY-FIFTH MANNER — *El moheundi* (the seducer). The woman lying on her back, the man sits between her legs, with his croupe on his feet; then he raises and separates the woman's thighs, placing her legs under his arms, or over his

34

shoulders; he then takes her round the waist, or seizes her shoulders.

The preceding descriptions furnish a large number of procedures, that cannot well be all put to the proof; but with such a variety to choose from, the man who finds one of them difficult to practise, can easily find plenty of others more to his convenience.

I have not made mention of positions which it appeared to me impossible to realize, and if there be anybody who thinks that those which I have described are not exhaustive, he has only to look for new ones.

It cannot be gainsaid that the Indian have surmounted the greatest difficulties in respect to coition. As a grand exploit, originating with them, the following may be cited:

The woman being stretched out on her back, the man sits down on her chest, with his back turned to her face, his knees turned forward and his nails gripping the ground; he then raises her hips, arching her back until he has brought her vulva face to face with his member, which he then inserts, and thus gains his purpose.

This position, as you perceive, is very fatiguing and very difficult to attain. I even believe that the only realization of it consists in words and designs. With regard to the other methods described above, they can only be practised if both man and woman are free from physical defects, and of analogous construction; for instance, one or the other of them must not be humpbacked, or very little, or very tall, or too obese. And I repeat, that both must be in perfect health.

Assuredly the Indian writers have in their works described a great many ways of making love, but the majority of them do not yield enjoyment, and give more pain than pleasure. That which is to be looked for in coition, the crowning point of it, is the enjoyment, the embrace, the kisses. This is the distinction between the coitus of men

35

and that of animals. No one is indifferent to the enjoyment which proceeds from the difference between the sexes, and the man finds his highest felicity in it.

If the desire of love in man is roused to its highest pitch, all the pleasure of coition becomes easy for him, and he satisfies his yearning in any way.

It is well for the lover of coition to put all these manners to the proof, so as to ascertain which is the position that gives the greatest pleasure to both combatants. Then he will know which to choose for the tryst, and in satisfying his desires retain the woman's affection.

Many people have essayed all the positions I have described, but none has been as much approved of as the *Dok el arz*.

A story is told on this subject of a man who had a wife of incomparable beauty, graceful and accomplished. He used to explore her in the ordinary manner, never having recourse to any other. The woman experienced none of the pleasure which ought to accompany the act, and was consequently generally very moody after the coition was over.

The man complained about this to an old dame, who told him, 'Try different ways in uniting yourself to her, until you find the one which best satisfies her. Then work her in this fashion only, and her affection for you will know no limit.'

He then tried upon his wife various manners of coition, and when he came to the one called *Dok el arz* he saw her overcome by violent transports of love, and at the crisis of pleasure he felt her womb grasp his verge energetically; and she said to him, biting his lips: 'This is the veritable manner of making love!'

These demonstrations proved to the lover, in fact, that his mistress felt in that position the most lively pleasure, and he always thenceforward worked with her in that way. Thus he attained his end, and caused the woman to love him to folly.

Therefore try different manners; for every woman likes one in preference to all other for her pleasure. The majority of them have, however, a predilection for the *Dok el arz*, as, in the application of the same, belly is pressed to belly, mouth glued to mouth, and the action of the womb is rarely absent.

I have now only to mention the various movements practised during coitus, and shall describe some of them.

FIRST MOVEMENT – *Neza el dela* (the bucket in the well). The man and woman join in close embrace after the introduction. Then he gives a push, and with-draws a little; the woman follows him with a push, and also retires. So they continue their alternate movement, keeping proper time. Placing foot against foot, and hand against hand, they keep up the motion of a bucket in a well.

SECOND MOVEMENT – *El netahi* (the mutual shock). After the introduction, they each draw back, but without dislodging the member completely. Then they both push tightly together, and thus go on keeping time.

THIRD MOVEMENT – *El motadani* (the approach). The man moves as usual, and then stops. Then the woman, with the member in her receptacle, begins to move like the man, and then stops. And they continue this way until the ejaculation comes.

FOURTH MOVEMENT – *Khiate el heub* (Love's tailor). The man, with his member being only partially inserted in the vulva, keeps up a sort of quick friction with the part that is in, and then suddenly plunges his whole member in up to its root. This is the movement of the needle in the hands of the tailor, of which the man and woman must take cognizance.

Such a movement only suits those men and women who can at will retard the crisis. With those who are otherwise constituted it would act too quickly.

FIFTH MOVEMENT – *Souak el feurdj* (the toothpick in the vulva). The man introduces his member between the walls of the vulva, and then drives it up and down, and right and left. Only a man with a very vigorous member can execute this movement.

SIXTH MOVEMENT – *Tâchik el heub* (the boxing up of love). The man introduces his member entirely into the vagina, so closely that his hairs are completely mixed up with the woman's. In that position he must now move forcibly, without withdrawing his tool in the least.

This is the best of all the movements, and is particularly well adapted to the position *Dok el arz*. Women prefer it to any other kind, as it procures them the extreme pleasure of seizing the member with their womb; and appeases their lust most completely.

Those women called *tribades* always use this movement in their mutual caresses. And it provokes prompt ejaculation both with man and woman.

Without kissing, no kind of position or movement procures the fullest pleasure; and those positions in which the kiss is not practicable are not entirely satisfactory, considering that the kiss is one of the most powerful stimulants to the work of love.

I have said in verse:

> The languishing eye
> Puts in connection soul with soul,
> And the tender kiss
> Takes the message from member to vulva.

The kiss is assumed to be an integral part of coition. The best kiss is the one impressed on humid lips combined with the suction of the lips and tongue, which latter particularly provokes the flow of sweet and fresh saliva. It is for the man to bring this about by slightly and softly nibbling his partner's tongue, when her saliva will flow sweet and exquisite, more pleasant than refined honey, and which will not mix with the saliva of her mouth. This manœuvre will give the man a trembling sensation, which will run all through his body, and is more intoxicating than wine drunk to excess.

A poet has said:

In kissing her, I have drunk from her mouth
Like a camel that drinks from the *redir*;
Her embrace and the freshness of her mouth
Give me a languor that goes to my marrow.

The kiss should be sonorous; it originates with the tongue touching the palate, lubricated by saliva. It is produced by the movement of the tongue in the mouth and by the displacement of the saliva, provoked by the suction.

The kiss given to the superficial outer part of the lips, and making a noise comparable to the one by which you call your cat, gives no pleasure. It is well enough thus applied to children and hands.

The kiss I have described above is the one for coitus and is full of voluptuousness.

A vulgar proverb says:

A humid kiss
Is better than a hurried coitus.

I have composed on this subject the following lines:

You kiss my hand – my mouth should be the place!
O woman, thou who art my idol!
It was a fond kiss you gave me, but it is lost,
The hand cannot appreciate the nature of a kiss.

The three words, *Kobla*, *letsem*, and *bouss* are used indifferently to indicate the kiss on the hand or on the mouth. The word *ferame* means specially the kiss on the mouth.

An Arab poet has said:

The heart of love can find no remedy
In witching sorcery nor amulets,
Nor in the fond embrace without a kiss,
Nor in a kiss without coitus.

And the author of the work, 'The Jewels of the Bride and the Rejoicing of Souls,' has added to the above, as complement and commentary, the two following verses:

Nor in converse, however unrestrained,
But in the placing of legs on legs (coition).

39

Remember that all caresses and all sorts of kisses, as described, are of no account without the introduction of the member. Therefore abstain from them, if you do not want action; they only fan a fire to no purpose. The passion which is excited resembles in fact a fire which is being lighted; and just as water only can extinguish the latter, so only the emission of the sperm can calm the lust and appease the heat.

The history of Djoâidi and Fadehat el Djemal

I was in love with a woman who was all grace and perfection, beautiful of shape, and gifted with all imaginable charms. Her cheeks were like roses, her forehead lily white, her lips like coral; she had teeth like pearls, and breasts like pomegranates. Her mouth opened round like a ring; her tongue seemed to be incrusted with precious gems; her eyes, black and finely slit, had the languor of slumber, and her voice the sweetness of sugar. With her form pleasantly filled out, her flesh was mellow like fresh butter, and pure as the diamond.

As to her vulva, it was white, prominent, round as an arch; the centre of it was red, and breathed fire, without a trace of humidity; for, sweet to the touch, it was quite dry. When she walked it showed in relief like a dome or an inverted cup. In reclining it was visible between her thighs, looking like a kid couched on a hillock.

This woman was my neighbour. All the others played and laughed with me, jested with me, and met my suggestions with great pleasure. I revelled in their kisses, their close embraces and nibblings, and in sucking their lips, breasts, and necks. I had coition with all of them, except my neighbour, and it was exactly her I wanted to possess in preference to all the rest; but instead of being kind to me, she avoided me rather. When I contrived to take her aside to trifle with her and try to rouse her gaiety, and spoke to

40

her of my desires, she recited to me the following verses, the sense of which was a mystery to me.

> Among the mountain tops I saw a tent placed
>   firmly,
> Apparent to all eyes high up in mid-air.
> But, oh! the pole that held it up was gone.
> And like a vase without a handle it remained,
> With all its cords undone, its centre sinking in,
> Forming a hollow like that of a kettle.

Every time I told her of my passion she answered me with these verses, which to me were void of meaning, and to which I could make no reply, which, however, only excited my love all the more. I therefore inquired of all those I knew – amongst wise men, philosophers, and savants – the meaning, but not one of them could solve the riddle for me, so as to satisfy my heat and appease my passion.

Nevertheless I continued my investigations, when at last I heard of a savant named Abou Nouass, who lived in a far-off country, and who, I was told, was the only man capable of solving the enigma. I betook to him, apprised him of the discourses I had with the woman, and recited to him the above-mentioned verses.

Abou Nouass said to me, 'This woman loves you to the exclusion of every other man. She is very corpulent and plump.' I answered, 'It is exactly as you say. You have given her likeness as if she were before you, excepting what you say in respect of her love for me, for, until now, she has never given me any proof of it.'

'She has no husband.'

'This is so,' I said.

Then he added, 'I have reason to believe that your member is of small dimensions, and such a member cannot give her pleasure nor quench her fire; for what she wants is a lover with a member like that of an ass. Perhaps it may not be so. Tell me the truth about this!' When I had reassured him on that point, affirming that my member, which began to rise at the expression of his doubtings, was full-sized, he told me that in that case all difficulties would disappear, and explained to me the sense of the verses as follows:'

The *tent*, firmly planted, represents the vulva of grand dimension and placed well forward, the *mountains*, between which it rises, are the thighs. The *stake* which supported its centre and has been torn up, means that she has no husband, comparing the stake or pole that supports the tent to the virile member holding up the lips of the vulva. *She is like a vase without a handle*; this means if the pail is without a handle to hang it up by it is good for nothing, the pail representing the vulva, and the handle the verge. *The cords are undone and its centre is sinking in*; that is to say, as the tent without a supporting pole caves in at the centre, inferior in this respect to the vault which remains upright without support, so can the woman who has no husband not enjoy complete happiness. From the words, *It forms a hollow like that of a kettle*, you may judge how lascivious God has made that woman in her comparisons; she likens her vulva to a kettle, which serves to prepare the *tserid*. Listen; if the *tserid* is placed in the kettle, to turn out well it must be stirred by means of a *medeleuk* long and solid, whilst the kettle is steadied by the feet and hands. Only in that way can it be properly prepared. It cannot be done with a small spoon; the cook would burn her hands, owing to the shortness of the handle, and the dish would not be well prepared. This is the symbol of this woman's nature, O Djoâidi. If your member has not the dimensions of a respectable *medeleuk*, serviceable for the good preparation of the *tserid*, it will not give her satisfaction, and, moreover, if you do not hold her close to your chest, enlacing her with your hands and feet, it is useless to solicit her favours; finally if you let her consume herself by her own fire, like the bottom of the kettle which gets burnt if the *medeleuk* is not stirred upon it, you will not gratify her desire by the result.

You see now what prevented her from acceding to your wishes; she was afraid that you would not be able to quench her flame after having fanned it.

'But what is the name of this woman, O Djoâidi?'

'Fadehat el Djemal (the sunrise of beauty),' I replied.

'Return to her,' said the sage, 'and take her these verses, and your affair will come to a happy issue, please God! You will then come back to me, and inform me of what will have come to pass between you two.'

I gave my promise, and Abou Nouass recited to me the following lines:

Have patience now, O Fadehat el Djemal,
I understand your words, and all shall see how I obey
    them.
O you! beloved and cherished by whoever
Can revel in your charms and glory in them!
O apple of my eye! You thought I was embarrassed
About the answer which I had to give you.
Yes, certainly! It was the love I bore you.
Made me look foolish in the eyes of all you know.
They thought I was possessed of a demon;
Called me a Merry Andrew and buffoon.
For God! What of buffoonery I've got,
        Should it be that
No other member is like mine? Here! see it, measure it!
What woman tastes it falls in love with me,
In violent love. It is a well known fact
That you from far may see it like a column.
If it erects itself it lifts my robe and shames me.
Now take it kindly, put it in your tent,
Which is between the well known mountains placed.
It will be quite at home there, you will find it
Not softening while inside, but sticking like a nail;
Take it to form a handle to your vase.
Come and examine it, and notice well

43

How vigorous it is and long in its erection!
If you but want a proper *medeleuk*,
A *medeleuk* to use between your thighs,
Take this to stir the centre of your kettle.
It will do good to you, O mistress mine!
Your kettle be it plated will be satisfied!

Having learnt these verses by heart, I took my leave of Abou Nouass and returned to Fadehat el Djemal. She was, as usual, alone. I gave a slight knock at her door; she came out at once, beautiful as the rising sun, and coming up to me, she said, 'Oh! enemy of God, what business has brought you here to me at this time?'

I answered her, 'O my mistress! a business of great importance.'

'Explain yourself, and I will see whether I can help you,' she said.

'I shall not speak to you about it until the door is locked,' I answered.

'Your boldness today is very great,' she said.

And I, 'True, O my mistress! boldness is one of my qualities.'

She then addressed me thus, 'O enemy of yourself! O you most miserable of your race! If I were to lock the door, and you have nothing wherewith to satisfy my desires, what should I do with you? face of a Jew!'

'You will let me share your couch, and grant me your favours.'

She began to laugh; and after we had entered the house, she told a slave to lock the house door. As usual, I asked her to respond to my proposals; she then recited to me again the above mentioned verses. When she had finished I began to recite to her those which Abou Nouass had taught me.

As I proceeded I saw her more and more moved, I observed her giving way, to yawn, to stretch herself, to sigh. I knew now I should arrive at the desired result. When I had finished my member was in such a state of erection that it became like a pillar, still lengthening. When Fadehat el Djemal saw it in that condition she precipitated herself upon it, took it into her hands, and drew it towards her thighs. I then said, 'O apple of my eyes! this may not be done here, let us go into your chamber.'

She replied, 'Leave me alone, O son of a debauched woman! Before God! I am losing my senses in seeing your member getting longer and longer, and lifting your robe. Oh, what a member! I never saw a finer one! Let it penetrate into this delicious, plump vulva, which maddens all who heard it described; for the sake of which so many died of love; and of which your superiors and masters themselves could not get possession.'

I repeated, 'I shall not do it anywhere else than in your chamber.'

She answered, 'If you do not enter this minute this tender vulva I shall die.'

As I still insisted upon repairing to her room, she cried, 'No, it is quite impossible; I cannot wait so long!'

I saw in fact her lips tremble, her eyes filling with tears. A general tremor ran over her, she changed colour, and laid herself down upon her back, baring her thighs, the whiteness of which made her flesh appear like crystal tinged with carmine.

Then I examined her vulva – a white cupola with a purple centre, soft and charming. It opened like that of a mare on the approach of a stallion.

At that moment she seized my member and kissed it, saying, 'By the religion of my father! it must penetrate into my vulva!' and drawing nearer to me she pulled it towards her vagina.

I now hesitated no longer to assist her with my member, and placed it against the entrance to her vulva. As soon as the head of my member touched the lips, the whole body of Fadehat el Djemal trembled with excitement. Sighing and sobbing, she held me pressed to her bosom.

Again I profited by this moment to admire the beauties of her vulva. It was magnificent, its purple centre setting off its whiteness all the more. It was round, and without any imperfection; projecting like a splendidly curved dome over her belly. In one word, it was a masterpiece of creation as fine as could be seen. The blessing of God, the best creator, upon it.

And the woman who possessed this wonder had in her time no superior.

Seeing her then in such transports, trembling like a bird, the throat of which is being cut, I pushed my dart into her. But thinking she might not be able to take in the whole of my member, I had entered cautiously, but she moved her buttocks furiously, saying to me, 'This is not enough for my contentment.' Making a strong push, I lodged my member completely in her, which made her utter a painful cry, but the moment after she moved with greater fury than before. She cried, 'Do not miss the corners, neither high nor low, but above all things do not neglect the centre! The centre!' she repeated. 'If you feel it coming, let it go into my matrix so as to extinguish my fire.' Then we moved alternately in and out, which was delicious. Our legs were interlaced, our muscles unbent, and so we went on with kisses and claspings until the crisis came upon us simultaneously. We then rested and took breath after this mutual conflict.

I wanted to with-draw my member, but she would not consent to this and begged of me not to take it out. I acceded to her wish, but a moment later she took it out herself, dried it, and replaced it in her vulva. We renewed our game, kissing, pressing, and moving in rhythm. After a short time, we rose and entered her chamber, without having this time accomplished the enjoyment. She gave me now a piece of an aromatic root, which she recommended me to keep in my mouth, assuring me that as long as I had it there my member would remain on the alert. Then she asked me to lie down, which I did. She mounted upon me, and taking my member into her hands, she made it enter entirely into her vagina. I was astonished at the vigour of her vulva and at the heat emitted from it. The opening of her matrix in particular excited my admiration. I never had any experience like it; it closely clasped my member and pinched the gland.

With the exception of Fadehat el Djemal no woman had until then taken in my member to its full length. She was able to do so, I believe, owing to her being very plump and corpulent, and her vulva being large and deep.

Fadehat el Djemal, astride upon me, began to rise and descend; she kept crying out, wept, went slower, then accelerated her movements again, ceased to move altogether; when part of my member became visible she looked at it, then took it out altogether to examine it closely, then plunged it in again until it had disappeared completely. So she continued until the enjoyment overcame her again. At last, having dismounted from me, she now laid herself down, and asked me to get on to her. I did so, and she introduced my member entirely into her vulva.

We thus continued our caresses, changing our positions in turns, until night came on. I thought it proper to show a wish to go now, but she would not agree to this, and I had to give her my word that I would remain. I said to myself. 'This woman will not let me go at any price, but when daylight comes God will advise me.' I remained with her, and all night long we kept caressing each other, and took but scanty rest.

I counted that during that day and night, I accomplished twenty-seven times the act of coition, and I became afraid that I should nevermore be able to leave the house of that woman.

Having at last made good my escape, I went to visit Abou Nouass again, and informed him of all that happened. He was surprised and stupefied, and his first words were, 'O Djoâidi, you can have neither authority nor power over such a woman, and she would make you do penance for all the pleasure you have had with other women!'

However, Fadehat el Djemal proposed to me to become her legitimate husband, in order to put a stop to the vexatious rumours that were circulating about her conduct. I, on the other hand, was only on the look-out for adultery. Asking the advice of Abou Nouass about it, he told me, 'If you marry Fadehat el Djemal you will ruin your health, and God will with-draw his protection from you, and the worst of all will be that she will cuckold you, for she is insatiable with respect to the coitus, and would cover you with shame.' And I answered him, 'Such is the nature of women; they are insatiable as far as their vulvas are concerned, and so long as their lust is satisfied they do not care whether it be with a buffoon, a negro, a valet, or even with a man that is despised and reprobated by society.'

On this occasion Abou Nouass depicted the character of women in the following verses:

Women are demons, and were born as such;
No one can trust them, as is known to all;
If they love a man, it is only out of caprice;
And he to whom they are most cruel loves them most.
Beings full of treachery and trickery, I aver
The man that loves you truly is a lost man;
He who believes me not can prove my word
By letting woman's love get hold of him for years!
If in your own generous mood you have given them
Your all and everything for years and years,
They will say afterwards, 'I swear by God! my eyes
Have never seen a thing he gave me!'
After you have impoverished yourself for their sake,
Their cry from day to day will be for ever 'Give!
Give man, Get up and buy and borrow.'
If they cannot profit by you they'll turn against you;
They will tell lies about you and calumniate you.
They do not recoil to use a slave in the master's absence,
If once their passions are aroused, and they play tricks;
Assuredly, if once their vulva is in rut,
They only think of getting in some member in erection.

Preserve us, God! from woman's trickery;
And of old women in particular. So be it.

The history of Zohra

The *Cheikh*, the protector of religion (God, the Highest,
be good to him!) records, that there lived once in remote
antiquity an illustrious King, who had numerous armies and
immense riches.

This King had seven daughters remarkable for their
beauty and perfections. These seven had been born one
after another, without any male infant between them.

The Kings of the time wanted them in marriage, but
they refused to be married. They wore men's clothing,
rode on magnificent horses covered with gold-embroidered
trappings, knew how to handle the sword and the spear, and
bore men down in single combat. Each of them possessed
a splendid palace with the servants and slaves necessary for
such service, for the preparation of meat and drink, and
other necessities of that kind.

Whenever a marriage-offer for one of them was presented
to the King, he never failed to consult with her about it; but
they always answered. 'That shall never be.'

Different conclusions were drawn from these refusals;
some in a good sense, some in a bad one.

For a long time no positive information could be gathered
of the reasons for this conduct, and the daughters persevered
in acting in the same manner until the death of their father.
Then the oldest of them was called upon to succeed him,
and received the oath of fidelity from all his subjects.
This accession to the throne resounded through all the
countries.

The name of the eldest sister was Fouzel Djemal (the
flower of beauty); the second was called Soltana el Agmar
(the queen of moons); the third, Bediâat el Djemal (the
incomparable in beauty); the fourth, Ouarda (the rose); the

fifth, Mahmouda (the praiseworthy); the sixth, Kamela (the perfect); and, finally, the seventh, Zohra (the beauty).

Zohra, the youngest, was at the same time the most intelligent and judicious.

She was passionately fond of the chase, and one day as she was riding through the fields she met on her way a cavalier, who saluted her, and she returned his salute; she had some twenty men in her service with her. The cavalier thought it was the voice of a woman he had heard, but as Zohra's face was covered by a flap of her *haïk*, he was not certain, and said to himself, 'I would like to know whether this is a woman or a man.' He asked one of the princess's servants, who dissipated his doubts. Approaching Zohra, he then conversed pleasantly with her till they made a halt for breakfast. He sat down near her to partake of the repast.

Disappointing the hopes of the cavalier, the princess did not uncover her face, and, pleading that she was fasting, ate nothing. He could not help admiring secretly her hand, the gracefulness of her waist, and the amorous expression of her eyes. His heart was seized with a violent love.

The following conversation took place between them:

The Cavalier: 'Is your heart insensible for friendship?'

Zohra: 'It is not proper for a man to feel friendship for a woman; for if their hearts once incline towards each other, libidinous desires will soon invade them, and with Satan enticing them to do wrong, their fall is soon known by everyone.'

The Cavalier: 'It is not so, when the affection is true and their intercourse pure without infidelity or treachery.'

Zohra: 'If a woman gives way to the affection she feels for à man, she becomes an object of slander for the whole world, and of general contempt, whence nothing arises but trouble and regrets.'

The Cavalier: 'But our love will remain secret, and in this retired spot, which may serve us as our place of meeting, we shall have intercourse together unknown to all.'

50

Zohra: 'That may not be. Besides, it could not so easily be done, we should soon be suspected, and the eyes of the whole world would be turned upon us.'

The Cavalier: 'But love, love is the source of life. The happiness, that is, the meeting, the embraces, the caresses of lovers. The sacrifice of the fortune, and even of the life for your love.'

Zohra: 'These words are impregnated with love, and your smile is seductive; but you would do better to refrain from similar conversation.'

The Cavalier: 'Your word is emerald and your counsels are sincere. But love has now taken root in my heart, and no one is able to tear it out. If you drive me from you I shall assuredly die.'

Zohra: 'For all that you must return to your place and I to mine. If it pleases God we shall meet again.'

They then separated, bidding each other adieu, and returned each of them to their dwelling.

The cavalier's name was Abou el Heïdja. His father, Kheiroun, was a great merchant and immensely rich, whose habitation stood isolated beyond the estate of the princess, a day's journey distant from her castle. Abou el Heïdja returned home, could not rest, and put on again his *temeur* when the night fell, took a black turban, and buckled his sword on under his *temeur*. Then he mounted his horse, and, accompanied by his favourite negro, Mimoun, he rode away secretly under the cover of night.

They travelled all night without stopping until, on the approach of daylight, the dawn came upon them in sight of Zohra's castle. They then made a halt among the hills, and entered with their horses into a cavern which they found there.

Abou el Heïdja left the negro in charge of the horses, and went in the direction of the castle, in order to examine its approaches; he found it surrounded by a very high wall. Not being able to get into it, he retired to some distance to watch those who came out. But the whole day passed away and he saw no one come out.

After sunset he sat himself down at the entrance of the cavern and kept on the watch until midnight; then sleep overcame him.

He was lying asleep with his head on Mimoun's knee, when the latter suddenly awakened him. 'What is it?' he asked. 'O my master,' said Mimoun, 'I have heard some noise in the cavern, and I saw the glimmer of a light.' He rose at once, and looking attentively, he perceived indeed a light, towards which he went, and which guided him to a recess in the cavern. Having ordered the negro to wait for him while he was going to find out where it proceeded from, he took his sabre and penetrated deeper into the cavern. He discovered a subterranean vault, into which he descended.

The road to it was nearly impracticable, on account of the stones which encumbered it. He contrived, however, after much trouble to reach a kind of crevice, through which the light shone which he had perceived. Looking through it, he saw the princess Zohra, surrounded by about a hundred virgins. They were in a magnificent palace dug out in the heart of the mountain, splendidly furnished and resplendent with gold everywhere. The maidens were eating and drinking and enjoying the pleasures of the table.

Abou el Heïdja said to himself, 'Alas! I have no companion to assist me at this difficult moment.' Under the influence of this reflection, he returned to his servant, Mimoun, and said to him, 'Go to my brother before God, Abou el Heïloukh, and tell him to come here to me as quickly as he can.' The servant forthwith mounted upon his horse, and rode through the remainder of the night.

Of all his friends, Abou el Heïloukh was the one whom Abou el Heïdja liked best; he was the son of the Vizir. This young man and Abou el Heïdja and the negro, Mimoun, passed as the three strongest and most fearless men of their time, and no one ever succeeded in overcoming them in combat.

When the negro Mimoun came to his master's friend, and had told him what had happened, the latter said, 'Certainly, we belong to God and shall return to him.' Then he took his sabre, mounted his horse, and taking his favourite negro with him, he made his way, with Mimoun, to the cavern.

Aboul el Heïdja came out to meet him and bid him welcome, and having informed him of the love he bore to Zohra, he told him of his resolution to penetrate forcibly into the palace, of the circumstances under which he had taken refuge in the cavern, and the marvellous scene he had witnessed while there. Abou el Heïloukh was dumb with surprise.

At nightfall they heard singing, boisterous laughter, and animated talking. Abou el Heïdja said to his friend, 'Go to the end of the subterranean passage and look. You will then make excuse for the love of your brother.' Abou el Heïloukh stealing softly down to the lower end of the grotto, looked into the interior of the palace, and was enchanted with the sight of these virgins and their charms. 'O brother,' he asked, 'which among these women is Zohra?'

Abou el Heïdja answered, 'The one with the irreproach-able shape, whose smile is irresistible, whose cheeks are roses, and whose forehead is resplendently white, whose head is encircled by a crown of pearls, and whose garments sparkle with gold. She is seated on a throne incrusted with rare stones and nails of silver, and she is leaning her head upon her hand.'

'I have observed her of all the others,' said Abou el Heïloukh, as though she were a standard or a blazing torch. But, O my brother, let me draw your attention to a matter which appears not to have struck you.' 'What is it?' asked Abou el Heïdja. His friend replied, 'It is very certain, O my brother, that licentiousness reigns in this palace. Observe that these people come here only at night time, and that this is a retired place. There is every reason to believe that it is exclusively consecrated to feasting, drinking, and debauchery, and if it was your idea that you could have come to her you love by any other way than the one on which we are now, you would have found that you had deceived yourself, even if you had found means to communicate with her by the help of other people.' 'And why so?' asked Abou el Heïdja. 'Because,' said his friend, 'as far as I can see, Zohra solicits the affection of young girls, which is a proof that she can have no inclination for men, nor be responsive to their love.'

'O Abou el Heïloukh,' said Abou el Heïdja, 'I know the value of your judgment, and it is for that I have sent for you. You know that I have never hesitated to follow your advice and counsel!' 'O my brother,' said the son of the Vizir, 'if God had not guided you to this entrance of the palace, you would never have been able to approach Zohra. But from here, please God! we can find our way.'

Next morning, at sunrise, they ordered their servants to make a breach in that place, and managed to get everything out of the way that could obstruct the passage. This done they hid their horses in another cavern, safe from wild beasts and thieves; then all the four, the two masters and the two servants, entered the cavern and penetrated into the palace, each of them armed with sabre and buckler. They then closed up again the breach, and restored its former appearance.

Now they found themselves in darkness, but Abou el Heïloukh, having struck a match, lighted one of the candles, and they began to explore the palace in every sense. It seemed to them the marvel of marvels. The furniture was magnificent. Everywhere there were beds and couches of all kinds, rich candelabras, splendid lustres, sumptuous carpets, and tables covered with dishes, fruits and beverages.

When they had admired all these treasures, they went on examining the chambers, counting them. There was a great number of them, and in the last one they found a secret door, very small, and of appearance which attracted their attention. Abou el Heïloukh said, 'This is very probably the door which communicates with the palace. Come, O my brother, we will await the things that are to come in one of these chambers.' They took their position in a cabinet difficult of access, high up, and from which one could see without being seen.

So they waited till night came on. At that moment the secret door opened, giving admission to a negress carrying a torch, who set alight all the lustres and candelabra, arranged the beds, set the plates, placed all sorts of meats upon the tables, with cups and bottles, and perfumed the air with the sweetest scents.

Soon afterwards the maidens made their appearance. Their gait denoted at the same time indifference and languor. They seated themselves upon the divans, and the negress offered them meat and drink. They ate, drank, and sang melodiously.

Then the four men, seeing them giddy with wine, came down from their hiding place with their sabres in their hands, brandishing them over the heads of the maidens. They had first taken care to veil their faces with the upper part of their *haïk*.

'Who are these men,' cried Zohra, 'who are invading our dwelling under cover of the shades of the night? Have you risen out of the ground, or did you descend from the sky? What do you want?'

'Coition!' they answered.

'With whom?' asked Zohra.

'With you, O apple of my eye!' said Abou el Heïdja, advancing.

Zohra: 'Who are you?'

'I am Abou el Heïdja.'

Zohra: 'But how is it you know me?'

'It is I who met you while out hunting at such and such a place.'

Zohra: 'But what brought you hither?'

'The will of God the Highest!'

At this answer Zohra was silent, and set herself to think of a means by which she could rid herself of these intruders.

Now among the virgins that were present there were several whose vulvas were like iron barred, and whom no one had been able to deflower; there was also present a woman called Mouna (she who appeases the passion), who was insatiable as regards coition. Zohra thought to herself, 'It is only by a stratagem I can get rid of these men. By means of these women I will set them tasks which they will be unable to accomplish as conditions for my consent.' Then turning to Abou el Heïdja, she said to him, 'You will not get possession of me unless you fulfil the conditions which I shall impose upon you.' The four cavaliers at once consented to this without knowing them, and she continued, 'But, if you do not fulfil them, will you pledge your word that you will be my prisoners, and place yourselves entirely at my disposition?' 'We pledge our words!' they answered.

She made them take their oath that they would be faithful to their word, and then, placing her hand in that of Abou el Heïdja, she said to him, 'As regards you, I impose upon you the task of deflowering eighty virgins without ejaculating. Such is my will!' He answered, 'I accept.'

She let him then enter a chamber where there were several kinds of beds, and sent to him the eighty virgins in succession. Abou el Heïdja deflowered them all, and so ravished in a single night the maidenhood of eighty young girls without ejaculating the smallest drop of sperm. This extraordinary vigour filled Zohra with astonishment, and likewise all those who were present.

The princess, turning then to the negro Mimoun, asked, 'And this one, what is his name?' They said, 'Mimoun.' 'Your task shall be,' said the princess, pointing to Mouna, 'to do this woman's business without resting for fifty consecutive days; you need not ejaculate unless you like; but if the excess

56

of fatigue forces you to stop, you will not have fulfilled your obligations.' They all cried out at the hardness of such a task; but Mimoun protested, and said, 'I accept the condition, and shall come out of it with honour!' The fact was that this negro had an insatiable appetite for the coitus. Zohra told him to go with Mouna to her chamber, impressing upon the latter to let her know if the negro should exhibit the slightest trace of fatigue.

'And you, what is your name?' she asked the friend of Abou el Heïdja. 'Abou el Heïloukh,' he replied. 'Well, then, Abou el Heïloukh, what I require of you is to remain here, in the presence of these women and virgins, for thirty consecutive days with your member during this period always in erection during day and night.'

Then she said to the fourth, 'What is your name?'

'Felah (good fortune),' was his answer. 'Very well, Felah,' she said, 'you will remain at our disposition for any services which we may have to demand of you.'

However, Zohra, in order to leave no motive for any excuse, and so that she might not be accused of bad faith, had asked them, first of all, what regimen they wished to follow during the period of their trial. Aboul el Heïdja had asked for the only drink – excepting water – camel's milk with honey, and, for nourishment, chick-peas cooked with meat and abundance of onions; and, by means of these aliments he did, by the permission of God, accomplish his remarkable exploit. Abou el Heïloukh demanded, for his nourishment, onions cooked with meat, and, for drink, the juice pressed out of pounded onions mixed with honey. Mimoun, on his part, asked for yolks of eggs and bread.

However, Abou el Heïdja claimed of Zohra the favour of copulating with her on the strength of the fact that he had fulfilled his engagement. She answered him, 'Oh, impossible! the condition which you have fulfilled is inseparable from those which your companions have to comply with. The agreement must be carried out in its entirety, and you will find me true to my promise. But if one amongst you should fail in his task, you will all be my prisoners by the will of God!'

Abou el Heïdja gave way in the face of this firm resolve, and sat down amongst the girls and women, and ate and drank with them, whilst waiting for the conclusion of the tasks of his companions.

At first Zohra, feeling convinced that they would soon all be at her mercy, was all amiability and smiles. But when the twentieth day had come she began to show signs of distress; and on the thirtieth she could no longer restrain her tears. For on that day Abou el Heïloukh had finished his task, and having come out of it honourably, he took his seat by the side of his friend amongst the company, who continued to eat tranquilly and to drink abundantly.

From that time the princess, who had now no other hope than in the failure of the negro Mimoun, relied upon his becoming fatigued before he finished his work. She sent every day to Mouna for information, who sent word that the negro's vigour was constantly increasing, and she began to despair, seeing already Abou el Heïdja and Abou el Heïloukh coming off as victors in their enterprises. One day she said to the two friends, 'I have made inquiries about the negro, and Mouna has let me know that he was exhausted with fatigue.' At these words Abou el Heïdja cried, 'In the name of God! if he does not carry out his task, aye, and if he does not go beyond it for ten days longer, he shall die the vilest of deaths!'

But his zealous servant never during the period of fifty days took any rest in his work of copulation, and kept going on, besides, for ten days longer, as ordered by his master. Mouna, on her part, had the greatest satisfaction, as this feat had at last appeased her ardour for coition. Mimoun, having remained victor, could then take his seat with his companions.

Then said Abou el Heïdja to Zohra. 'See, we have fulfilled

all the conditions you have imposed upon us. It is now for you to accord me the favours which, according to our agreement, was to be the price if we succeeded.' 'It is but too true!' answered the princess, and she gave herself up to him, and he found her excelling the most excellent.

As to the negro, Mimoun, he married Mouna. Abou el Heïloukh chose, amongst all the virgins, the one whom he had found most attractive.

They all remained in the palace, giving themselves up to good cheer and all possible pleasures, until death put an end to their happy existence and dissolved their union. God be merciful to them as well as to all Mussulmans! Amen!

It is to this story that the verses cited previously make allusion. I have given it here, because it testifies to the efficacy of the dishes and remedies, the use of which I have recommended, for giving vigour for coition, and all learned men agree in acknowledging their salutary effects.

There are still other beverages of excellent virtue. I will describe the following: Take one part of the juice pressed out of pounded onions, and mix it with two parts of purified honey. Heat the mixture over a fire until the onion-juice has disappeared and the honey only remains. Then take the residue from the fire, let it get cool, and preserve it for use when wanted. Then mix of the same one *aoukia* with three *aouak* of water, and let chickpeas be macerated in this fluid for one day and one night.

This beverage is to be partaken of during winter and on going to bed. Only a small quantity is to be taken, and only for one day. The member of him who has drunk of it will not give him much rest during the night that follows. As to the man who partakes of it for several consecutive days, he will constantly have his member rigid and upright without intermission. A man with an ardent temperament ought not to make use of it, as it may give him a fever. Nor should the medicine be used three days in succession except by old or

cold-tempered men. And lastly, it should not be resorted to
in summer.

I certainly did wrong to put this book together;
But you will pardon me, nor let me pray in vain,
O God! award no punishment for this on judgment day
And thou, oh reader, hear me conjure thee to say:
    So be it!

from MEMOIRS OF A WOMAN OF PLEASURE

John Cleland

Popularly known as 'Fanny Hill', John Cleland's famous erotic novel, Memoirs of a Woman of Pleasure, *contains the following scene which is part of Fanny's grooming for her career as a whore.*

We went down the back-stairs very softly, and opening the door of a dark closet, where there was some old furniture kept, and some cases of liquor, Phoebe drew me in after her, and fastening the door upon us, we had no light but what came through a long crevice in the partition between ours and the light closet, where the scene of action lay; so that sitting on those low cases, we could, with the greatest ease, as well as clearness, see all objects (ourselves unseen), only by applying our eyes close to the crevice, where the moulding of a panel had warped, or started a little on the other side.

The young gentleman was the first person I saw, with his back directly towards me, looking at a print. Polly was not yet come: in less than a minute tho', the door opened, and she came in; and at the noise the door made he turned

61

about, and came to meet her, with an air of the greatest tenderness and satisfaction.

After saluting her, he led her to a couch that fronted us, where they both sat down, and the young Genoese help'd her to a glass of wine, with some Naples biscuit on a salver.

Presently, when they had exchanged a few kisses, and questions in broken English on one side, he began to unbutton, and, in fine, stript to his shirt.

As if this had been the signal agreed on for pulling off all their clothes, a scheme which the heat of the season perfectly favoured, Polly began to draw her pins, and as she had no stays to unlace, she was in a trice, with her gallant's officious assistance, undress'd to all but her shift.

When he saw this, his breeches were immediately loosen'd, waist and knee bands, and slipped over his ankles, clean off; his shirt collar was unbuttoned too: then, first giving Polly an encouraging kiss, he stole, as it were, the shift off the girl, who being, I suppose, broke and familiariz'd to this humour, blush'd indeed, but less than I did at the apparition of her, now standing stark-naked, just as she came out of the hands of pure nature, with her black hair loose and afloat down her dazzling white neck and shoulders, whilst the deepen'd carnation of her cheeks went off gradually into the hue of glaz'd snow: for such were the blanded tints and polish of her skin.

This girl could not be above eighteen: her face regular and sweet-featur'd, her shape exquisite; nor could I help envying her two ripe enchanting breasts, finely plump'd out in flesh, but withal so round, so firm, that they sustain'd themselves, in scorn of any stay: then their nipples, pointing different ways, mark'd their pleasing separation; beneath them lay the delicious tract of the belly, which terminated in a parting or rift scarce discernible, that modestly seem'd to retire downwards, and seek shelter between two plump fleshy thighs: the curling hair that overspread its delightful front, clothed it with the richest sable fur in the universe: in short, she was evidently a subject for the painter to court her sitting to them for a pattern of female beauty, in all the true pride and pomp of nakedness.

The young Italian (still in his shirt) stood gazing and transported at the sight of beauties that might have fir'd a dying hermit; his eager eyes devour'd her, as she shifted attitudes at his discretion: neither were his hands excluded their share of the high feast, but wander'd, on the hunt of pleasure, over every part and inch of her body, so qualified to afford the most exquisite sense of it.

In the meantime, one could not help observing the swell of his shirt before, that bolster'd out, and shewed the condition of things behind the curtain: but he soon remov'd it, by slipping his shirt over his head; and now, as to nakedness, they had nothing to reproach one another.

The young gentleman, by Phoebe's guess, was about two and twenty; tall and well limb'd. His body was finely form'd, and of a most vigorous make, square-shoulder'd, and broad-chested: his face was not remarkable in any way, but for a nose inclining to the Roman, eyes large, black, and sparkling, and a ruddiness in his cheeks that was the more a grace, for his complexion was of the brownest, not of that dusky dun colour which excludes the idea of freshness, but of that clear, olive gloss, which, glowing with life, dazzles perhaps less than fairness, and yet pleases more, when it pleases at all. His hair, being too short to tie, fell no lower than his neck, in short easy curls; and he had a few sprigs about his paps, that garnish'd his chest in a style of strength and manliness. Then his grand movement, which seem'd to rise out of a thicket of curling hair that spread from the root all round thighs and belly up to the navel, stood stiff and upright, but of a size to frighten me, by sympathy, for the small tender part which was the object of its fury, and which now lay expos'd to my fairest view; for he had, immediately on stripping off his shirt, gently push'd her down on the couch, which stood conveniently to break her willing fall. Her thighs were spread out to their utmost extension, and discovered between them the mark of the sex, the red-centred cleft of flesh, whose lips, vermilioning inwards, exprest a small ruby line in sweet miniature, such as *Guido's* touch or colouring could never attain to the life or delicacy of.

Phoebe, at this, gave me a gentle jog, to prepare me for a whispered question: whether I thought my little maiden-head was much less? But my attention was too much engross'd, too much enwrapp'd with all I saw, to be able to give her any answer.

By this time the young gentleman had changed her posture from lying breadth to length-wise on the couch: but her thighs were still spread, and the mark lay fair for him, who, now kneeling between them, display'd to us a side-view of that fierce erect machine of his, which threaten'd no less than splitting the tender victim, who lay smiling at the uplifted stroke, nor seem'd to decline it. He looked upon his weapon himself with some pleasure, and guiding it with his hand to the invisible slit, drew aside the lips, and lodg'd it (after some thrust, which Polly seem'd even to assist) about half way; but there it stuck, I suppose from its growing thickness: he draws it again, and just wetting it with spittle, re-enters, and with ease sheath'd it now up to the hilt, at which Polly gave a deep sigh, which was quite another tone than one of pain; he thrusts, she heaves, at first gently, and in a regular cadence; but presently the transport began to be too violent to observe any order or measure; their motions were too rapid, their kisses too fierce and fervent for nature to support such fury long: both seem'd to me out of themselves: their eyes darted fires: 'Oh! . . . oh! . . . I can't bear it . . . It is too much . . . I die . . . I am going . . .' were Polly's expressions of ecstasy: his joys were more silent; but soon broken murmurs, sighs heart-fetch'd, and at length a dispatching thrust, as if he would have forced himself up her body, and then motionless languor of all his limbs, all shewed that the die-away moment was come upon him; which she gave signs of joining with, by the wild throwing of her hands about, closing her eyes, and giving a deep sob, in which she seemed to expire in an agony of bliss.

When he had finish'd his stroke, and got from off her, she lay still without the last motion, breathless, as it should seem, with pleasure. He replaced her again breadth-wise on the couch, unable to sit up, with her thighs open, between which I could observe a kind of white liquid, like froth, hanging about the outward lips of that recently opened wound, which now glowed with a deeper red. Presently she gets up, and throwing her arms round him, seemed far from undelighted with the trial he had put her to, to judge at least by the fondness with which she ey'd and hung upon him.

For my part, I will not pretend to describe what I felt all over me during this scene; but from that instant, adieu all fears of what man could do unto me; they were now changed into such ardent desires, such ungovernable longings, that I could have pull'd the first of that sex that should present himself, by the sleeve, and offered him the bauble, which I now imagined the loss of would be a gain I could not too soon procure myself.

Phoebe, who had more experience, and to whom such sights were not so new, could not however be unmoved at so warm a scene; and drawing me away softly from the peep-hole, for fear of being overheard, guided me as near the door as possible, all passive and obedient to her least signal.

Here was no room either to sit or lie, but making me stand with my back towards the door, she lifted up my petticoats, and with her busy fingers fell to visit and explore that part of me, where now the heat and irritations were so violent, that I was perfectly sick and ready to die with desire; the bare touch of her finger, in that critical place, had the effect of a fire to a train, and her hand instantly made her sensible to what a pitch I was wound up and melted by the sight she had thus procured me.

from THE DELIGHTS OF VENUS

Meursius

Naked I lay, clasp'd in my Callus' arms,
  Dreading, yet longing for his sweet'ning charms;
Two burning tapers spread around their light,
And chas'd away the darkness of the night,
When Callus from my panting bosom flew,
And with him from the bed, the bed cloaths drew.
I to conceal my naked body try'd,
And what he wish'd to see, I strove to hide;
But what I held, with force he pull'd away,
I blush'd, but yet my thoughts were pleas'd to find
Myself so laid, and him I loved, so kind.
Struggling I lay, exposed to his eyes;
He view'd my breast, my belly, and my thighs,
And ev'ry part that there adjacent lies.
No part, or limb, his eager eyes escap'd,
Nay my plump buttocks too he saw and clasp'd.
He dally'd thus, thus rais'd the lustful fire
'Till modesty was vanquish'd by desire.
I then look'd up, which yet I had not done,
And saw his body naked as my own;
I saw his prick with active vigour strong,
Thick as my arm, and, 'faith, almost as long,
Of cruel smart I knew I should not fail,
Because his prick so large, my cunt so small.
He soon perceiv'd my blushings and surprize.

And straight my hand unto his prick did seize;
Which bigger grew, and did more stiffly stand,
Feeling the warmth of my enliv'ning hand.
Thus far I've told of the pleasing sight;
You know that prick our darling favorite.
    It is defin'd, a hollow boneless part
Of better use, and nobler than the heart;
With mouth, but without eyes; it has a head,
Soft as the lips, and as the cherry red;
The balls hang dangling in their hairy cods
From whence proceed the spring of tickling floods,
Good pricks should be both thick as well as tall,
Your French dildoes are a size too small.
At first they're hardly in our cunts contain'd;
For maidenheads are by much labour gain'd;
But men, well furnish'd with stout pricks, are wont
To force their passage thro' a bleeding cunt.
Man's unesteem'd, a hated monster made,
When his prick's short, and can't for favour plead.
Women do not the man, but pintle wed;
For marriage joys are centred in the bed.
Now Callus strok'd and kiss'd my milk-white breast,
He fell, and saw the beauties of the rest;
Stroking my belly down, he did descend
To the lov'd place where all his joys must end.
He seiz'd my cunt, and gently pull'd the hair;
At that I trembled; there began my fear.
My soft and yielding thighs he open forc'd;
And quite into my cunt his finger thrust;
With which he grop'd, and search'd my cunt all round,
And of a maid the certain tokens found.
Then wide as could be stretch'd, my thighs he spread,
Under my buttocks too a pillow laid,
And told me then the fairest mark was made.
Then prostrate threw himself upon my breast
That groan'd with such unusual weight opprest.
My cunt's plump lips his finger drew aside,
And then to enter, but in vain, he try'd:
His body nimbly up and down he mov'd,
Against my cunt his tarse stood.

Sharp was the pain I suffer'd, yet I bor't,
Resolving not to interrupt the sport;
When suddenly I felt the tickling seed
O'erflow my cunt, my belly, and the bed.
I saw his prick, when Callus from me rose,
Limber and weak hang down his snotty nose;
For when they fuck, their stiffness then they lose,
But soon my Callus fix'd his launce upright,
Rais'd by my hand, again prepared to fight;
Tho' then within my cunt he could not spend,
Oft times he swore the error he would mend,
And the warm juice thro' every passage send.
About my cunt I felt a burning pain,
Yet long'd with more success to try again.
Callus once more new mounted to begin,
Gave me his prick, and begg'd I'd put it in.
At first against such impudence I rail'd,
But he with moving arguments prevail'd.
He kiss'd and pray'd and would not be deny'd,
And said pricks blind, and needs must have a guide.
Where there's no path, no track, he runs astray;
But in a beaten road can find his way.
I put it in, and made the passage stretch,
Whilst he push'd on, t'enlarge the narrow breach,
His prick bore forward with such strength and pow'r,
That 'twould have made a cunt had there been none
    before.
When half was in, and but one half remain'd,
I sigh'd aloud, and of the smart complain'd
As he push'd down, the pain I sharper found,
And drew his weapon from my bleeding wound.
Callus is vex'd to lose his half-won prize,
And spews his juicy seed upon my thighs.
My hand upon my mangled cunt I laid
To feel the monstrous wound his prick had made.

Then from the window he an ointment brought,
Which his too hasty passion had forgot.
His prick smelt sweet with what he rubb'd upon't,
And seem'd as fitting for my mouth as cunt.
As soon as this was done, he made me rise,

69

And place myself upon my hands and thighs.
My head down stooping on the bed did lie,
But my round buttocks lifted were on high,
Just like a cannon plac'd against the sky.
My bloody smock he then turn'd up behind,
As if to bugger me he had design'd:
Then with his sweet and slipp'ry prick drew near,
And vig'rously he charg'd me in the rear.
His prick, as soon as to my cunt apply'd,
Up to the hilt into my cunt did slide.
He fucked, and ask'd me if my cunt was sore?
Or his prick hurt me as it did before:
    I answer'd, No, my dear; no, do not cease;
But oh! do thus as long as e'er you please.
This stroke did fully answer our intent
For at one moment both together spent
Just as we fuck'd, I cry'd, I faint, I die,
And fell down in a blissful extasy,
Kind Callus then drew out his prick, and said,
There, pretty fool, you've lost your maidenhead:

Now Callus had his rampant Fury laid,
And limber prick hung down his dangling head.
Since made a perfect woman, prick and I
Arriv'd at much familiarity.
But languishing poor prick could do no more;
Tho' not for want of will, but want of pow'r.

Tullia replies, my dear Octavia, you,
That I can teach, shall ev'ry secret know.
Come this way, I've a pretty engine here,
Which us'd to ease the torments of the fair;
And next those joys which charming Man can give,
This best a woman's passion can relieve.
This dildo 'tis, with which I oft was wont
T'asswage the raging of my lustful cunt.
For when cunts swell, and glow with strong desire,
'Tis only pricks can quench the lustful fire;
And when that's wanting, dildoes must supply
The place of pricks upon necessity.
Then on your back lie down upon the bed,

And lift your petticoats above your head;
I'll shew you a new piece of lechery,
For I'll the man, you shall the woman be.
Your thin transparent smock, my dear remove
That last bless'd cover to the scene of love,
What's this I see, you fill me with surprize,
Your charming beauties dazzle quite my eyes!
Gods! what a leg is here! what lovely thighs!
A belly too, as polish'd iv'ry white,
And then a cunt would charm an anchorite!
Oh! now I wish I were a man indeed,
That I might gain thy pretty maidenhead,
But since, my dear, I can't my wish obtain,
Let's now proceed t'instruct you in the game;
That game that brings the most substantial bliss;
For swiving of all games the sweetest is.
Ope wide your legs, and throw them round my back,
And clasp your snowy arms about my neck.
Your buttocks then move nimbly up and down,
Whilst with my hand I thrust the dildo home.
You'll feel the titulation by and by;
Have you no pleasure yet, no tickling joy?
Oh! yes, yes, now I faint, I die.

from THE MEMOIRS OF GIACOMO CASANOVA DE SEINGALT

The following account of Casanova's youthful affair with a nun, proves him to be the most rakish to roam the earth.

A man never reasons so well as when his purse is full, never shows to such advantage in society, and is never so sure to win as when it is not of vital importance to him that he should do so. The moment I regained courage and confidence I regained my luck, and whenever I gambled I was sure to win. I paid my debts to all, including the usurer, redeemed my jewels, and was once more able to make a decent figure in the world.

My head was quite full of my dear C.C. I commissioned a Piedmontese, a young artist whom I met at the fair in Venice, to paint my portrait – it was a very small miniature; he then painted a Saint Catherine of the same dimensions, and a clever Venetian jeweller mounted them both in a ring. One could only see the Saint Catherine, but, with a pin, press an almost imperceptible blue dot on the white enamel which surrounded it, and back flew a spring, and my portrait was revealed!

The messenger from the convent brought me a letter, which I read eagerly. C.C. told me that if on a certain day I would go to Murano and post myself outside the convent church I should see her mother, and that I had better speak to her.

Following her instructions, I saw the good lady appear and enter the church. I passed in with her, and kneeling at her side, I told her I should always be faithful to her daughter, and asked her if she was going to see her.

'I am going to see her on Sunday,' she replied, 'and I will speak of you to her. She will be pleased, I know, to hear of you.'

'Will you give her this ring? It is the picture of her patron saint; and tell her to wear it always, tell her to pray to it every day, for without that she can never be my wife. Tell her that for my part I pray to Saint James and recite a *Credo* while thinking of her.'

The good lady was enchanted with my pious sentiments, and promised to do what I asked. I gave her ten sequins, which I begged her to remit to C.C. as pocket-money: she accepted them, at the same time mentioning that her father provided C.C. with everything needful.

My greatest pleasure in life now was the Wednesday letter, which the old messenger, Laura, brought me faithfully. After a rather serious malady from which she had suffered, and which, with the aid of Laura, she had been able to keep from the knowledge of the Mother Superior, C.C. was more beautiful than ever, old Laura assured me. I longed for a sight of her. An unexpected chance presented itself. One of the novices was to take the veil, a ceremony which always attracted spectators from the outside world. As the nuns on these occasions receive many visitors, it was probable that the boarders also might be allowed to go to the parlour. I ran no risk of being especially remarked. I should pass in

73

the crowd. So without saying a word to anyone, I presented myself at the convent church and after the investiture walked into the parlour with the rest. I got within four paces of my dear little wife and had the pleasure of seeing her eyes fixed on me in a kind of ecstasy. I noticed that she was taller and more womanly, and consequently more beautiful, than before. After this I attended Mass at her church regularly on Sundays and feast-days. I could not see her, but I knew that she saw me, and that the sight gave her great happiness. There was not much danger of my being recognised, as the church was attended only by the people from Murano; nevertheless, I was on my guard, for I knew her father wished her to forget me, and that he would remove her to the ends of the earth if he discovered that I knew her whereabouts.

I was not afraid of the 'bon bourgeois' of Murano; but I little knew the craft and subtlety of the holy daughters of the Lord! Nor did I think that there was anything particularly noticeable about me, or attractive to the inhabitants of a convent. I was still unversed in the ways of womanly curiosity, and the little machinations indulged in by vacant hearts and intelligences. I soon learnt to know them better.

My beloved C.C. wrote to me one day and informed me that I had become the puzzle of the whole community, that one and all, boarders and nuns, even the oldest among them, were busy guessing who I could possibly be. They waited for my appearance, they made signs to each other when I came in, when I took holy water, when I knelt down or stood up, my slightest action was of interest to them. They noticed that I never tried to peer behind the grating where they were, or paid attention to any woman in the church; from which the old ones gathered that I was in terrible trouble, and the young ones that I was melancholy or misanthropical.

It was a fact that I was withering and pining away under the ascetic regimen it had pleased me to impose on myself. I was made to make some woman happy, and

74

to be happy with her. I threw myself into play and won as a rule; nevertheless, I grew thinner and thinner, a daily prey to *ennui*.

On All Saints' Day 1753, after having heard Mass, I was getting into my gondola to return to Venice when a woman rather like old Laura passed close to me, looked at me, and dropped a letter. When she saw that I had picked it up she went on quietly. There was no address on it, and the seal represented a running knot. It was as follows:

'A nun, who for the last two months has seen you in her convent church, wishes to make your acquaintance. A pamphlet which you lost has come by chance into her hands, and leads her to believe that you speak French, but if you prefer you can answer this in Italian. If you care to be presented to her she will give you the name of a certain lady who will bring you to the parlour. If you would rather, the nun will appoint a place in Murano where you can meet her any night you choose. You can sup with her, or you can leave after a quarter of an hour's conversation, as you will; or if you prefer to invite her to sup with you in Venice, fix an hour and a place and she will meet you. She will be masked, and you must come masked also, and alone. You must understand that were she not convinced of the generosity of your heart, and the elevation of your sentiments, she would never have ventured to take a step which might lead you to take an unfavourable view of her.'

The tone of the letter, which I give word for word, surprised me more than the proposition itself. It seemed to bespeak a mad woman, yet its strangeness and a sort of dignity there was about it attracted me. It occurred to me that the writer might be the nun who gave French lessons to my friend, and of whom she had often spoken, describing her as beautiful, rich, and generous. My dear C.C. might have been indiscreet – perhaps this was a trap? A thousand theories occurred to me, but I discarded all those unfavourable to a project which, as a matter of fact, pleased me mightily. This is how I replied:

'I answer you in French, madam, hoping my letter will be as clear to you as yours to me. What you say is interesting, but you will understand, madam, that not being a coxcomb, I am a little apprehensive of your being about to practise some mystification on me, prejudicial to my honour. If it be really true that you consider me worthy of the honour of knowing you personally, I will hasten to obey your command. Of the three means you offer me, I choose the first; I will accompany the lady to the parlour, but as she will not know me, she cannot present me to you. Do not judge me harshly, madam, if I tell you I must conceal my name from you. I will not seek to know yours until you think fit to disclose it to me. I may mention by the way that I am a Venetian, and free in every sense of the word. I beg you to believe in my sincerity, and to measure my impatience by your own. I will go tomorrow at the same hour to the place where I received your first letter, in hope of a reply to this.'

The next day my female Mercury handed me the following:

'I see, sir, that I have not been mistaken in you. Of my three propositions you have chosen the one which does the most honour to your head and heart. I respect the reasons which prevent you from making yourself known to me. I enclose a note for the Countess of S—, which I beg you to read before presenting. She will tell you when you can accompany her here. She will not put any questions to you, but you will learn my name; and our acquaintance once made, you can come here masked as her friend, and ask for me whenever you choose. If this arrangement suits you, tell the messenger that there is no answer.'

The note to the countess, which she enclosed, was very brief:

'My dear friend, come and see me when you have

time, and tell the masked bearer of this note when you intend coming, so that he may accompany you. Your convenience will be his, Adieu. You will immensely oblige.   YOUR FRIEND.

I was lost in admiration of the high development of the spirit of intrigue which pervaded the nun's letter. She was so sure that, having seen her once, I should be desirous of seeing her again that I was convinced she must be young and pretty. She was too clever in intrigue to be a novice, and I was anxious to see what manner of nun this could be who offered so casually to sup with me in Venice. I could not understand how she could violate the sanctity of her cloister with such ease.

At three o'clock that afternoon I called on the countess. She asked me to fetch her the next day at the same hour, after which we bowed gravely to one another and parted. The countess was a most distinguished-looking woman, a little past her prime, but still beautiful. The next day being Sunday I went to Mass, dressed with much elegance and with my hair carefully arranged. I was already faithless in imagination to my dear C.C., for I thought more of this opportunity of showing myself off to my unknown nun than to my charming little wife. In the afternoon I called, wearing a mask, for the countess. We took a two-oared gondola and arrived at the convent without having spoken of anything but the weather.

The countess asked for 'M.M.' at the convent gate. This name astonished me, for it was that of a well-known person. We were shown into a parlour, and in a few moments a nun appeared at the grating: she pressed a button and a sort of window opened, through which the two friends embraced. The countess sat facing the nun, and I remained a little in the back-ground. In this way I was able to observe at my ease one of the most lovely women I have ever seen. She was about twenty-two or twenty-three years old, considerably above the average height; her complexion was fair, almost

77

to pallor; her manners full of dignity and decision, yet at the same time modest and reserved; her great eyes were a brilliant blue, and her teeth like two rows of pearls; her hand and arm, which were bare to the elbow, were exquisitely moulded. The two friends talked together in a low voice for about a quarter of an hour. I could not hear what they said, for delicacy compelled me to remain at some distance from them; then, having embraced each other again, the nun turned on her heel and walked away without looking at me.

On the way back to Venice the countess said: 'M.M. is very lovely, and very clever too.'

'So I could see, and I could imagine.'

'She did not say a word to you?'

'As I did not ask you to present me, she punished me by pretending not to see that I was there.'

When we reached the countess's house she made me a deep curtsy, saying, 'Farewell, sir,' in a tone meant to convey to me that I must not seek to continue her acquaintance. I did not particularly wish to do so; and I left her to wonder over this strange adventure and its possible *dénouement*.

I was at a loss to account for the complete liberty enjoyed by my beautiful nun. A casino at Murano, the power to sup alone at Venice with a young man! She must have an official lover; I was only her caprice! I loved C.C. still; and it seemed to me that an infidelity of this kind, should it ever come to pass, ought to be readily condoned by her, since it would effectually palliate the *ennui* in which I languished for her sake, and preserve me to her against her liberation. Among my intimate friends at this time was Countess Coronini, a relation of M. Dandolo's; this lady, who had been a celebrated beauty in her day, had retired to the Convent of Saint Justine. She still maintained relations with the world; and was visited by all the foreign ambassadors and principal personages of Venice. Within the walls of her convent the countess managed to be aware of everything that went on in the city, and sometimes more. I was sure that I should learn something from her about M.M., if I questioned her adroitly. So I resolved to pay my respects the day after I had seen the beautiful nun.

After a few ordinary remarks I led the conversation to the different Venetian convents. We spoke of a certain nun called Celsi, who had so much intelligence and tact that, although she was ugly, she exerted an immense influence; from her we passed to others who were credited with a taste for intrigue. I spoke of M.M., saying that she must certainly be of this category, but that no one knew for certain. The countess replied with a smile that some people were better informed than others. 'I cannot understand,' she said, 'why she should have taken the veil. She was beautiful, young, rich, free, cultivated, and a good, clear reasoner; there was no physical or moral reason for such a step; it was pure caprice.'

'Do you think she is happy, madame?'

'Yes, if she has not already rued the step she took, or if she does not rue it some day; but if that happens I believe she will be discreet enough to conceal her unhappiness.'

I was sure from the mysterious manner of the countess that she knew more than she would say, and I determined to pay another visit to the convent at Murano, masked, of course. I rang the bell with a beating heart, and asked if I could see M.M., as I had a message to deliver to her from the Countess S. I waited for more than an hour, then a toothless old nun came and told me that Mother M.M. was engaged for the whole day!

A rake is exposed to these sudden and terrible checks. Such moments are humiliating, they are deadly. My concentrated despair nearly approached madness. I saw that I had been tricked, and that M.M. must be either the most impudent or the most foolish of women, for the two letters I had in her own hand were enough to ruin her. In this disposition I wrote her several missives, all of which, however, I had the good sense to destroy. When I was calmer I sent her a few lines, saying that she would not see me again at Mass, for reasons she could easily divine. I enclosed her two letters to me, and despatched the packet by a *fourlan*, a sort of confidential commissioner, much employed in Venice in those days, on whose discretion and despatch one could rely, as one used to count on Savoyards of Paris. I also wrote to C.C., telling her that imperative reasons prevented me from ever going to Mass again at her convent.

Ten days after, as I was leaving the opera, the same *fourlan* accosted me.

'God be praised! I have found you; I took your letter, and I have one to give you in exchange, but as you left me no address, I have been looking for you ever since; I only recognised you now by the buckles of your shoes.'

'Where is the letter?'

'At home, under lock and key, for I am afraid of losing it, if you will wait for me an instant in the café I will fetch it.'

I entered the café, and he returned with a big packet, which contained, first, the two letters I had returned, and secondly, a long letter from M.M. She told me that the old nun had not delivered the message correctly; she should have said, 'Mother M.M. *is ill*,' not 'engaged': she explained why she had thought it better not to speak to me in the presence of her friend, and begged me, whatever I might think of her, not to condemn her unheard, but to grant her at least one more interview. And this precious letter had been lying for ten days at the *fourlan's* lodgings!

I ordered him to take my answer to Murano before dawn next day, so that M. M. might have it when she awoke. I told her that at eleven o'clock that morning I would be at her feet, imploring her pardon for having misjudged her.

I was punctual next day. As soon as I saw M.M. at the grating I threw myself on my knees, but she begged me to rise. She was blushing deeply, and looked more beautiful than when I had first seen her.

'Our friendship,' she said, 'has begun stormily, let us hope that in the future it will enjoy peace. This is the first time that we have spoken to each other, but after what has passed, we seem like old friends.'

'When may I have the pleasure of expressing, freely and unrestrainedly, my sentiments towards you?'

'We will have supper together at my little countryhouse whenever you like, only you must let me know two days in advance; or if you prefer, I will sup with you in Venice, if that is more convenient for you.'

'You are an angel; let us be frank with one another. Let me tell you that I am in easy circumstances, and that so far from fearing expense, I delight in it; and furthermore, that everything I have belongs to the woman I adore.'

'This confidence, dear friend, is very flattering; let me tell you in my turn that I, too, am rich, and all my wealth is at my lover's service.'

'And – have you no lover but me?'

'I have a friend who is also absolutely my master – it is to him I owe my wealth. The day after tomorrow I will tell you more. Is there not also a woman whom you love?'

'Yes; but, alas! she was violently torn from me, and for six months I have lived a life of absolute celibacy.'

'Do you still love her?'

'Yes; when I think of her. She is like you, charming and attractive; yet I foresee that you will make me forget her.'

'I warn you that if you once allow me to take her place in your heart no power on earth can tear me from thence.'

'And what will your lover say?'

'He will be happy to see me happy. He is like that. Now answer me. What sort of life do you lead in Venice?'

'Society, the play, gaming-tables, where I fight with fortune, sometimes winning, sometimes losing.'

'Do you go to any of the foreign ministers' houses?'

'I knew them abroad. For instance, I met the Spanish ambassador in Parma, the Austrian ambassador in Vienna, and I knew the French ambassador in Paris about two years ago.'

She interrupted me, saying quickly: 'It is noon, my dear friend, we must part. Come the day after tomorrow at the same time, and I will arrange for us to sup together that evening.'

She came to the opening in the grating. I stood where the Countess S. had stood, and I kissed her passionately and left her.

I passed the next two days in a state of feverish impatience, which prevented me from sleeping or eating. Over and above birth, beauty, and wit, my new conquest possessed an additional charm. She was forbidden fruit. I was about to become the rival of the Church.

Had my reason not been overcome by passion, I should have known that this nun in nowise differed from the other women that I had loved, but for the moment she queened it over them all.

Animal nature secures for itself instinctively the three means necessary for its perpetuation.

With these three instinctive needs nature has endowed all creatures: First, the instinct of selfnourishment. Secondly, the instinct of propagation. Thirdly, the instinct of destruction. Outside these general laws, however, each species has its own special idiosyncrasy. These three sensations – hunger, desire, and hatred – are habits, merely, with animals. Man alone is endowed with perfect organs, capable of perfect pleasure. He can seek, foresee, compose, perfect, and extend by reflection and recollection.

Dear reader, be patient with me, who am today only the shadow of the gay, the fascinating, the dashing Casanova that was. I love to dwell on memories of myself.

Man becomes like an animal when he gives way to these three instincts without reference to reason and judgment; but when mind controls matter, then these instincts procure for us the most complete happiness we are capable of

82

knowing. The voluptuous but intelligent man disdains gluttony, rejects luxury with contempt; the brutal lusts of vengeance, which are evoked by a paroxysm of rage, are repulsive to him; he is dainty, satisfies his appetite in accordance with his temperament; he is amorous, but happy only if happiness is mutual. He seeks to be revenged for insult, but plans the method of it carefully, and in cold blood. If he is sometimes more cruel than the brute, he is also sometimes more noble, and finds vengeance in forgiveness. These three operations are the work of the soul, which for its own pleasure becomes the minister of the passions. We endure hunger the better to enjoy the satisfaction of our appetite; we put off the perfect enjoyment of love to make it more intense; we postpone a reprisal to make it the more sure. It is also true that we sometimes die from indigestion, that we are mistaken in our affections, and that the individual we wish to exterminate escapes us; but nothing is perfect in this world, and we must accept all risks.

M.M. Again

I rang the convent bell as the clock struck ten, the hour appointed for our meeting.

'Good heavens! my friend,' were the beautiful nun's first words, 'are you ill?'

'I can neither eat nor sleep, and if our appointment tonight is put off I will not answer for my life.'

'It will not be put off. Here is the key of my little house; you will find someone there, for we cannot do without servants, but no one will speak to you, and you need speak to no one. You will go masked, and two hours after sunset. There is a staircase opposite the entrance, and at the top of the stairs you will see, by the light of a lanthorn, a green door, which you will open, it will lead you into a suite of apartments where, if I am not already there, you must wait for me. You will find fire and lights and some entertaining books; take off your mask and make yourself comfortable.'

I asked this strange woman, as I took the key she offered me, if she would come dressed in her religious habit.

'I always go out dressed as a nun,' she answered, 'but I have a complete wardrobe in my casino, and can transform myself into a woman of the world when I choose.'

'I hope you will keep on your habit.'

'Why, may I ask?'

'Because I like to see you in it.'

'Ha! ha! I understand. You think I have a cropped head, it frightens you; but be easy, I have a wig which looks perfectly natural.'

'Heavens! don't mention it; the thought of a wig is terrible. Never fear but what I shall find you charming in any guise, but I beseech you not to put that cruel wig on in my presence. Ah! now I have offended you. I was a fool to speak of it. Tell me, how do you propose to leave the convent?'

'I have the key of a room which opens on to the banks of the river, and I have confidence in the lay sister who waits on me.'

'And the gondoliers?'

'They are the servants of my friend, and he is responsible for their fidelity.'

'What a strange man your friend must be! I fancy he is very old?'

'You are mistaken. He is not yet forty, and most attractive. He has birth, beauty, breeding, wit, sweetness of character – he is all a woman could possibly wish. It is a year since he assumed possession of me, and you are the first caprice I have permitted myself. He knows about you, for I showed him your letters and mine. He was surprised at first, and then he laughed. He believes you are a Frenchman, though you say you are a Venetian; but do not be alarmed, he will take no steps to find out who you are until you tell him yourself.'

I followed her instructions carefully, and found all as she had said: the quiet secluded cottage – casino, as we Venetians call it – with lights shining from the windows, and door obedient to the key, but no servants to be seen. At the top of the stairs was the green door she had spoken of. I pushed it open, and after crossing two ante-rooms I found her waiting for me in a little salon. She was most elegantly attired, in the fashion of the day, and wore her hair dressed in a superb chignon, but as the recollection of the wig was still in my mind, I refrained from speaking of it. The room was lighted by wax candles in girandoles, and by four superb candelabra placed on a table among a quantity of handsome books. She seemed to me of a loveliness far other than that which I had admired beneath her nun's coif. I flung myself on my knees at her feet, kissing her hands, telling her in broken accents of my gratitude and devotion. M.M. thought it necessary to make some show of resistance. How charming such refusals are! As a tender, respectful, but audacious lover did I meet her protestations, and as I kissed her beautiful mouth, my very soul seemed to pass from me to her.

At last she said, laughing, 'Dear friend, you will be surprised to hear that I am hungry; I believe I could do justice to supper, if you would keep me company.'

She rang the bell, and a middle-aged woman of respectable appearance answered the summons. She set the table for two, putting the wine, dessert, and sweetmeats on a sideboard. She then brought in eight hot meats, served in Sèvres china, set on silver chafing dishes, and left us once more alone. The supper was dainty and abundant: I recognised at once the French mode of cooking. We had excellent burgundy and champagne. My companion mixed the salad dexterously; indeed, in everything she did, I admired her graceful ease. Her friend was evidently a connoisseur, and had instructed her in the art of good living. I was curious to know him, and when we were

taking punch after supper I said that if she would satisfy my curiosity in this particular I would tell her my
own name.

'All in good time, my friend,' said she; 'let us not be in
a hurry.'

Among the charms hanging at her side I noticed a little
flask in rock crystal, exactly like one I wore on my own
chain: like mine, it was filled with cotton saturated with
essence of rose.

'This is a rare perfume,' said I, 'and very costly.'

'It is next to impossible to procure,' she answered.

'You are right, the maker of this essence is a crowned head,
the King of France himself. He made one pound of it, and it
cost him thirty thousand francs.'

'What I have here was given by the king to my lover,'
said M.M.

'And mine is some of a small quantity sent by Madame
de Pompadour to the Venetian ambassador in Paris, M.
de Mocenigo, by favour of M. de Bernis, who is French
ambassador here at the present moment.'

'Do you know him?' she asked curiously.

'I have dined with him. He is a favourite with Dame
Fortune, but he deserves it. He is well born, and has a
right to call himself Comte de Lyon. He is so handsome
his nickname is "*Belle Babet*". But see, it is night, the hour
when all living things seek rest.'

'What! are you so tired?'

'No, but I am sure that you must be. Rest here. I will sit
beside you, and watch you sleep; or, if you prefer, I will
go away.'

She took a handkerchief and bound it round my head,
asking me to render her the same service. I must own
that I shrank instinctively from the wig, but was agreeably
surprised to feel instead the most beautiful natural hair,
long, fine, waving, and of a reddish gold. At my cry of
astonishment and admiration she laughed heartily, then

86

explained to me that a nun is only obliged to hide her hair from the vulgar gaze, not to sacrifice it entirely.

We were disturbed by a noisy alarum, hidden somewhere in the room.

'What is that?' cried I.

'It is time for me to go back to my convent.'

She rang, and the woman who had served us at supper, and who was doubtless her confidante and secret minister, appeared. Having dressed her hair, she assisted her to change her satin corset for the dimity one of a nun; the jewels and fine clothes were carefully locked up; the Mother M.M. stood before me. Her confidante having left the room to call the gondoliers, she kissed me, saying: 'I shall expect you the day after tomorrow.'

Next day Laura gave me a letter from C.C. It ran as follows:

'DEAR, Don't be angry with me, but give me credit for being able to keep a secret, young as I am. I am sure of your love, and I don't want you to tell me more than you think proper of your affairs, and I am glad of anything which can alleviate the pains of separation for you, only – listen! Yesterday I was crossing the hall, when I dropped something and moved a footstool to recover it. The footstool was just beside a crack in the wall of the parlour. I looked through – I am so dull here that I can't help being anxious – and I saw you, dear, in earnest converse with my friend, Mother M.M. I put the footstool back quietly and went away. Tell me all, dear, and make me happy. Does she know you, and how did you make her acquaintance? She is my bosom friend, the woman of whom I have often spoken, but without telling you her name. It is she who lends me books and teaches me things very few women know. She knows I have a lover, just as I know she has one, but we never ask each other questions. She is a wonderful woman. You love each other, I know, you could not help it, and as I am not jealous, I deserve your whole confidence. I am sorry for you both, for I don't see how you can possibly manage to meet. Everybody in the convent thinks you ill, and I am dying to see you. Come once at any rate. Adieu.'

This truly noble letter frightened me – not on account of C.C., she was true as steel, but because of others. Honour and delicacy forbade me telling her the facts. I lied boldly to C.C., saying that I had heard such wonderful things of M.M. that I had made an opportunity of seeing her, but that there was nothing whatever between us.

Saint Catherine's Day was C.C.'s birthday, and I thought it beseemed me to give the pretty recluse, who was imprisoned for my sake, a chance of seeing me. But I had discovered that I was watched and followed, and I thought it wiser not to visit Murano any more, except at night or masked.

The following day I was in the convent parlour betimes. M.M. did not keep me waiting long. She congratulated me on the good effect of my reappearance at church; the nuns, she said, were delighted to see me again after an absence of three weeks; even the abbess had expressed her pleasure, and at the same time her determination to find out who I was. This made me remember that the day before a man had dogged my footsteps so resolutely and so importunately that I had seized the fellow by the throat, and should certainly have shaken the life out of him had he not managed to slip through my hands. I mentioned the incident to M.M., and we both agreed that it was probably a spy the holy mother had set at my heels. From this we concluded that it would be best for me to discontinue my visits to the chapel altogether. She told me all about the tell-tale chink in the boards, of which she had, she said, been warned by a young novice who was devoted to her. This was, of course, my obedient C.C., but I took care not to seem curious about her.

'And now, dear one,' I said, 'tell me when you will come again?'

88

'The newly professed sister has invited me to supper in her room, and I have no plausible pretext for refusing.'

'Can you not confide in her?'

'No. If I am not present at her supper I shall make an enemy of her.'

'Are you the only one to pay surreptitious visits to the outside world?'

'Yes, of that I am sure. It is gold alone which here, as elsewhere, works miracles. But tell me, when can you meet me tomorrow – two hours after sunset?'

'Can I not meet you at your casino?'

'No, for it is my lover himself who is going to escort me to Venice.'

'Your lover! Incredible!'

'But none the less true.'

'I will wait for you there, in the Square of St John and St Paul, behind the statue of Bartholomew of Bergamo.'

'I don't know the square or the statue except from pictures, but no matter, I will be there, unless the weather prevents me.'

I had no time to lose, if I wished to find a place to receive my beautiful guest in, but I soon found the very thing I was looking for, a charming casino in the environs of Venice. It had formerly belonged to the English ambassador, but when he left Venice he had abandoned it to his cook. The new proprietor let it to me until Easter for a hundred sequins, which I paid him in advance, on condition that he himself cooked for me. There were five rooms, furnished in the best possible taste. The meals were served in the dining-room through a buttery hatch, so that there was no need for servant and master to see each other. The salon was ornamented with superb mirrors and lustres in rock crystal and gilded bronze. A magnificent picture hung over the white marble chimney-piece that was inlaid with Chinese plaques. An octagonal-shaped room led out of the salon; its walls, floor, and ceiling were entirely covered with

89

Venetian mirrors. There was a boudoir which might have been furnished for the Queen of Love herself, and a bath of Carrara marble.

I ordered a sumptuous supper, with exquisite wines, to be prepared for that night, at the same time warning the landlord that he was to be sure that no one watched my ingoings and outgoings. The servants were to remain absolutely invisible. I then went and bought the most beautiful pair of slippers I could find, and a cap in *point d'Alençon* lace.

Two hours after sunset I returned to my casino. The French cook was much astonished at seeing me alone, and as he had neglected to light up the rooms, I reproached him severely, after which I told him to serve supper. It came up by a lift, through the door in the wall, and in very good style. I commented on every dish, but, as a matter of fact, I found all excellent. Game, sturgeon, oysters, truffles, wine, dessert, all was good, and all well served in fine Dresden china and silver-gilt plate. When I told him he had forgotten the hard-boiled eggs, the anchovies, and dressing for salad the poor cook raised hands and eyes to heaven as though he had been guilty of a terrible misdemeanour.

I was at St John's Square an hour before the appointed time. The night was cold, but I did not notice it. By and by I saw a two-oared boat come up, and a masked figure stepped ashore. My heart beat wildly, but as it drew nearer I saw it was a man, and wished I had brought my pistols. The mask walked once round the statue, and then came up to me, extending a friendly hand. It was my angel! She laughed heartily at my surprise, and taking my arm, we walked away to my casino, which was about a hundred steps from St Moïse. Everything was in perfect order. We went quickly upstairs, and I flung away my cloak and mask. M.M. was delighted with the rooms, and examined every corner. She was not sorry either to afford me an opportunity of admiring . her beautiful figure, and the richness of her apparel, which did her lover's generosity credit. The mirrors reflected her charming person a thousand times over, and this system of multiplied portraits were evidently new to her. She stood still and looked at herself; I sat on a stool and watched her. She wore a coat of rose-coloured velvet, embroidered with gold spangles, a hand-embroidered waistcoat to match, black satin breeches, diamond buckles, a valuable solitaire on the little finger of one hand, and on the other a ring with a crystal set over white satin. Her mask, of black blonde, was remarkably fine in design and quality. She came and stood in front of me, that I might better admire all these fine things. I turned out her pockets and found in them a gold snuff-box, a *bonbonnière* set with pearls, a gold needle-case, a superb opera-glass, two fine cambric handkerchiefs simply soaked with perfume, two richly wrought gold watches with chains and bunches of charms sparkling with diamonds. I also found a pocket-pistol – a little English pistol in exquisitely engraved steel.

'All these, my beautiful one,' said I, 'are not half good enough for you, yet I cannot help expressing my admiration for the astounding being – I had almost said the *adorable* being – who hopes by such offerings to convince you of his affection.'

'That is much what he said to me when I begged him to escort me to Venice and leave me there. "Be happy," he said to me, "and I only hope the lucky man whom you honour will be worthy of your condescension."'

'He is a most astounding being! I repeat it. He is simply unique. I fear that I no more resemble him than I deserve the happiness whose prospect dazzles me.'

She asked my leave to unmask herself in a room apart. In a quarter of an hour she came back to my side, her hair dressed like a man's, tied with a black ribbon; it came down to her knees.

'Adorable creature!' I exclaimed, 'you were not made for mortal man, and I fear you will never be mine. Some miracle

91

will tear you from me at the very moment when I think that I hold you. Your divine spouse will perhaps be jealous of a mere man, and will destroy me with his lightning. Who knows, but in a quarter of an hour I may have ceased to exist!'

'Nonsense! I am yours now, this very moment!'

I proposed to ring for supper. She shuddered at the idea of being seen, but was pacified when I showed her the ingenious method by which we could be served without the servants entering the room.

'When I tell my lover of this,' she said, 'he will say you are no novice in the art of love-making! And I see well that I am not the only person whom you receive in this discreet little nest.'

'You are the first woman who ever came to me here, adorable creature! Though you are not my first love, you will surely be my last!'

'I shall be content if I make you happy. My lover is satisfied with me; he is gentle, kind, and amiable, but he has never filled my heart.'

'Nor can you have filled his, or he would not permit you such liberty.'

'He loves me as I love you, and you believe that I love you, don't you?'

'I like to believe it.'

The fatal alarum sounded all too quickly, and after a hasty cup of coffee I took her back to the square of St John, promising to visit her in two days. She had put the beautiful lace cap in her pocket to keep as a souvenir.

When, however, I next presented myself in the convent parlour she told me her friend had just announced his visit, and that I must postpone mine.

'He is going to Padua until Christmas,' she said; 'but in the meantime he has arranged for us to sup at his casino whenever we please.'

'Why not at mine?'

'He has begged me not to go to Venice during his absence. He is prudent, and I intend to do as he bids me.'

'Then I must fain be content as well. When shall we meet?'

'On Sunday.'

'I will go there in the twilight, and read till you come. But remember that nine days before Christmas there will be no more masking, and I shall then have to go to your casino by water, for fear of being recognised by the spy you know of.'

'But I hope you will be able to come during Lent, too, for all Heaven insists that during that time we should mortify the flesh! Isn't it strange that it should please the Lord that at one time we should amuse ourselves wildly and abstain at another? How can a mere anniversary affect Him, who is independent of our doings? It seems to me that if the Lord could have created us virtuous by inclination and did not choose to do so, then it is His own fault if we go wrong. Imagine the Lord keeping Lent!'

'My dear, who taught you to reason like this?'

'My friend, who lent me books, and opened my mind. I think for myself and don't listen to the priests.'

On Sunday, while I was waiting for my divinity, I amused myself with examining the books in the boudoir, which, she said, had made her a freethinker. They were not numerous, but they were well chosen, and worthy of the place. Among them was everything that had been written against religion, and everything the most voluptuous pens had written about pleasure. Several richly bound folios contained engravings, whose merit lay all in the correctness of their drawing and the fineness of their execution. There were the illustrations of the *Portier des Chartreux*, engraved in England, those of Meunius, Aloysia, Sigea Toletana, and others, all of remarkable beauty. A quantity of little pictures hung on the walls, all *chefs-d'œuvre* of the same style.

I studied these volumes till my beautiful mistress in her nun's habit arrived.

We decided that while her lover was absent I should live at the casino; and during the ten days he was away I had the happiness of receiving her four times.

While there I amused myself by reading, and writing to C.C., but my love for her had dwindled away a good deal. What most interested me in her letters was her enthusiasm for her teacher, the Mother M.M., with whom she was most anxious I should become acquainted! She blamed me for lack of interest in her friend, and for not trying to make her acquaintance in the parlour. I answered that I was afraid of being recognised, and enjoined her to maintain the strictest secrecy.

I do not think it is possible to love two people at the same time, in the same degree, neither can one maintain a vigorous affection by over-nourishment, or a paucity of it, for the matter of that. My passion for M.M. was kept at fever heat because I felt as if every meeting might be the last.

'It is certain,' I said to her, 'that some time or other, some one of the nuns will want to speak to you while you are absent from your room.'

'No,' said she, 'there is no danger, for nothing is more strictly respected in the convent than the right of each nun to make herself inaccessible to all the others, even the abbess. There is nothing to fear but fire, and then it would indeed seem strange for a nun to remain locked up in her cell. I have won over a lay sister, and the gardener, and one other nun. It is gold and the skill of my lover combined which have worked this miracle. He is responsible, too, for the fidelity of the cook and his wife at the casino, and of the two gondoliers, though we know that one of the latter is a spy in the service of the State Inquisitors.'

On Christmas Eve she wrote me that her lover would be

back next day and that they intended to go to the opera together.

'I shall expect you, dear friend,' she wrote, 'on New Year's Eve, and in the meantime I beg you to read the enclosed at your leisure, and at your own house.'

So, to make room for the other, I packed up my baggage and went off to the Bragadin Palace, where I read her letter:

'I was piqued somewhat, dear friend, when you said *à propos* of the mystery with which I am obliged to surround my lover, that so long as you possessed my heart, you were content to leave me mistress of my mind. This division of the heart and mind seems to me purely sophistical, and if it does not seem so to you also, it must be because you do not love me absolutely. You cannot separate me from my soul, or cherish my body, if my mind is not in harmony with it!

'However, lest you should some day think I have been wanting in frankness towards you, I have determined to tell you a secret concerning my friend, although I know he counts on my discretion. I am going to commit treason, but you will not love me the less for it, because, forced as I am to choose between you, and to deceive either one or the other, love has gained the day. It is not *you* who will be betrayed, so do not punish me for it. I am not acting blindly, and you can weigh the motives which have tipped the scales in your favour carefully.

'When I felt I must yield to my desire to know you I took my friend into my confidence. We formed a high opinion of your character from your first letter to me, because you selected the convent parlour as the place for our first interview, and his casino at Murano for second. But in return for his complaisance he begged me to allow him to be present at our interview, to conceal him in a small dressing-room, from which one can see and hear everything which goes on in the other room. You have not yet seen this hiding-place, but I will show it you when next we meet. Tell me, dearest, could I refuse this strange satisfaction to a man who was so lenient to me? I consented, and naturally I hid the fact from you. Now you know my friend witnessed all we said and did that first night, but this need not trouble you, for he approved you. I was afraid, when the conversation turned on him, that you might say something wounding to his vanity; but as it happened your remarks were flattering enough. This, then, is the sincere confession of my treason; but you are wise, and I think you will forgive it, more especially as it has done you no harm. My friend is anxious to know who you are.

'On the night in question you behaved quite naturally; but would you have done so had you known you were watched? Probably not. But now that we know each other, and that you do not doubt my love for you, I am going to risk everything for everything. On the last night of the old year my lover will be at the casino, and he will not leave until the next day. We shall not see him, but he will see us. As you will not be supposed to know that he is there, you must be as natural as you were the first time, otherwise he would guess I had told you. One thing you must be careful about, your subjects of conversation. My friend has all the virtues except the theological virtue called faith. So on this point you will have a free hand. You can speak of literature, travels, politics, everything you like, and you need not restrict yourself in personal anecdote. You are sure to meet with his approbation. Tell me frankly, do you object? Yes or no? I shall not close my eyes till I get your answer. If it is *no* I will find some excuse, but I hope it will be *yes*.'

This letter astonished me, but on reflection I saw that, if anything, the leading part had been assigned to me, and so could afford to laugh.

I answered, assuring her that I would do her pleasure, and would be careful not to let him see I knew his secret.

I spent the six intervening days with my friends in Venuice, and on the seventh, New Year's Eve, I repaired to the casino, where I found M.M. awaiting me. She was dressed with the most extreme elegance.

'My friend is not here yet,' she said; 'as soon as he is I will make you a sign.'

'Where is this mysterious cupboard?'

'Here; look at the back of this sofa, which is set in the wall; all the flowers which are carved in relief have a hole in the middle, the dressing-room is behind, there is a couch in it, a table, and all that is needful to pass the night in comfort.'

I complimented M.M. on her costume, remarking that it was the first time I had seen her wearing rouge. I liked the way she had put it on, as the court ladies at Versailles put on theirs. The charm lies in the negligent way in which it is applied; no one tries to make it look natural; it pleases, inasmuch as it permits us to anticipate a greater carelessness and freedom. M.M. said she wore it to please her friend.

'I argue from that,' said I, 'that he is a Frenchman.'

At this moment she made me a little sign; the lover was at his post, and the comedy began.

We sat down to table, where a sumptuous supper was laid; she ate for two, and I for four. I had eaten nothing that day but a cup of chocolate and a salad of whites of eggs drowned in Lucca oil and *vinaigre des quatre voleurs*. The dessert was served in silvergilt dishes of the same pattern as the handsome candelabra which were on the table. To please the lover behind the screen, I alluded to these candelabra and admired them.

'They are a present from him,' she said, as I expected.

'A most magnificent present; did he give you snuffers with them?'

'No.'

'From that I imagine he is a *grand seigneur*.'

'Why should you think so?'

'Because a *grand seigneur* does not even know that candles need snuffing.'

My beloved M.M. had expressed a wish to have my

portrait; I sent for the artist who had painted me in miniature for C.C., and after three sittings he produced a masterpiece. It was rather larger than the one I had had done for C.C., and made so as to be worn in a locket. The portrait was hidden by an ivory medallion of the same size, on which was an Annunciation, the Angel Gabriel represented as a dark young man, and the Blessed Virgin as a fair woman. (The famous painter Mengs imitated this idea in the Annunciation which he painted in Madrid twelve years later.) The two were mounted by an expert jeweller in the most exquisite taste, and I hung them on a gold chain, of the pattern known as 'Spanish links', six ells long.

Two days after offering this present to my divinity I received from her a gold snuff-box, the lid of which contained her portrait in her nun's costume. The bottom of the box was hinged, and on being pressed in a certain manner it opened and revealed another portrait, in which she appeared lying full length on a black satin couch, smiling at Cupid, who, his bow at his feet, was seated near her.

On Twelfth Night we went together to the opera, and afterwards to the Ridotto, where M.M. was much amused at the patrician ladies, who alone had the privilege of promenading up and down unmasked; we then passed into the larger gambling saloon, where my companion, having lost all her money, began to play with mine, with such extraordinary luck that she broke the bank. On counting our gains after supper, in our little casino, we found that my share alone amounted to a thousand sequins.

Shortly after Twelfth Night I received a letter from C.C.:

'Ah! my dear little husband, I am quite, quite sure that you are in love with my charming friend M.M. She wears a locket containing a picture of the Annunciation, which is evidently by the artist who painted the miniature I have in my ring, and I feel certain that your portrait is underneath; besides which, Mother M.M. is very curious about my ring, and asked me the other day if St Catherine did not conceal the picture of my lover. I am sorry to have to be reserved and deceitful towards her, but believe me when I say that it will not hurt me in the least if you tell me you care for her. I am fond of her, and she has been too good for me for me to endure this deceit for long; let us be quite frank with each other; it must be terrible to have to make love through an iron grating!'

I replied that she had guessed rightly so far as the locket was concerned; it was a present I had made to M.M., and contained my portrait, but she must keep the secret, and at the same time feel assured that the friendship I had for M.M. did not in any way interfere with my feeling for her.

I knew well enough that my letter was somewhat shifty, but I was weak enough to wish to continue an intrigue which my better sense told me was drawing to its inevitable close; it could not possibly continue, if an intimacy was once established between the two rivals.

I had learned from Laura that there was to be a ball in the big parlour of the convent, and I determined to go, disguised so that my two friends should not recognise me. In Venice these innocent amusements are permitted in convents in carnival time; the public dances in the parlours, and the sisters watch them through the gratings; the ball winds up early, everyone goes home, and the poor recluses have something to think of during the long dull months that follow. I decided to dress as a Pierrot. This costume, which is comparatively uncommon in Italy, has the advantage of hiding peculiarities of figure and bearing; the large cap covers the hair, and the white gauze stretched over the face prevents the eyes and eyebrows from being recognisable. I started for Murano without taking a cloak, and with nothing in my pockets but a handkerchief, my purse, and the key of my casino. The parlour was crowded, but I was the only Pierrot among numberless harlequins, punchinellos, pantaloons, and scaramouches. Behind the grating, among the nuns and boarders, I saw my two friends, their eyes fixed on the dancers. I attached myself to a pretty columbine, and together we danced a minuet. She danced divinely, and we were frantically applauded. Then I danced twelve *forlanes* straight off, and then, falling down, I pretended to be asleep, and everyone respected the sleep of Pierrot. After a *contredanse*, which lasted an hour, a harlequin came up, and with the impertinence which is part of the character, attempted to rob me of my partner. He struck and worried me with his wand, till I quickly caught him by the waistband and carried him round the room; then I put him down and seized his columbine. I packed her on to my shoulder and chased him. Then I had a fight with another, and knocked him down; then, in the midst of the laughter and clapping of the spectators and the nuns, who had never seen such a spectacle, I gained the door and disappeared.

It was still two hours to the time appointed for meeting M.M. at my casino, and these hours I spent gambling, winning at every stroke. With my pockets full of gold, and gloating over the thought of M.M.'s surprise when she should recognise me in the applauded Monsieur Pierrot, I arrived at our casino, and entered the sanctuary. There was my divinity leaning against the chimney-piece. She was dressed as a nun. I approached on tiptoe, looked at her, and stood petrified!

For it was not M.M.; it was C.C., in the costume of her friend. The poor girl did not heave a sigh, or proffer a word, or make a movement. I flung myself into a chair. I was stupefied, bodily and mentally, and sat there for half an hour, thinking over M.M.'s perfidy, for, sure, it was she had played me this trick.

But I could not remain all night in dead silence; I must do and say something. C.C., so far, knew me only for the Pierrot she had seen dancing at the convent; or perhaps she had guessed. I owed her something; I had given her the right to call me husband. I was wretched. I took the covering off my face, and C.C. sighed out, 'I felt it was you.'

After lavishing on her such caresses as I could command at the moment, I begged her to tell me how she came there.

'I hardly know myself,' she answered; 'it is like a dream. After having laughed at the tricks of the Pierrot, whom we little thought was you, dear friend, M.M. and I left the parlour and went to her room. She asked me if I would do something for her, and I said, "Yes, with all my heart." She opened her wardrobe and dressed me as you see; she then said she was going to confide a great secret to my keeping, but that she knew she could trust me. "Know," said she, "that I was about to leave the convent, and stay away until tomorrow morning, but fate has decreed it should be you who are to follow this programme in my stead. In an hour's time a lay sister will come for you; follow her across the garden to the river, where you will find a gondola. Say to the boatman, 'To the casino.' In five minutes you will come to a little house; go in and upstairs; there you will find a comfortable room and a good fire; wait. I must not tell you more than this, but be sure that nothing unpleasant will happen." I looked upon it all as an amusing escapade, I followed her instructions, and here I am. I had been here three-quarters of an hour when you came in. In spite of your disguise, my heart told me at once it was you; but when you recoiled from me I was thunderstruck, for I knew then that though you expected someone, it was not me. But now kiss me. You know I am reasonable, and glad you are happy with M.M.; she is the only woman in the world I could bear to share you with. Kiss me!'

I embraced her again tenderly, at the same time telling her that I thought her friend had played us an ugly trick.

'I will not conceal from you,' I said, 'that I am in love with M.M. You must not judge me too harshly; remember you have been shut up for eight months in your convent, and during that time I have had to console myself as best

101

I could. I do not love you any the less, but I have become attached to M.M., and she knows it; she has accepted my homage, and now she has given me a mark of her disdain, for if she cared for me as I care for her she would not have thought of sending you in her place.'

The loyal and generous C.C. took up the defence of her friend, and strove to persuade me she had been actuated only by the kindest motives. M.M., she argued, was as devoid of jealousy and small-mindedness as she was herself. M.M. was unable to keep her appointment; it was only natural that she should send the friend who was her other self instead.

But I was very angry with M.M. 'It is not the same thing at all,' I said. 'I love M.M., and I can never marry her. As for you, dear, you are to be my wife, and propinquity will give fresh life to our love. But it is not so with M.M. It is humiliating to think that I have only inspired her with a fleeting caprice, is it not?'

We continued arguing in this strain until midnight, when the prudent concierge brought us supper. My heart was too heavy to eat, although I made a pretence of doing so. I could not help seeing that C.C. had improved and developed. Nevertheless, I remained indifferent to her, though the poor thing was full of tact. She continued to be tender without being passionate, and perfectly sweet in every way. Two hours before daybreak, as we were seated before the fire, she asked me what she should say to M.M. on her return to the convent.

'Tell her all,' I said; 'hide nothing from her, and above all, tell her that she has made me very unhappy. Believe me, dear friend, I love you with all my heart, but I am in a most difficult position.'

The alarum sounded. I had hoped that M.M. would appear during the course of that long night and justify herself, but no! With tears in our eyes we parted, C.C. to return to her expectant friend, and I to Venice.

It was bitterly cold, and a strong wind was blowing; there

was neither boat nor boatman to be seen along the quay, the rain beat through my linen dress. I could not go back to the casino, for in a fit of temper I had given the key to C.C. to remit to M.M. My pockets and purse were full of gold pieces, and Murano is celebrated for its thieves, who rob and assassinate with impunity; they are indeed granted many a privilege because of their skill in the glass factories; the Government has even made them citizens to keep them there. I had not even the little knife about me which in my dear country every honest citizen must carry to defend his life. I wandered about until I came to a cottage, through whose window a light was shining. With much difficulty and much bribing I induced the proprietor to get up, and, accompanied by his son, row me back to the city. The storm had by this time increased in fury, and several times we were within an ace of drowning; one of the men fell overboard, but scrambled back into the gondola; we lost an oar, and were all drenched to the skin; at last, however, we got into the Beggar's Canal, and from there to the Bragadin Palace.

Five or six hours later, when M. de Bragadin and his friends came to see me, they found me in bed, in a high fever and delirious, but they could not help laughing at the sight of the dripping Pierrot costume on the sofa. By the evening I was better, though still very ill, and when the faithful Laura came in the morning I could not read the letters she brought me; it was many days before I could do so.

The two charming creatures each wrote to me protestations of esteem and affection, and expressed their desire that we should form a trio of friends. They implored me to think better of my determination to abandon the casino.

M.M. had indeed been present during my stormy interview with C.C., but she had prudently refrained from interfering with our hoped-for reconciliation. Then sleep had overtaken her, and she had not waked until the noise of the alarum roused her. C.C. had given her the key, which she now sent back to me, and together they had fled out into the storm, and back to the convent, where they changed their dresses, and M.M. went to bed, while C.C. sat at her pillow and listened to her confession, how she had seized the opportunity of C.C. being called away to examine her ring, and with a pin had moved and disclosed the spring. Then she had guessed that they both loved the same man. In spite of this disclosure, M.M. had not changed her manner to C.C., but had thought only of how she should prove her generosity to the other two. She had thought herself so clever when she had substituted C.C. for M.M., but 'our lover', as they called me, had, alas, taken the matter in bad part. Then C.C.'s aunt had come in and had told them a long story of the Pierrot and an accident to the boat, which terrified them. But the aunt was able to assure them that the Pierrot was saved and was a son of M. de Bragadin. When she had gone, M.M. turned to C.C. and asked her if I was really a son of M. de Bragadin, for he had never been married? Then C.C. told her the whole story, and how I was in treaty with her father for her hand. They hoped to meet me at the casino soon, either together or singly.

How could I resist this? As soon as I was well enough I wrote explaining the reason of my long silence, and fixing a rendezvous with M.M.

On the 4th of February 1754 I again found myself tête-à-tête with her. We fell spontaneously into each other's arms, and our reconciliation was complete. I asked her if we were really alone. She took a candle, and opening a large wardrobe, which I had already suspected of being practicable in some way, she shot a bolt, and behold, a small apartment with a sofa, and over that sofa three or four little holes through which the occupants of the chamber we were in could be observed.

'You want to know,' she said, 'if I was alone on the fatal

night when you met C.C. here? I was not; my friend was with me, and don't be angry, for he was delighted with you and with C.C. in her distress. How well she reasoned, he thought, and only fifteen!' Then we talked of my Pierrot disguise, and how it had led to their discovery of my real estate; and she admitted that she was glad I was not a patrician, as she had feared.

I knew perfectly well what she meant, but I pretended to be ignorant.

'I cannot speak to you openly,' she continued, 'until you promise to do what I am going to ask of you.'

'Speak, sweetheart, and count on me. I am sure you will ask nothing that could compromise my honour.'

'I want you to ask my friend to sup openly with us at the casino; he is dying to make your acquaintance. I have already told him who you are, as otherwise he would not have dared to suggest such a thing.'

'I imagine that your friend is a foreigner. One of the ministers, perhaps.'

'Precisely.'

'I hope he will do me the honour of not preserving his incognito on that occasion?'

'I shall present him to you in due form by his right name, and mention his political qualifications.'

'In that case then I consent; fix the day and I will be there.'

'Now that I am sure of your coming, I will tell you everything,' she said. 'My protector is M. de Bernis, the French ambassador.'

'I can now understand why you dreaded to hear that I was a patrician! The State Inquisitors would not have been long in showing their zeal! They would have soon interfered with us, and I shudder to think of the awful consequences which would surely have ensued. I should have been put in "The Leads", and you would have been dishonoured, and the abbess, and the convent! Great Heavens! what risks you

105

have run! As it is, we are safe, and nothing remains but to fix the date of the supper.'

'Four days from now we are going to the opera, and after the second ballet will come on here, if that is agreeable to you.'

After the departure of my beautiful nun I returned posthaste to Venice, where my first care was to send for my cook. I wanted the supper to be worthy of host and guests.

Four days after this, the time appointed by M.M., she appeared at the casino with the ambassador.

'I am delighted, sir,' he said, 'at this opportunity of renewing our acquaintance, for madame tells me we knew each other in Paris.' While saying this he looked at me keenly, as though trying to recall my face.

'I had the honour,' I answered, 'of dining with your Excellency at M. de Mocenigo's, but you were so occupied with Marshal Keith, the ambassador from the Court of Prussia, that I could not succeed in attracting your attention.'

'I remember you now,' he said, 'for I asked someone if you were not one of the secretaries of the Embassy. However, from this day forth we shall not forget each other, and I hope our intimacy will be a lasting one.'

We sat down to table, when of course I did the honours. The ambassador was a connoisseur, and found my wines excellent. The supper was delicate, abundant, and varied, and my manner towards the handsome couple was that of a private individual receiving his sovereign and royal favourite. I saw that M.M. was pleased at my attitude, and at the manner in which I talked with the ambassador, who listened to me with the greatest interest. Though we were naturally a little shy, the conversation was animated and amusing. Monsieur de Bernis was a thorough Frenchman, and could thrust and parry in conversation as only one of his nationality can. We spoke of the romantic manner in which our acquaintance had begun, and from thence

M.M. led me adroitly to speak of C.C. and my attachment to her; her description of my little friend so pleased the ambassador that he asked why she had not been invited to supper.

'Why,' said the artful nun, 'it might easily be managed another time, as she shares my room; I could bring her here without any difficulty – that is, if M. Casanova desires it.'

This offer astonished me somewhat, but it was not then the moment to show my surprise.

'If I am to be of the party,' said the ambassador, 'I think she ought to be warned beforehand.'

'I will tell her,' I said, 'to obey madame blindly; at the same time I must beg your Excellency to be indulgent towards a girl of fifteen, who is quite unversed in the ways of the world.'

The next morning I received a letter from M.M., in which she said that she could not rest until she was sure that the proposed *partie Carrée* was to my liking; if I had consented merely out of politeness she would undertake to postpone it indefinitely.

I could see then, when it was too late, that I had been the dupe of two cunning diplomats. There was no doubt of it! The ambassador admired C.C. and equally without doubt the complaisant M.M. had determined to further his ends. She could do nothing without my consent, and this she had obtained very cleverly. I had jumped at the bait; at the same time she had made it impossible for me to reproach her, by offering to quash the arrangement, and she knew very well that my vanity would not let anyone suppose me jealous; there was nothing left for me to do but to put a good face on it, and not appear stupid and ungrateful in the eyes of a man who, after all, had shown me the most unheard of condescension. I hastened therefore to reiterate my invitation, though I was now conscious that our ideal intercourse was drawing to a close.

The ambassador was the first to arrive on the fateful night.

He was most civil to me, and told me that had he known me in Paris he would have put me in the way of making my fortune. Now, when I look back on it all, I say to myself, 'Supposing he had done so, where and what should I be now?' Perhaps one of the victims of the revolution, as he himself would undoubtedly have been had not fate decreed he should die at Rome in the year 1794. He died very rich, but very miserable.

I asked him if he liked Venice, and he replied that it was delightful, and if one had plenty of money one could amuse oneself there better than anywhere else. 'But,' he added, 'I am afraid I shall not be here much longer; keep my secret, though, for I do not wish to sadden M.M.'

We continued this confidential talk until the arrival of M.M. and her young friend. C.C. looked perfectly ravishing, and during the supper, which was fit for a king, the ambassador was most attentive to her. Wit, gaiety, decency, and *bon ton* presided at the table, but did not exclude the Gallic salt which Frenchmen know well how to insinuate into any conversation. M.M. treated the ambassador like an intimate friend; to me she behaved politely, she might have been C.C.'s sister.

M. de Bernis thanked M.M. for the most delightful supper he had ever assisted at in his life, thus obliging her to invite us to another the week following. At this second supper, however, he did not appear. Just as we were ready to sit down to table the concierge came in with a letter, in which the ambassador said that a courier had brought him some unexpected despatches, and it was impossible for him to join us.

'It is not his fault,' said M.M., 'we must amuse ourselves as we best can, but let us make another rendezvous. Shall we say Friday?'

I acquiesced, not realising that once more I was walking into a trap; but the next day, in thinking over recent events, my eyes were opened, and I saw how I had played into the ambassador's hands; the story of the courier was an invention; the *Suisse* at the door of the ambassador's house told me that no despatches had been received for two months. He had voluntarily stayed away, so as to leave me with the two friends. I, in my turn, could not be less obliging; Friday night came, I must invent some excuse for absenting myself.

It was M.M.'s doing. She wanted me to believe in her love, and she was able to assume all those virtues a man best prefers – honour, delicacy, and loyalty – but she was still a libertine at heart, and yearned to make me her accomplice. She had subdued the spirit to the flesh to such an extent, and her conscience to such a pitch of flexibility, that it no longer reproached her. She had manipulated events to her liking, and she relied on a sense of false shame in me to stand her ally.

De Bernis and she knew well enough that C.C. was a weak woman, and that once deprived of my moral support, she would not be able to withstand them. I was sorry for C.C., but I felt that I could never marry her now.

C.C. wrote and described the supper to me; it made me laugh. She liked the ambassador, but she tried to persuade me that she loved me. M.M.'s letter was still more singular. She told me that C.C. had become a freethinker like ourselves, and was now superior to prejudices. M.M. herself had been under no delusion as to my polite fiction. I had, she thought, magnificently returned the ambassador's civility. I said to myself, '*George Dandin, tu l'as voulu*,' and I had the effrontery and courage to write to C.C., congratulating her on her new conquest, and bidding her emulate and imitate M.M. in everything.

On Shrove Tuesday we all four supped together, and this was the last evening I ever spent in C.C.'s company. She was very lively, but having decided on a line of conduct, I devoted myself entirely to M.M. The ambassador proposed after supper that we should play a game of faro; having cut

109

the cards, and put an hundred double louis on the table, we managed so that C.C. should win the whole sum. She was dazzled at the sight of so much gold, and begged her friend to take care of it for her until she should leave the convent to get married.

Now, although her infidelity had led me to look upon her in a totally different light to that in which I had hitherto regarded her, I could not help feeling that it was owing to me that she had wandered so far astray, and that consequently I must always remain her sincere friend. Had I reasoned as clearly in those days as I do now, I should probably have acted otherwise. I should have said, 'It was I who first set the example of infidelity; I told her to follow the advice of M.M., when I knew that her counsels must be vicious; why should I expect a poor weak girl to be stronger than a man who is twice her age?' Following this line of argument. I should have condemned my own conduct rather than hers, and should not have changed towards her, but the fact is that, while I thought myself supremely broad-minded and above all prejudices, I was nearly as limited and as much a slave to custom as most men who expect immaculate virtue in their wives, while insisting on absolute licence for themselves and their mistresses.

On Good Friday, when I arrived at the casino, I found de Bernis and his mistress plunged in sorrow; supper was served, but he ate nothing; M.M. was like a marble statue. Discretion and good breeding forbade me questioning them, but when M.M. left us, de Bernis told me that he had orders to leave for Vienna within fifteen days. 'I may as well tell you,' he said, 'that I do not think there is any likelihood of my returning, but do not let her know this, it would only add to her grief. I am going to work with the Austrian Cabinet on a treaty which will make all Europe talk. Write to me as a friend, and without reserve, and if you really care for our mutual friend, look after her, and above all be careful of her honour; be strong to resist temptations which may expose you to what would be fatal to you both. You know what happened to Madame de Riva, who was a nun at the convent of S—? As soon as the scandal became public she disappeared, and her protector, M. de Frulai, my predecessor, went mad, and died shortly after. J. J. Rousseau told me that his madness was the effect of poison, but Rousseau always sees the darkest side of things. I think he died of grief at being unable to help the unhappy lady, whom the Pope has since dispensed from her vows. She lives now at Parma, married, but without respect or consideration. Let loyal and prudent friendship be stronger than love; see M.M. sometimes in the convent, but do not meet here, for the gondoliers will surely betray you as soon as I am gone. So for God's sake be careful in the future, and above all keep me informed, for I shall always be interested in her and her fate, from duty and from sentiment.'

The minister then sent for the concierge, and drew up a deed in his presence, which he made him sign. By this deed he made over the casino and everything in it to me, and ordered the concierge to treat me in everything as his master.

We were to have one farewell supper together; but when, on the appointed evening, I entered the casino I found M.M. alone, as pale as death, and almost as cold.

'He has gone,' she said, 'and he commends me to you. I shall perhaps never see him again. Fatal man! I thought I only cared for him as a friend, but now that I have lost him I see all that he was to me. Before knowing him I was not happy, but I was not miserable, as I am now, and as I shall be for the rest of my life.'

During that long and wretched night her character was completely revealed to me. She was a creature of the moment, as wildly transported with joy over good fortune as she was cast down and overcome by sorrow when things went against her. Today, when years have bleached my hair, and calmed the ardour of my senses, I can judge her dispassionately, and I feel that my beautiful nun sinned against modesty, that most worthy attribute of her sex. But if this unique woman was wanting in that virtue – I then thought the lack of it admirable – she was equally free from the frightful venom called jealousy, a miserable passion which burns and dries up its victims, and the objects of their hate.

For some time we faithfully followed de Bernis's injunctions, and only saw each other in the convent parlour; then, giving way to our feelings, we disobeyed him, and appointed a meeting at the casino.

'I am sure,' said M.M., 'I can rely on the gardener's wife, she will let me in and out of a small door at the bottom of the garden; all that we need is a gondola and a boatman. Surely, if you pay him well enough you can find one who will serve us faithfully.'

'Listen,' said I, 'I will be the boatman myself, you will let me in through the little door, and I will stay with you here, and the following day as well, if you think you can hide me.'

'No,' said she, 'your project is too dangerous; let me know as nearly as possible the time you will come in your boat, and I will be waiting for you. We will go to our dear casino; after all, it is the safest place for us to meet in.'

I bought a boat, and a boatman's costume, hired a *cabane* in which to keep them, and after having made one or two trial trips round the island I went one hour before sunset to the little door in the garden wall. It opened an instant after my arrival, and M.M. came out, wrapped in an immense cloak.

It must be owned that my first experience as *barcarolo* was not encouraging, and would certainly have cooled the ardour of lovers less infatuated than we were. The nights were short, and M.M. had to return to her convent before three in the morning, which gave us but little time to be

112

together. Once, an hour or so before it was time for her to start on her homeward journey, a frightful storm broke; and we were obliged to sit out in driving wind and rain; although I was a strong and competent oarsman, I had not the skill of a professional. I do not know what would have happened to us if we had not had the luck to be overtaken by a four-oared barque, which, for two sequins, consented to tow us to our destination. If salvation had not come to us in the shape of the barque we should have had to elope together, and my life would have been irrevocably bound to hers. Then I should not have been sitting here at Dux, at the age of seventy-two, writing these Memoirs.

For three months we contrived to see each other weekly, and always by the same means. I, of course, grew more skilful in the management of my boat, and in all this time we did not meet with the slightest accident.

The false M.M.

De Bernis having left Venice, I became intimate with Murray, the English resident minister. He was a fine fellow, learned, and very fond of women. He kept Ancilla, one of my old loves, and she died in his arms, a hideous sight, of the illness which killed Francis the First of France. Murray cynically bragged about his heroism in loving her to the end. He did not replace her for some time, but flew like a bee from flower to flower. Some of the prettiest women in Venice passed through his hands. Two years later he left for Constantinople, where he represented the Cabinet of St James with the Sublime Porte.

About this time fate threw in my way a patrician named Mark Anthony Zorzi, a man of some talent, celebrated for his witty couplets; he was devoted to the drama, and produced a comedy which the public dared to hiss. The piece was condemned for its want of merit, but he was convinced that its failure was due to influence of the Abbé

113

Chiari, the titular poet of the Theatre St Angelo. From that moment Zorzi looked on the abbé as his enemy, and vowed vengeance against him. He hired a set of ruffians, who attended the theatre nightly, to hiss, without rhyme or reason, every one of the unfortunate Chiari's comedies. I did not care for Chiari, either as a man or author, and Zorzi's house was an agreeable one to frequent: he had an excellent cook and a charming wife. I repaid his hospitality by criticising his enemy's productions, about which I wrote *martelliers*, a form of doggerel verse much in vogue. Zorzi had these verses printed and distributed. My poor lines became one of the factors in my subsequent misfortunes. They gained me the dislike of M. Condulmer, a person of much political influence. This good gentleman was over sixty, but was still alert and vigorous; he was fond of money and play. It was said he practised usury on the sly, but he was careful to maintain a good reputation, and passed for a saint, as he went to daily Mass at St Mark's, and he had been seen on many occasions weeping before the crucifix. He had another reason to dislike me besides my lampoons. Before I appeared on the scene he was first in the good graces of the wife of Zorzi, who after my advent grew cool towards him; he was also part proprietor of the theatre of St Angelo, and the nonsuccess of the poetical abbé's pieces affected his pocket painfully.

Unfortunately for me, he was appointed Councillor of State, and in this quality served for eight months as inquisitor, in which eminent and diabolical position it was easy for him to insinuate to his colleagues that it would be a good thing to put me in prison. The notorious 'Leads' – *I Piombi* – were made for disturbers of the public peace and repose, like myself.

At the beginning of the winter came the astonishing news of the treaty of alliance between the houses of France and Austria. This treaty totally changed the political face of Europe, and had hitherto been considered by the powers as impossible. All Italy rejoiced at the alliance, for had the slightest friction arisen between France and Austria, her fair fields would have become the theatre of war. The marvellous treaty was conceived and concluded by a young minister who until then had been looked upon merely in the light of a *bel esprit*. The whole thing was planned in secret, in the year 1750, by Madame de Pompadour, the Comte de Kaunitz, and the Abbé de Bernis, who was not made ambassador to Venice till the following year.

For two hundred and forty years the houses of Hapsburg and Bourbon had been at enmity; the reconciliation between them, which was brought about by de Bernis, lasted barely forty years, but was probably as durable a one as could possibly be made between kingdoms so essentially opposed to one another. After the signing of the treaty de Bernis was made Minister of Foreign Affairs. Three years later he re-established the French Parliament, and as a reward received a cardinal's hat, but almost immediately after this honour he was disgraced and practically exiled to Rome.

What both he and I had foreseen came to pass: he was not able to return to Venice, and in him I lost a most devoted and powerful protector. He signified to M.M. in a letter, breaking the fact to her in the most affectionate and delicate manner, that their separation was a final one. I have never seen a human being so heartbroken; her grief was such that I believe she would have succumbed to it, had I not fortunately prepared her for the blow some time before it fell. I received instructions from de Bernis to sell the casino and all that it contained, and to hand the proceeds to M.M.; only the books and engravings were to be sent to Paris in charge of the concierge. Truly they constituted a pretty breviary for a future cardinal!

So by the middle of January we had no casino. I could now only see M.M. at the convent grating. She came to me there, one day early in February, looking like a dying woman. She told me she thought she would not live long,

115

and gave me her jewel-case, containing her diamonds and the greater part of her money; she reserved only a small sum for herself. She also gave me all the curious books she possessed, and her love-letters; if she recovered I was to return them to her, but in case of her death I was to keep everything. I promised her that I would live at Murano till she was better, and old Laura found me a furnished room and lent me her pretty daughter, Tonine, as a servant. I was terribly afraid Tonine would console me to her own destruction. I meant to ask Laura to provide me someone plainer, but I thought better – or worse – of it, and Tonine stayed and devoted herself to my comfort.

A few days later I heard through C.C. that her friend was delirious, and had raved loudly for over three days, in French fortunately, or she would certainly have put the decorous nuns to flight. This was the worst day of her illness. The moment her senses returned to her, she asked C.C. to write and tell me that she would be sure to recover if I would promise to carry her off as soon as her health would allow of a long journey. I said she might count on me, that my own life depended on it. From that time she began to mend; by the end of March she was out of danger. She was not to leave her room till after Easter. I went on living at Murano, and Tonine, my pretty servant, made the time pass pleasantly for me. M.M.'s letters were loving, but they had ceased to interest me. It was difficult and tiresome to me to answer them.

At the end of April I saw M.M. at the convent grating. She was very thin and much changed. I flatter myself that my behaviour inspired her with confidence, and that she did not notice the change which a new love had worked in me. I dared not take the hope of the projected elopement from her, lest she fell ill again. I kept my casino, which didn't cost much, and went to see M.M. twice a week, and on other days I stopped at the casino and made love to Tonine.

One evening when I was supping at the casino of Mr Murray, the English resident, with my friend Dr Righellini, I purposely turned the conversation on a beautiful nun, M.E., whom we had seen that afternoon at the Convent of the Virgins, a religious house under the jurisdiction of the Doge.

'Between Masons,' said the Englishman, 'I think if you asked M.E. to supper, and offered her a handsome present, she would come.'

'Someone has been hoaxing you, my dear friend,' I answered, 'or you would not say such a thing. It is anything but easy to gain access to the most beautiful nun in Venice.'

'She is not the most beautiful nun in Venice. Mother M.M. of Murano is far better looking.'

'I have heard of her,' said I. 'I have even seen her – once. But I do not think that she could be bribed.'

'I think she could,' said he, smiling; 'and I am not over-credulous.'

'I will wager anything you are mistaken.'

'You would lose your wager. As you have only seen her once, you would perhaps not recognise her portrait.'

'Indeed I should. Her appearance made a great impression on me.'

He took half a dozen miniatures out of a table drawer.

'If you recognise any of them,' said he, 'I hope you will be discreet.'

'You can count on my silence,' said I. 'Here are three whom I know, and one who is certainly like M.M., but so many women have traits in common.'

He persisted, and even went so far as to tell me, under the seal of secrecy, that M.M. had supped with him in her nun's dress, and had accepted a purse containing five hundred sequins. He had never been to see her at the convent, he said, for fear of arousing the suspicions of her official lover, the French ambassador. Although I could not stifle

117

the rising doubts in my mind, I still had sufficient faith in M.M. to wager Murray five hundred sequins that he was mistaken, and we determined to decide the wager as follows. He was to make a rendezvous with the supposed M.M. through Capsucefalo, the man who had introduced him to her. As soon as she arrived at the appointed place he would leave her for an hour or so, and then he and I were to go to the convent of Murano and summon M.M. to the parlour. If the answer came that she was ill, or busy, I was to admit that I had lost the wager. He was, moreover, to take his nun, whether she was M.M. or no, to my casino. My pretty Tonine was to prepare a cold supper and to keep out of the way on the fateful night.

We dined there first, Righellini, Murray, and I, and Tonine waited on us. Murray and Righellini were delighted with her. She confided to me afterwards her amazement at seeing the Englishman walk away as fresh and steady as possible with six bottles of my good wine in him. He looked like a handsome Bacchus, limned by Rubens.

When he came to the convent gate I was more dead than alive, though I did not love M.M. any longer. I entered the parlour with my Englishman. It was lighted by four candles, and after a few moments of the most horrible suspense my dear M.M. appeared, with a lay sister, holding small flat candle-sticks in their hands. Murray looked very serious, and did not even smile when M.M., brilliant and beautiful, addressed him.

'I am afraid,' she said, 'that I am making you miss the first act of the opera?'

'I had rather see you, for one moment, madame, than the best opera in the world.'

'You are English, I think, sir?'

'Yes, madame.'

'The English nation is now the first in the world, for it is as free as it is powerful. Gentlemen, I am your very humble servant.'

118

So we were dismissed! As soon as we were outside the door of my casino – 'Well,' said I, 'are you convinced?'

'Come along, and hold your tongue. We will talk about this when we get home; meantime, you must come in here with me. What should I do left alone for four hours with the creature in there? Capsucefalo is to fetch the pretended nun at midnight, and I promise you some fun. I shall throw them both out of the window.'

When I entered the room with Murray the false nun flung a handkerchief over her face, her mantle and her mask were on the bed. She began to abuse Murray for introducing a third person, but he silenced her by brutally calling her by her right name. We found a pair of pistols and a dagger hidden in the folds of her dress, which we took from her, threatening her with imprisonment if she made the slightest disturbance. After some protest she decided that it would be better to make friends with us, if possible, and told us the whole story. Capsucefalo had told her that there was a lot of money to be made out of Murray if she were only clever enough to play the game under his directions. She had studied the rôle until he had pronounced her perfect in it; but she was only a poor courtesan from Venice, whose name was Innocente.

We sat down to supper and supped well. We thought fit to utterly neglect the creature, and did not even offer her a glass of wine. Shortly after mid-night we heard someone knocking gently at the door. Murray opened it, and admitted Capsucefalo, who did not change countenance when he saw me, but said, 'Oh, it is you, is it? Well, you know how to keep your mouth shut.'

Murray, who was playing carelessly with the fair one's pistols, asked him quietly, where he was going when he left us, and where he intended to take his protégée.

'Back to the convent.'

'I hardly think so. I fancy it is more likely you will keep each other company in prison.'

119

'I think not,' said the other, in no wise disconcerted, 'for the affair would make too much noise, and the laugh would not be altogether on your side.'

'Come,' said he, addressing his companion, 'it is time we were off.'

Murray, calm and cold as became an Englishman, poured Capsucefalo out some chambertin, and the scoundrel had the impudence to drink his health.

'That is a fine ring you have on,' said Murray; 'may I look at it more closely? It is a good diamond; what did you give for it?'

'Four hundred sequins,' answered Capsucefalo, somewhat abashed.

'I will keep it at that price,' said Murray, putting it into his pocket, 'and we will cry quits, eh, procurer of nuns?'

Capsucefalo remained for a moment speechless, then with a low bow he left the room, followed by his companion.

I congratulated Murray on the neat way in which he had outwitted the knave. He laughed, and shrugging his shoulders, said, 'That is how legends grow; but for you I should have been firmly convinced that the nuns of Venice are as immoral as they are lovely.'

I told the whole story to M.M., and it was curious to note her change of expression – fear, anger, indignation, and pleasure – when I told her that the gentleman who accompanied me to the parlour was the English consul. She expressed disdain when I told her that he had said he would willingly give a hundred guineas a month for the privilege of seeing her from time to time, even with the grating between them. She teased me about Tonine, and I confessed. She told me that I owed it to her, however, to have Capsucefalo put away, and I was obliged to promise her that if the resident did not get rid of him I would. However, two or three days later, when I was dining with Lady Murray (English women, when they are the daughters of titled people, retain the parental title after marriage), Murray told me that he had spoken to the Secretary of the Inquisition about the affair, and that Capsucefalo had been sent back to Cephalonia, and forbidden to re-enter Venice on pain of death. As for the courtesan, no one knew what became of her.

About this time M. de Bernis wrote to me, and to M.M., begging us to think seriously before putting our project of running away together into execution. He said that I must talk sense to our nun, and point out to her that if we went to Paris it would be impossible for him to protect us, and that not all his influence could guarantee safety. We agreed with him and wept, but indeed M.M. was growing convinced and I had very little more trouble with her.

I think that in every man's life there are distinct periods governed by good or bad luck. I was now entering upon one of these latter. I was unsuccessful in whatever I undertook. I had had a long run of luck in love and at cards both. I had won steadily for many months, but now, though love still smiled upon me, chance forsook me altogether. I lost not only my own money but also M.M.'s. At her request I sold her diamonds, but their price went the way of our other possessions. It could now no longer be a question of eloping together. We had nothing to elope on.

One day Murray made me a proposal with regard to Tonine, which I did not feel I should be justified in keeping from her. I loved her, but I knew well enough that we should not be able to spend the rest of our lives together. If I would give her up he offered to establish her in well-furnished apartments where he could see her when he chose. She was to have a maid, a cook, and thirty sequins a month for table expenses, excepting wine, which Murray would attend to himself. He would allow her an annuity of two hundred crowns a year, to which she would be entitled after she had been a year with him. Tonine cried, though she liked the Englishman well enough, except when he tried to speak Venetian, which made her die of laughing. She made me talk of it to her mother; such details were, she said, a little

121

delicate to be spoken of between mother and daughter. Her mother was delighted, however, so that was settled.

Then I went to see M.M. She was sad, for C.C.'s father had died, and her people had removed her from the convent, and were trying to marry her to a lawyer. C.C. had left a letter for me, swearing eternal fidelity. I answered honestly that I had no prospects, and left her free. All the same, C.C. did not marry till after my escape from 'The Leads', when she knew that I could never again set foot in Venice. I saw her twenty-nine years later, a sad little widow. If I were in Venice now I certainly would not offer to marry her, it would be an impertinence at my age, but I would share my little all with her, and we would live together like brother and sister.

The reader will remember my satires on the Abbé Chiari. He had answered them in a pamphlet in which I was roughly handled. I replied to this pamphlet, and threatened the abbé with the bastinado if he were not more careful in his way of speaking in future. He took no public notice of this threat, but I received an anonymous letter bidding me mind myself and leave the abbé alone. About this same time a man named Manuzzi (whom I afterwards found out to be a vile spy in the pay of the inquisitors) offered to get me some diamonds on credit, and on this pretended business obtained admission to my rooms. While there he began to turn over my books and manuscripts, showing special interest in those which dealt with magic. Like a fool, I showed him some books dealing with elementary spirits. My readers will do me the justice to believe that I was not the dupe of this nonsense. I merely amused myself with it, as one may amuse oneself with a clever toy. A few days later the traitor told me that a certain person, whose name he was not at liberty to mention, would give me a thousand sequins for five of my books, provided he was convinced of their authenticity. I confided them to him, and in twenty-four hours he brought them back, saying that the would-be purchaser feared they were forgeries. Some years afterwards I learnt that he had taken them to the Secretary of the State Inquisitors, and the fact of my having such books in my possession was sufficient to convince this official that I was a magician.

Everything went against me in this fatal month. A certain Madame Memno took it into her head that I was teaching her son the precepts of atheism. She appealed to the uncle of M. de Bragadin to check me in my nefarious career, and naturally the old man was only too glad of an excuse to attack me, for like all de Bragadin's family, he was jealous of me. He declared I had obtained an undue influence over his nephew by means of my *cabbala*.

This was growing serious; an *auto-da-fé* might even have become possible, for the things I was accused of concerned the Holy Office, and the Holy Office is a ferocious beast with whom it is dangerous to meddle. There were certain circumstances connected with me, however, which made it difficult for them to shut me up in the ecclesiastical prisons of the Inquisition, and because of this it was finally decided that the State Inquisitors should deal with me. I learnt afterwards that a paid denunciator, supported by two witnesses, had been found to solemnly declare that I did not believe in God, and worshipped the devil. As a proof of this it was alleged that when I lost at play I was never heard to curse Satan! I was also accused of not observing Fridays and other days of abstinence. I was suspected of being a Freemason, and was known to be intimate with foreign ministers, who doubtless, said my traducers, paid me large sums of money for information I obtained from my patrician friends. This was a long and serious list of charges against me. It was obvious that I was looked on with disfavour by many influential personages, and several of my real friends, who were truly interested in me, advised me to travel for a time, but I was too obstinate to listen to their counsels. I knew I was innocent, and therefore I thought I had no cause for fear, besides which the actual troubles and anxieties with which I was beset prevented me from attending to what I considered imaginary difficulties. I was heavily in debt, and had pawned all my valuables. Fortunately I had confided my miniatures, papers, and letters to my old friend, Madame Manzoni. How necessary this precaution was my readers will soon see. On returning from the theatre one night I found my door had been forced; the Grand Inquisitor himself, my landlady told me, accompanied by a body of police, had paid me a domiciliary visit, and had turned over everything in my apartment. They told the woman they were looking for a large case of salt, which was an article of contraband; of course they did not find the pretended object of their search, and after a thorough investigation of my belongings, retired, seemingly empty-handed.

'The case of salt,' said my old friend, de Bragadin, 'is nothing but a pretext. I was a state inquisitor for several months, and I know something of their ways. They do not break open doors in search of contraband goods. Believe me, when I tell you, you must leave Venice at once. Go to Fusina, and from thence to Florence, and do not return till I tell you you can do so without risk.'

Blind and presumptuous as I was, I would not listen to his advice. He then, and as a last resource, begged me to take up my abode in the palace with him, for a patrician's palace is sacred, and the archers of the police do not dare to cross the threshold without a special order from the tribunal. Such an order is rarely or never given.

I am ashamed to say I refused even this request from the dear and worthy old man to whom I owed so much love and gratitude; had I listened to him, I should have saved myself much misery, and him much grief. Long and earnestly he urged me to take some precautions for my safety, but in vain. I was moved when I saw him actually weeping; but as I did not want to yield, I begged him to spare me the sight of his tears. With a strong effort, he controlled himself, made a few casual remarks, and then with a kind, affectionate smile embraced me, saying, 'Perhaps this is the last time we shall see each other, but *Fata viam invenient*.'

I returned his embrace and left him; his prediction was fulfilled. I never saw him again; he died eleven years later.

I was not in the least concerned about my safety, but I was troubled about my debts. On leaving the Bragadin Palace that last time I went to see one of my principal creditors, to persuade him to grant me a delay of eight days before forcing me to pay what I owed him. After a painful interview with this man I went home to bed.

The next morning, before it was light, the door of my room was flung open and the terrible Grand Inquisitor entered.

'Are you Jacques Casanova?' he asked.

He then commanded me to rise and dress myself, and to give him all the papers and documents in my possession, whether written by myself or by others.

'In the virtue of whose order?' I asked.

'The order of the State Tribunal,' he replied, and I knew there was nothing for me to do but to obey.

TO HIS COY MISTRESS

Andrew Marvell

Had we but world enough, and time,
This coyness, Lady, were no crime.
We would sit down, and think which way
To walk, and pass our long love's day.
Thou by the Indian Ganges' side
Shouldst rubies find: I by the tide
Of Humber would complain. I would
Love you ten years before the flood:
And you should, if you please, refuse
Till the conversion of the Jews.
My vegetable love should grow
Vaster than empires, and more slow.
An hundred years should go to praise
Thine eyes, and on thy forehead gaze.
Two hundred to adore each breast:
But thirty thousand to the rest.
An age at least to every part.
And the last age should show your heart:
For, Lady, you deserve this state;
Nor would I love at lower rate.
   But at my back I always hear
Time's winged chariot hurrying near:
And yonder all before us lie
Deserts of vast eternity.
Thy beauty shall no more be found;

Nor, in thy marble vault, shall sound
My echoing song: then worns shall try
That long preserved virginity:
And your quaint honour turn to dust;
And into ashes all my lust.
The grave's a fine and private place,
But none, I think, do there embrace.
Now, therefore, while the youthful hue
Sits on thy skin like morning dew,
And while thy willing soul transpires
At every pore with instant fires,
Now let us sport us while we may;
And now, like amorous birds of prey,
Rather at once our time devour,
Than languish in his slow-chapped power.
Let us roll all our strength, and all
Our sweetness, up into one ball:
And tear our pleasures with rough strife,
Thorough the iron gates of life.
Thus, though we cannot make our sun
Stand still, yet we will make him run.

THE IMPERFECT ENJOYMENT

John Wilmot, Earl of Rochester

Naked she lay, claspt in my longing Arms,
I fill'd with Love, and she all over charms,
Both equally inspir'd with eager fire,
Melting through kindness, flaming in desire;
With *Arms, Legs, Lips*, close clinging to embrace,
She clips me to her *Breast*, and sucks me to her *Face*.
The nimble *Tongue* (*Love's* lesser Lightning) plaid
Within my *Mouth*, and to my thoughts conveyed
Swift Orders, that I shou'd prepare to throw,
The *All-dissolving Thunderbolt* below.
My flutt'ring *Soul*, sprung with the pointed kiss,
Hangs hov'ring o're her *Balmy Brinks* of Bliss.
But whilst her busie hand, wou'd guide that part,
Which shou'd convey my *Soul* up to her *Heart*,
In liquid *Raptures*, I dissolve all o're,
Melt into Sperme, and spend at ev'ry Pore:
A touch from any part of her had don't,
Her Hand, her Foot, her very look's a *Cunt*.
Smiling, she chides in a kind murm'ring *Noise*,
And from her *Body* wipes the clammy joys;
When with a Thousand Kisses, wand'ring o're
My panting *Bosome*, – is there then no more?
She cries. All this to Love, and *Rapture's* due,
Must we not pay a debt to pleasure too?
But I the most forlorn, lost *Man* alive,

To shew my wisht Obedience vainly strive,
I sigh alas! and Kiss, but cannot Swive.
Eager desires, confound my first intent,
Succeeding shame, does more success prevent,
And *Rage*, at last, confirms me impotent.
Ev'n her fair Hand, which might bid heat return
To frozen *Age*, and make cold *Hermits* burn,
Apply'd to my dead *Cinder*, warms no more,
Than Fire to *Ashes*, cou'd past Flames restore.
Trembling, confus'd, despairing, limber, dry,
A wishing, weak, unmoving lump I ly.
This *Dart* of love, whose piercing point oft try'd,
With *Virgin blood*, *Ten thousand Maids* has dy'd;
Which *Nature* still directed with such *Art*,
That it through ev'ry *Cunt*, reacht ev'ry *Heart*.
Stiffly resolv'd, twou'd carelessly invade,
Woman or *Man*, nor ought its fury staid,
Where e're it pierc'd, a *Cunt* it found or made.
Now languid lies, in this unhappy hour,
Shrunk up, and Sapless, like a wither'd *Flow'r*.
Thou treacherous, base, deserter of my flame,
False to my passion, fatal to my *Fame*;
Through what mistaken *Magick* dost thou prove,
So true to lewdness, so untrue to love?
What *Oyster*, *Cinder*, *Beggar*, common *Whore*,
Didst thou e're fail in all thy Life before?
When *Vice*, *Disease* and *Scandal* lead the way,
With what officious hast dost thou obey?
Like a Rude roaring *Hector*, in the *Streets*,
That Scuffles, Cuffs, and Ruffles all he meets;
But if his *King*, or *Country*, claim his Aid,
The *Rakehell Villain*, shrinks, and hides his head:
Ev'n so thy *Brutal Valor*, is displaid,
Breaks ev'ry *Stew*, does each small *Whore* invade,
But when great *Love*, the onset does command,
Base Recreant, to thy *Prince*, thou darst not stand.
Worst part of me, and henceforth hated most,
Through all the *Town*, a common *Fucking Post*;
On whom each *Whore*, relieves her tingling *Cunt*,
As *Hogs*, on *Gates*, do rub themselves and grunt.

May'st thou to rav'nous *Shankers*, be a *Prey*,
Or in consuming *Weepings* waste away.
May *Strangury*, and *Stone*, thy *Days* attend,
May'st thou ne're Piss, who didst refuse to spend,
When all my joys, did on false thee depend.
And may *Ten thousand* abler *Pricks* agree,
To do the wrong'd *Corinna*, right for thee.

from THE MEMOIRS OF HARRIETTE WILSON

written by herself

Harriette Wilson rose from being a mere shopkeeper's daughter to being the mistress to the Duke of Wellington. Witty and charming, Wilson recounts her days and experiences as a much sought-after courtesan.

I shall not say why and how I became, at the age of fifteen, the mistress of the Earl of Craven. Whether it was love, or the severity of my father, the depravity of my own heart, or the winning arts of the noble Lord, which induced me to leave my paternal roof and place myself under his protection, does not now much signify: or if it does, I am not in the humour to gratify curiosity in this matter.

I resided on the Marine Parade, at Brighton; and I remember that Lord Craven used to draw cocoa trees, and his fellows, as he called them, on the best vellum paper, for my amusement. Here stood the enemy, he would say; and here, my love, are my fellows: there the cocoa trees, etc. It was, in fact, a dead bore. All these cocoa trees and fellows, at past eleven o'clock at night, could have no peculiar interest for a child like myself, so lately in the habit of retiring early to rest. One night, I recollect, I fell asleep; and, as I often dream, I said, yawning, and half awake, Oh, Lord! oh, Lord! Craven has got me into the West Indies again. In short, I soon found that I had made but a bad speculation by going from my father to Lord Craven. I was even more afraid of the latter than I had been of the former; not that there was any particular harm in the man, beyond his cocoa trees; but we never suited nor understood each other.

I was not depraved enough to determine immediately on a new choice, and yet I often thought about it. How, indeed, could I do otherwise, when the Honourable Frederick Lamb was my constant visitor, and talked to me of nothing else? However, in justice to myself, I must declare that the idea of the possibility of deceiving Lord Craven, while I was under his roof, never once entered my head. Frederick was then very handsome; and certainly tried, with all his soul and with all his strength, to convince me that constancy to Lord Craven was the greatest nonsense in the world. I firmly believe that Frederick Lamb sincerely loved me, and deeply regretted that he had no fortune to invite me to share with him.

Lord Melbourne, his father, was a good man. Not one of your stiff-laced moralizing fathers, who preach chastity and forbearance to their children. Quite the contrary; he congratulated his son on the lucky circumstance of his friend Craven having such a fine girl with him. 'No such thing,' answered Frederick Lamb; 'I am unsuccessful there. Harriette will have nothing to do with me.' – 'Nonsense!' rejoined Melbourne, in great surprise; 'I never heard anything half so ridiculous in all my life. The girl must be mad! She looks mad: I thought so the other day, when I met her galloping about, with her feathers blowing and her thick dark hair about her ears.'

'I'll speak to Harriette for you,' added His Lordship, after a long pause; and then continued repeating to himself, in an undertone, 'Not have my son, indeed! six feet high! a fine, straight, handsome, noble young fellow! I wonder what she would have!'

In truth, I scarcely knew myself; but something I determined on: so miserably tired was I of Craven, and his cocoa trees, and his sailing boats, and his ugly cotton nightcap. Surely, I would say, all men do not wear those shocking cotton nightcaps; else all women's illusions had been destroyed on the first night of their marriage!

I wonder, thought I, what sort of a nightcap the Prince of Wales wears? Then I went on to wonder whether the Prince of Wales would think me so beautiful as Frederick Lamb did? Next I reflected that Frederick Lamb was younger than the Prince; but then, again, a Prince of Wales!!!

I was undecided: my heart began to soften. I thought of my dear mother, and wished I had never left her. It was too late, however, now. My father would not suffer me to return; and as to passing my life, or any more of it, with Craven, cotton nightcap and all, it was death! He never once made me laugh, nor said nor did anything to please me.

Thus musing, I listlessly turned over my writing-book, half in the humour to address the Prince of Wales. A sheet of paper, covered with Lord Craven's cocoa trees, decided me; and I wrote the following letter, which I addressed to the Prince.

Brighton.

I am told that I am very beautiful, so, perhaps, you would like to see me; and I wish that, since so many are disposed to love me, one, for in the humility of my heart I should be quite satisfied with one, would be at the pains to make me love him. In the mean time, this is all very dull work, Sir, and worse even than being at home with my father: so, if you pity me, and believe you could make me in love with you, write to me, and direct to the post-office here.

By return of post, I received an answer nearly to this effect: I believe, from Colonel Thomas.

Miss Wilson's letter has been received by the noble

133

individual to whom it was addressed. If Miss Wilson will come to town, she may have an interview, by directing her letter as before.

I answered this note directly, addressing my letter to the Prince of Wales.

Sir,

To travel fifty-two miles, this bad weather, merely to see a man, with only the given number of legs, arms, fingers, etc., would, you must admit, be madness, in a girl like myself, surrounded by humble admirers, who are ever ready to travel any distance for the honour of kissing the tip of her little finger; but if you can prove to me that you are one bit better than any man who may be ready to attend my bidding, I'll e'en start for London directly. So, if you can do anything better, in the way of pleasing a lady, than ordinary men, write directly: if not, adieu, Monsieur le Prince.

I won't say Yours,
By day or night, or any kind of light;
Because you are too impudent.

It was necessary to put this letter into the post office myself, as Lord Craven's black footman would have been somewhat surprised at its address. Crossing the Steyne, I met Lord Melbourne, who joined me immediately.

'Where is Craven?' said His Lordship, shaking hands with me.

'Attending to his military duties at Lewes, my Lord.'

'And where's my son Fred?' asked His Lordship.

'I am not your son's keeper, my Lord,' said I.

'No! By the bye,' inquired His Lordship, 'how is this? I wanted to call upon you about it. I never heard of such a thing, in the whole course of my life! What the Devil can you possibly have to say against my son Fred?'

'Good heavens! my Lord, you frighten me! I never recollect to have said a single word against your son, as long as I have lived. Why should I?'

'Why, indeed!' said Lord Melbourne. 'And since there is nothing to be said against him, what excuse can you make for using him so ill?'

'I don't understand you one bit, my Lord.' (The very idea of a father put me in a tremble.)

'Why,' said Lord Melbourne, 'did you not turn the poor boy out of your house, as soon as it was dark; although Craven was in town, and there was not the shadow of an excuse for such treatment?'

At this moment, and before I could recover from my surprise at the tenderness of some parents, Frederick Lamb, who was almost my shadow, joined us.

'Fred, my boy,' said Lord Melbourne, 'I'll leave you two together; and I fancy you'll find Miss Wilson more reasonable.' He touched his hat to me, as he entered the little gate of the Pavilion, where we had remained stationary from the moment His Lordship had accosted me.

Frederick Lamb laughed long, loud, and heartily at his father's interference. So did I, the moment he was safely out of sight; and then I told him of my answer to the Prince's letter, at which he laughed still more. He was charmed with me for refusing His Royal Highness. 'Not,' said Frederick, 'that he is not as handsome and graceful a man as any in England; but I hate the weakness of a woman who knows not how to refuse a prince, merely because he is a prince.' – 'It is something, too, to be of royal blood,' answered I frankly; 'and something more to be so accomplished: but this posting after a man! I wonder what he could mean by it!!'

Frederick Lamb now began to plead his own cause. 'I must soon join my regiment in Yorkshire,' said he (he was, at that time, aide-de-camp to General Mackenzie); 'God knows when we may meet again! I am sure you will not long continue with Lord Craven. I foresee what will happen, and yet, when it does, I think I shall go mad!'

For my part, I felt flattered and obliged by the affection

Frederick Lamb evinced towards me; but I was still not in love with him.

At length the time arrived when poor Frederick Lamb could delay his departure from Brighton no longer. On the eve of it, he begged to be allowed to introduce his brother William to me.

'What for?' said I.

'That he may let me know how you behave,' answered Frederick Lamb.

'And if I fall in love with him?' I inquired.

'I am sure you won't,' replied Fred. 'Not because my brother William is not likeable; on the contrary, William is much handsomer than I am; but he will not love you as I have done, and do still; and you are too good to forget me entirely.'

Our parting scene was rather tender. For the last ten days, Lord Craven being absent, we had scarcely been separated an hour during the whole day. I had begun to feel the force of habit; and Frederick Lamb really respected me, for the perseverance with which I had resisted his urgent wishes, when he would have had me deceive Lord Craven. He had ceased to torment me with such wild fits of passion as had, at first, frightened me; and by these means he had obtained much more of my confidence.

Two days after his departure for Hull, in Yorkshire, Lord Craven returned to Brighton, where he was immediately informed, by some spiteful enemy of mine, that I had been, during the whole of his absence, openly intriguing with Frederick Lamb. In consequence of this information, one evening, when I expected his return, his servant brought me the following letter, dated Lewes:

A friend of mine has informed me of what has been going on at Brighton. This information, added to what I have seen with my own eyes, of your intimacy with Frederick Lamb, obliges me to declare that we must separate. Let me add, Harriette, that you might have done anything with me, with only a little more conduct. As it is, allow me to wish you happy; and further, pray inform me, if, in any way, *a la distance*, I can promote your welfare.

Craven.

This letter completed my dislike of Lord Craven. I answered it immediately, as follows:

My lord,

Had I ever wished to deceive you, I have the wit to have done it successfully; but you are old enough to be a better judge of human nature than to have suspected me of guile or deception. In the plenitude of your condescension, you are pleased to add, that I 'might have done anything with you, with only a little more conduct', now I say, and from my heart, the Lord defend me from ever doing any thing with you again! Adieu.

Harriette.

My present situation was rather melancholy and embarrassing, and yet I felt my heart the lighter for my release from the cocoa trees, without its being my own act and deed. It is my fate! thought I; for I never wronged this man. I hate his fine carriage, and his money, and everything belonging to, or connected with him. I shall hate cocoa as long as I live; and, I am sure, I will never enter a boat again, if I can help it. This is what one gets by acting with principle.

The next morning, while I was considering what was to become of me, I received a very affectionate letter from Frederick Lamb, dated Hull. He dared not, he said, be selfish enough to ask me to share his poverty, and yet he had a kind of presentiment, that he should not lose me.

My case was desperate; for I had taken a vow not to remain another night under Lord Craven's roof. John, therefore, the black, whom Craven had, I suppose, imported, with his cocoa trees from the West Indies, was desired to secure me a place in the mail for Hull.

It is impossible to do justice to the joy and rapture which brightened Frederick's countenance, when he flew to receive

137

me, and conducted me to his house, where I was shortly visited by his worthy general, Mackenzie, who assured me of his earnest desire to make my stay in Hull as comfortable as possible.

We continued here for about three months, and then came to London. Fred Lamb's passion increased daily; but I discovered, on our arrival in London, that he was a voluptuary, somewhat worldly and selfish. My comforts were not considered. I lived in extreme poverty while he contrived to enjoy all the luxuries of life; and suffered me to pass my dreary evenings alone, while he frequented balls, masquerades, etc. Secure of my constancy, he was satisfied -- so was not I! I felt that I deserved better from him.

I asked Frederick, one day, if the Marquis of Lorne was as handsome as he had been represented to me. 'The finest fellow on earth,' said Frederick Lamb, 'all the women adore him'; and then he went on to relate various anecdotes of His Lordship, which strongly excited my curiosity.

Soon after this, he quitted town for a few weeks, and I was left alone in London, without money, or, at any rate, with very little; and Frederick Lamb, who had intruded himself on me at Brighton, and thus become the cause of my separation from Lord Craven, made himself happy; because he believed me faithful, and cared not for my distresses.

This idea disgusted me; and, in a fit of anger, I wrote to the Marquis of Lorne, merely to say that, if he would walk up to Duke's Row, Somerstown, he would meet a most lovely girl.

This was his answer:

If you are but half as lovely as you think yourself, you must be well worth knowing; but how is that to be managed? not in the street! But come to No. 39, Portland-street, and ask for me.

L.

My reply was this:

No! our first meeting must be on the high road, in order that I may have room to run away, in case I don't like you.

Harriette.

The Marquis rejoined:

Well, then, fair lady, tomorrow, at four, near the turnpike, look for me on horseback; and then, you know, I can gallop away.

L.

We met. The Duke (he has since succeeded to the title) did not gallop away; and, for my part, I had never seen a countenance I had thought half so beautifully expressive. I was afraid to look at it, lest a closer examination might destroy all the new and delightful sensations his first glance had inspired in my breast. His manner was most gracefully soft and polished. We walked together for about two hours.

'I never saw such a sunny, happy countenance as yours in my whole life,' said Argyle to me.

'Oh, but I am happier than usual today,' answered I, very naturally.

Before we parted, the Duke knew as much of me and my adventures as I knew myself. He was very anxious to be allowed to call on me.

'And how will your particular friend, Frederick Lamb, like that?' inquired I.

The Duke laughed.

'Well, then,' said His Grace, 'do me the honour, some day, to come and dine or sup with me at Argyle House.'

'I shall not be able to run away, if I go there,' I answered, laughingly, in allusion to my last note.

'Shall you want to run away from me?' said Argyle; and there was something unusually beautiful and eloquent in his· countenance, which brought a deep blush into my cheek.

'When we know each other better?' added Argyle, beseechingly. '*En attendant*, will you walk with me tomorrow?' I assented, and we parted.

I returned to my home in unusual spirits; they were a little damped, however, by the reflection that I had been doing wrong. I cannot, I reasoned with myself, I cannot, I fear, become what the world calls a steady, prudent, virtuous woman. That time is past, even if I was ever fit for it. Still I must distinguish myself from those in the like unfortunate situations, by strict probity and love of truth. I will never become vile. I will always adhere to good faith, as long as anything like kindness or honourable principle is shown towards me; and, when I am ill-used, I will leave my lover rather than deceive him. Frederick Lamb relies in perfect confidence on my honour. True, that confidence is the effect of vanity. He believes that a woman who could resist him, as I did at Brighton, is the safest woman on earth! He leaves me alone, and without sufficient money for common necessaries. No matter, I must tell him tonight, as soon as he arrives from the country, that I have written to, and walked with Lorne. My dear mother would never forgive me, if I became artful.

So mused, and thus reasoned I, till I was interrupted by Frederick Lamb's loud knock at my door. He will be in a fine passion, said I to myself, in excessive trepidation; and I was in such a hurry to have it over, that I related all immediately. To my equal joy and astonishment, Frederick Lamb was not a bit angry. From his manner, I could not help guessing that his friend Lorne had often been found a very powerful rival.

I could see through the delight he experienced, at the idea of possessing a woman whom, his vanity persuaded him, Argyle would sigh for in vain; and, attacking me on my weak point, he kissed me, and said, 'I have the most perfect esteem for my dearest little wife, whom I can, I know, as safely trust with Argyle as Craven trusted her with me.'

'Are you quite sure?' asked I, merely to ease my conscience. 'Were it not wiser to advise me not to walk about with him?'

'No, no,' said Frederick Lamb; 'it is such good fun! bring him up every day to Somerstown and the Jew's Harp House, there to swallow cyder and sentiment. Make him walk up here as many times as you can, dear little Harry, for the honour of your sex, and to punish him for declaring, as he always does, that no woman who will not love him at once is worth his pursuit.'

'I am sorry he is such a coxcomb,' said I.

'What is that to you, you little fool?'

'True,' I replied. And, at that moment, I made a sort of determination not to let the beautiful and voluptuous expression of Argyle's dark blue eyes take possession of my fancy.

'You are a neater figure than the Marquis of Lorne,' said I to Frederick, wishing to think so.

'Lorne is growing fat,' answered Frederick Lamb; 'but he is the most active creature possible, and appears lighter than any man of his weight I ever saw; and then he is, without any exception, the highest-bred man in England.'

'And you desire and permit me to walk about the country with him?'

'Yes; do trot him often up here. I want to have a laugh against Lorne.'

'And you are not jealous?'

'Not at all,' said Frederick Lamb, 'for I am secure of your affections.'

I must not deceive this man, thought I, and the idea began to make me a little melancholy. My only chance, or rather my only excuse, will be his leaving me without the means of existence. This appeared likely; for I was too shy and too proud to ask for money; and Frederick Lamb encouraged me in this amiable forbearance!

The next morning, with my heart beating very unusually

high, I attended my appointment with Argyle. I hoped, nay, almost expected, to find him there before me. I paraded near the turnpike five minutes, then grew angry; in five more, I became wretched; in five more, downright indignant; and, in five more, wretched again – and so I returned home.

This, thought I, shall be a lesson to me hereafter, never to meet a man: it is unnatural; and yet I had felt it perfectly natural to return to the person whose society had made me so happy! No matter, reasoned I, we females must not suffer love or pleasure to glow in our eyes until we are quite sure of a return. We must be dignified! Alas! I can only be and seem what I am. No doubt my sunny face of joy and happiness, which he talked to me about, was understood, and it has disgusted him. He thought me bold, and yet I am sure I never blushed so much in any man's society before.

I now began to consider myself with feelings of the most painful humility. Suddenly I flew to my writing-desk; he shall not have the cut all on his side neither, thought I, with the pride of a child. I will soon convince him I am not accustomed to be slighted; and then I wrote to His Grace, as follows:

It was very wrong and very bold of me, to have sought your acquaintance, in the way I did, my Lord; and I entreat you to forgive and forget my childish folly, as completely as I have forgotten the occasion of it.

So far, so good, thought I, pausing; but then suppose he should, from this dry note, really believe me so cold and stupid as not to have felt his pleasing qualities? Suppose now it were possible that he liked me after all? Then hastily, and half ashamed of myself, I added these few lines:

I have not quite deserved this contempt from you, and, in that consolatory reflection, I take my leave – not in anger, my Lord, but only with the steady determination so to profit by the humiliating lesson you have given me, as never to expose myself to the like contempt again.

Your most obedient servant,
Harriette Wilson.

Having put my letter into the post, I passed a restless night; and, the next morning, heard the knock of the twopenny postman, in extreme agitation. He brought me, as I suspected, an answer from Argyle, which is subjoined.

You are not half vain enough, dear Harriette. You ought to have been quite certain that any man who had once met you, could fail in a second appointment, but from unavoidable accident – and, if you were only half as pleased with Thursday morning as I was, you will meet me tomorrow, in the same place, at four. Pray, pray, come.

Lorne.

I kissed the letter, and put it into my bosom, grateful for the weight it had taken off my heart. Not that I was so far gone in love, as my readers may imagine, but I had suffered severely from wounded pride, and, in fact, I was very much *tête montée*.

The sensations which Argyle had inspired me with, were the warmest, nay, the first of the same nature I had ever experienced. Nevertheless, I could not forgive him quite so easily as this, neither. I recollected what Frederick Lamb had said about his vanity. No doubt, thought I, he thinks it was nothing to have paraded me up and down that stupid turnpike road, in the vain hope of seeing him. It shall now be his turn: and I gloried in the idea of revenge.

The hour of Argyle's appointment drew nigh, arrived, and passed away, without my leaving my house. To Frederick Lamb I related everything – presented him with Argyle's letter, and acquainted him with my determination not to meet His Grace.

'How good!' said Frederick Lamb, quite delighted. 'We dine together today, at Lady Holland's; and I mean to ask him, before everybody at table, what he thinks of the air about the turnpike on Somerstown.'

The next day I was surprised by a letter, not, as I antici-
pated, from Argyle, but from the late Tom Sheridan, only
son of Richard Brinsley Sheridan. I had, by mere accident,
become acquainted with that very interesting young man,
when quite a child, from the circumstances of his having
paid great attention to one of my elder sisters.

He requested me to allow him to speak a few words to me,
wherever I pleased. Frederick Lamb having gone to Brocket
Hall, in Hertfordshire, I desired him to call on me.

'I am come from my friend Lorne,' said Tom Sheridan.
'I would not have intruded on you, but that, poor fellow,
he is really annoyed; and he has commissioned me to
acquaint you with the accident which obliged him to
break his appointment, because I can best vouch for the
truth of it, having, upon my honour, heard the Prince of
Wales invite Lord Lorne to Carlton House, with my own
ears, at the very moment when he was about to meet you in
Somerstown. Lorne,' continued Tom Sheridan, 'desires me
to say, that he is not coxcomb enough to imagine you cared
for him; but, in justice, he wants to stand exactly where he
did in your opinion, before he broke his appointment: he
was so perfectly innocent on that subject. I would write to
her, said he, again and again; but that, in all probability, my
letters would be shown to Frederick Lamb, and be laughed
at by them both. I would call on her, in spite of the devil,
but that I know not where she lives.

'I asked Argyle,' Tom Sheridan proceeded, 'how he
had addressed his last letters to you? To the post office,
in Somerstown, was his answer, and thence they were
forwarded to Harriette. He had tried to bribe the old
woman there, to obtain my address, but she abused him,
and turned him out of her shop. It is very hard,' continued
Tom, repeating the words of his noble friend, 'to lose the
goodwill of one of the nicest, cleverest girls I ever met
with in my life, who was, I am certain, civilly, if not kindly
disposed towards me, by such a mere accident. Therefore,'

144

continued Tom Sheridan, smiling, 'you'll make it up with Lorne, won't you?'

'There is nothing to forgive,' said I, 'if no slight was meant. In short, you are making too much of me, and spoiling me, by all this explanation; for, indeed, I had, at first, been less indignant; but that I fancied His Grace neglected me, because – ' and I hesitated, while I could feel myself blush deeply.

'Because what?' asked Tom Sheridan.

'Nothing,' I replied, looking at my shoes.

'What a pretty girl you are,' observed Sheridan, 'particularly when you blush.'

'Fiddlestick!' said I, laughing; 'you know you always preferred my sister Fanny.'

'Well,' replied Tom, 'there I plead guilty. Fanny is the sweetest creature on earth; but you are all a race of finished coquettes, who delight in making fools of people. Now can anything come up to your vanity in writing to Lorne, that you are the most beautiful creature on earth?'

'Never mind,' said I, 'you set all that to rights. I was never vain in your society, in my life.'

'I would give the world for a kiss at this moment,' said Tom; 'because you look so humble, and so amiable; but' – recollecting himself – 'this is not exactly the embassy I came upon. Have you a mind to give Lorne an agreeable surprise?'

'I don't know.'

'Upon my honour I believe he is downright in love with you.'

'Well?'

'Come into a hackney coach with me, and we will drive down to the Tennis Court, in the Haymarket.'

'Is the Duke there?'

'Yes.'

'But – at all events, I will not trust myself in a hackney coach with you.'

'There was a time,' said poor Tom Sheridan, with much drollery of expression, 'there was a time when the very motion of a carriage would – but now!' – and he shook his handsome head with comic gravity – 'but now! you may drive with me, from here to St Paul's, in the most perfect safety. I will tell you a secret,' added he, and he fixed his fine dark eye on my face while he spoke, in a tone, half merry, half desponding, 'I am dying; but nobody knows it yet!'

I was very much affected by his manner of saying this.

'My dear Mr Sheridan,' said I, with earnest warmth, 'you have accused me of being vain of the little beauty God has given me. Now I would give it all, or, upon my word, I think I would, to obtain the certainty that you would, from this hour, refrain from such excesses as are destroying you.'

'Did you see me play the Methodist parson, in a tub, at Mrs Beaumont's masquerade, last Thursday?' said Tom, with affected levity.

'You may laugh as you please,' said I, 'at a little fool like me pretending to preach to you; yet I am sensible enough to admire you, and quite feeling enough to regret your time so misspent, your brilliant talents so misapplied.'

'Bravo! Bravo!' Tom reiterated, 'what a funny little girl you are! Pray, Miss, how is your time spent?'

'Not in drinking brandy,' I replied.

'And how might your talent be applied, Ma'am?'

'Have not I just given you a specimen, in the shape of a handsome quotation?'

'My good little girl – it is in the blood, and I can't help it, – and, if I could, it is too late now. I'm dying, I tell you. I know not if my poor father's physician was as eloquent as you are; but he did his best to turn him from drinking. Among other things, he declared to him one day, that the brandy, Arquebusade, and eau de Cologne he swallowed, would burn off the coat of his stomach. Then, said my father, my stomach must digest in its waistcoat; for I cannot help it.'

'Indeed, I am very sorry for you,' I replied; and I hope he believed me; for he pressed my hand hastily, and I think I saw a tear glisten in his bright, dark eye.

'Shall I tell Lorne,' said poor Tom, with an effort to recover his usual gaiety, 'that you will write to him, or will you come to the Tennis Court?'

'Neither,' answered I; 'but you may tell His Lordship that, of course, I am not angry, since I am led to believe he had no intention to humble nor make a fool of me.'

'Nothing more?' inquired Tom.

'Nothing,' I replied, 'for His Lordship.'

'And what for me?' said Tom.

'You! what do you want?'

'A kiss!' he said.

'Not I, indeed!'

'Be it so, then; and yet you and I may never meet again on this earth, and just now I thought you felt some interest about me'; and he was going away.

'So I do, dear Tom Sheridan!' said I, detaining him; for I saw death had fixed his stamp on poor Sheridan's handsome face. 'You know I have a very warm and feeling heart, and taste enough to admire and like you; but why is this to be our last meeting?'

'I must go to the Mediterranean,' poor Sheridan continued, putting his hand to his chest, and coughing.

To die! thought I, as I looked on his sunk, but still very expressive dark eyes.

'Then God bless you!' said I, first kissing his hand, and then, though somewhat timidly, leaning my face towards him. He parted my hair, and kissed my forehead, my eyes, and my lips.

'If I do come back,' said he, forcing a languid smile, 'mind let me find you married, and rich enough to lend me an occasional hundred pounds or two.' He then kissed his hand gracefully, and was out of sight in an instant.

I never saw him again.

The next morning my maid brought me a little note from Argyle, to say that he had been waiting about my door an hour, having learned my address from poor Sheridan; and that, seeing the servant in the street, he could not help making an attempt to induce me to go out and walk with him. I looked out of the window, saw Argyle, ran for my hat and cloak, and joined him in an instant.

'Am I forgiven?' said Argyle, with gentle eagerness.

'Oh yes,' returned I, 'long ago; but that will do you no good, for I really am treating Frederick Lamb very ill, and therefore must not walk with you again.'

'Why not?' Argyle inquired. '*Apropos*,' he added, 'you told Frederick that I walked about the turnpike looking for you, and that, no doubt, to make him laugh at me?'

'No, not for that; but I never could deceive any man. I have told him the whole story of our becoming acquainted, and he allows me to walk with you. It is I who think it wrong, not Frederick.'

'That is to say, you think me a bore,' said Argyle, reddening with pique and disappointment.

'And suppose I loved you?' I asked, 'still I am engaged to Frederick Lamb, who trusts me, and — '

'If,' interrupted Argyle, 'it were possible you did love me, Frederick Lamb would be forgotten: but, though you did not love me, you must promise to try and do so, some day or other. You don't know how much I have fixed my heart on it.'

These sentimental walks continued more than a month. One evening we walked rather later than usual. It grew dark. In a moment of ungovernable passion, Argyle's ardour frightened me. Not that I was insensible to it: so much the contrary, that I felt certain another meeting must decide my fate. Still, I was offended at what, I conceived, shewed such a want of respect. The Duke became humble. There is a charm in the humility of a lover who has offended. The charm is so great that we like to prolong it. In spite of all he could say, I left him in anger. The next morning I received the following note:

> If you see me waiting about your door, tomorrow morning, do you not fancy I am looking for you; but for your pretty housemaid.

I did see him from a sly corner of my window; but I resisted all my desires, and remained concealed. I dare not see him again, thought I, for I cannot be so very profligate, knowing and feeling, as I do, how impossible it will be to refuse him anything, if we meet again. I cannot treat Fred Lamb in that manner! besides, I should be afraid to tell him of it: he would, perhaps, kill me.

But then, poor dear Lorne! to return his kisses, as I did last night, and afterwards be so very severe on him, for a passion which it seemed so out of his power to control!

Nevertheless we must part, now or never; so I'll write and take my leave of him kindly. This was my letter:

> At the first, I was afraid I should love you, and, but for Fred Lamb having requested me to get you up to Somerstown, after I had declined meeting you, I had been happy: now the idea makes me miserable. Still it must be so. I am naturally affectionate. Habit attaches me to Fred Lamb. I cannot deceive him or acquaint him with what will cause him to cut me, in anger and for ever. We may not then meet again, Lorne, as hitherto: for now we could not be merely friends: lovers we must be, hereafter, or nothing. I have never loved any man in my life before, and yet, dear Lorne, you see we must part. I venture to send you the inclosed thick lock of my hair; because you have been good enough to admire it. I do not care how I have disfigured my head, since you are not to see it again.
>
> God bless you, Lorne. Do not quite forget last night directly, and believe me, as in truth I am,
>
> Most devotedly yours,
Harriette.

This was his answer, written, I suppose, in some pique.

True, you have given me many sweet kisses, and a lock of your beautiful hair. All this does not convince me you are one bit in love with me. I am the last man on earth to desire you to do violence to your feelings, by leaving a man as dear to you as Frederick Lamb is; so farewell, Harriette. I shall not intrude to offend you again.

Lorne.

Poor Lorne is unhappy; and, what is worse, thought I, he will soon hate me. The idea made me wretched. However, I will do myself the justice to say, that I have seldom, in the whole course of my life, been tempted by my passions or my fancies, to what my heart and conscience told me was wrong. I am afraid my conscience has been a very easy one; but, certainly, I have followed its dictates. There was a want of heart and delicacy, I always thought, in leaving any man, without full and very sufficient reasons for it. At the same time, my dear mother's marriage had proved to me so forcibly, the miseries of two people of contrary opinions and character, torturing each other to the end of their natural lives, that, before I was ten years old, I decided, in my own mind, to live free as air from any restraint but that of my conscience.

Frederick Lamb's love was now increasing, as all men's do, from gratified vanity. He sometimes passed an hour in reading to me. Till then, I had no idea of the gratification to be derived from books. In my convent in France, I had read only sacred dramas; at home, my father's mathematical books, *Buchan's Medicine*, *Gil Blas*, and the *Vicar of Wakefield*, formed our whole library. The two latter I had long known by heart, and could repeat at this moment.

My sisters used to subscribe to little circulating libraries, in the neighbourhood, for the common novels of the day; but I always hated these. Fred Lamb's choice was happy – Milton, Shakespeare, Byron, the Rambler, Virgil, etc. I must know all about these Greeks and Romans, said I to myself. Some day I will go into the country quite alone, and study like mad. I am too young now.

In the meantime, I was absolutely charmed with Shakespeare. Music, I always had a natural talent for. I played well on the pianoforte; that is, with taste and execution, though almost without study.

There was a very elegant-looking woman, residing in my neighbourhood, in a beautiful little cottage, who had long excited my curiosity. She appeared to be the mother of five extremely beautiful children. These were always to be seen with their nurse, walking out, most fancifully dressed. Every one used to stop to admire them. Their mother seemed to live in the most complete retirement. I never saw her with anybody besides her children.

One day our eyes met: she smiled, and I half bowed. The next day we met again, and the lady wished me a good morning. We soon got into conversation. I asked her, if she did not lead a very solitary life? 'You are the first female I have spoken to for four years,' said the lady, 'with the exception of my own servants; but', added she, 'some day we may know each other better. In the meantime will you trust yourself to come and dine with me today?' – 'With great pleasure,' I replied, 'if you think me worthy of that honour.' We then separated to dress for dinner.

When I entered her drawing-room, at the hour she had appointed, I was struck with the elegant taste, more than with the richness of the furniture. A beautiful harp, draw-ings of a somewhat voluptuous cast, elegant needlework, Moore's poems, and a fine pianoforte, formed a part of it. She is not a bad woman – and she is not a good woman, said I to myself. What can she be?

The lady now entered the room, and welcomed me with an appearance of real pleasure. 'I am not quite sure', said she, 'whether I can have the pleasure of introducing you to Mr Johnstone today, or not. We will not wait dinner for him, if he does not arrive in time.' This was the first word I had heard about a Mr Johnstone, although I knew the lady was called by that name.

Just as we were sitting down to dinner, Mr Johnstone arrived, and was introduced to me. He was a particularly elegant handsome man, about forty years of age. His manner of addressing Mrs Johnstone was more that of a humble romantic lover than of a husband; yet Julia, for so he called her, could be no common woman. I could not endure all this mystery, and, when he left us in the evening, I frankly asked Julia, for so we will call her in future, why she invited a strange madcap girl like me to dinner with her?

'Consider the melancholy life I lead,' said Julia.

'Thank you for the compliment,' answered I.

'But do you believe', interrupted Julia, 'that I should have asked you to dine with me, if I had not been particularly struck and pleased with you? I had, as I passed your window, heard you touch the pianoforte with a very masterly hand, and therefore I conceived that you were not uneducated, and I knew that you led almost as retired a life as myself. *Au reste,*' continued Julia, 'some day, perhaps soon, you shall know all about me.'

I did not press the matter further at that moment, believing it would be indelicate.

'Shall we go to the nursery?' asked Julia.

I was delighted; and, romping with her lovely children, dressing their dolls, and teaching them to skip, I forgot my love for Argyle, as much as if that excellent man had never been born.

Indeed I am not quite sure that it would have occurred to me even when I went home, but that Fred Lamb, who was just at this period showing Argyle up all over the town as my amorous shepherd, had a new story to relate of His Grace.

Horace Beckford and two other fashionable men, who had heard from Frederick of my cruelty, as he termed it, and the Duke's daily romantic walks to the Jew's Harp House, had come upon him, by accident, in a body, as they were galloping through Somerstown. Lorne was sitting, in a very pastoral fashion, on a gate near my door, whistling. They saluted him with a loud laugh. No man could, generally speaking, parry a joke better than Argyle: for few knew the world better: but this was no joke. He had been severely wounded and annoyed by my cutting his acquaintance altogether, at the very moment when he had reason to believe that the passion he really felt for me was returned. It was almost the first instance of the kind he had ever met with. He was bored and vexed with himself, for the time he had lost, and yet he found himself continually in my neighbourhood, almost before he was aware of it. He wanted, as he has told me since, to meet me once more by accident, and then he declared he would give me up.

'What a set of consummate asses you are,' said Argyle to Beckford and his party; and then quietly continued on the gate, whistling as before.

'But r-e-a-l-l-y, r-e-a-l-l-y, ca-ca-cannot Tom She-She-She-Sheridan assist you, Marquis?' said the handsome Horace Beckford, in his usual stammering way.

'A very good joke for Fred Lamb, as the case stands now,' replied the Duke, laughing; for a man of the world must laugh in these cases, though he should burst with the effort.

'Why don't she come?' said Sir John Shelley, who was one of the party.

An odd mad-looking Frenchman, in a white coat and a white hat, well known about Somerstown, passed at this moment, and observed His Grace, whom he knew well by sight, from the other side of the way. He had, a short time before, attempted to address me, when he met me walking alone, and inquired of me, when I had last seen the Marquis of Lorne, with whom he had often observed me walking? I made him no answer. In a fit of frolic, as if everybody combined at this moment against the poor, dear, handsome Argyle, the Frenchman called, as loud as he

153

could scream, from the other side of the way, '*Ah! ah! oh! oh! vous voilà, Monsieur le Comte Dromedaire* (alluding thus to the Duke's family name, as pronounced Camel), *Mais où est donc Madame la Comtesse?*'

'D—d impudent rascal!' said Argyle, delighted to vent his growing rage on somebody, and started across the road after the poor thin old Frenchman, who might have now said his prayers, had not his spider-legs served him better than his courage.

Fred Lamb was very angry with me for not laughing at this story; but the only feeling it excited in me, was unmixed gratitude towards the Duke, for remembering me still, and for having borne all this ridicule for my sake.

The next day Julia returned my visit; and, before we parted, she had learned, from my usual frankness, every particular of my life, without leaving me one atom the wiser as to what related to herself. I disliked mystery so much that, but that I saw Julia's proceeded from the natural extreme shyness of her disposition, I had, by this time, declined continuing her acquaintance. I decided, however, to try her another month, in order to give her time to become acquainted with me. She was certainly one of the best mannered women in England, not excepting even those of the very highest rank. Her handwriting, and her style, were both beautiful. She had the most delicately fair skin, and the prettiest arms, hands, and feet, and the most graceful form, which could well be imagined; but her features were not regular, nor their expression particularly good. She struck me as a woman of very violent passions, combined with an extremely shy and reserved disposition.

Mr Johnstone seldom made his appearance oftener than twice a week. He came across a retired field to her house, though he might have got there more conveniently by the roadway. I sometimes accompanied her, and we sat on a gate to watch his approach to this field. Their meetings were full of rapturous and romantic delight. In his absence, she never received a single visitor, male or female, except myself; yet she always, when quite alone, dressed in the most studied and fashionable style.

There was something dramatic about Julia. I often surprised her, hanging over her harp so very gracefully, the room so perfumed, the rays of her lamp so soft, that I could scarcely believe this *tout ensemble* to be the effect of chance or habit. It appeared arranged for the purpose, like a scene in a play. Yet who was it to affect? Julia never either received or expected company!

Everything went on as usual for another month or two; during which time Julia and I met every day, and she promised shortly to make me acquainted with her whole history. My finances were now sinking very low. Everything Lord Craven had given me, whether in money or valuables, I had freely parted with for my support. Fred Lamb, I thought, must know that these resources cannot last for ever; therefore I am determined not to speak to him on the subject.

I was lodging with a comical old widow, who had formerly been my sister Fanny's nurse when she was quite a child. This good lady, I believe, really did like me, and had already given me all the credit for board and lodging she could possibly afford. She now entered my room, and acquainted me that she actually had not another shilling, either to provide my dinner or her own.

Necessity hath no law, thought I, my eyes brightening, and my determination being fixed in an instant. In ten minutes more, the following letter was in the post office, directed to the Marquis of Lorne.

If you still desire my society, I will sup with you tomorrow evening in your own house.

Yours, ever affectionately,
Harriette.

155

I knew perfectly well that on the evening I mentioned to His Grace, Fred Lamb would be at his father's country house, Brocket Hall.

The Duke's answer was brought to me by his groom, as soon as he had received my letter; it ran thus:

Are you really serious? I dare not believe it. Say, by my servant, that you will see me, at the turnpike, directly, for five minutes, only to put me out of suspense. I will not believe anything you write on this subject. I want to look at your eyes, while I hear you say yes.

> Yours, most devotedly and impatiently,
> *Lorne*.

I went to our place of rendezvous to meet the Duke. How different, and how much more amiable, was his reception than that of Fred Lamb in Hull! The latter, all wild passion; the former, gentle, voluptuous, fearful of shocking or offending me, or frightening away my growing passion. In short, while the Duke's manner was almost as timid as my own, the expression of his eyes and the very soft tone of his voice, troubled my imagination, and made me fancy something of bliss beyond all reality.

We agreed that he should bring a carriage to the old turnpike, and thence conduct me to his house. 'If you should change your mind!' said the Duke, returning a few steps after we had taken leave: '*mais tu viendras, mon ange? Tu ne seras pas si cruelle?*' Argyle is the best Frenchman I ever met with in England, and poor Tom Sheridan was the second best.

'And you,' said I to Argyle, 'suppose you were to break your appointment tonight?'

'Would you regret it?' Argyle inquired. 'I won't have your answer while you are looking at those pretty little feet,' he continued. 'Tell me, dear Harriette, should you be sorry?'

'Yes,' said I, softly, and our eyes met, only for an

156

instant. Lorne's gratitude was expressed merely by pressing my hand.

'*A ce soir, donc*,' said he, mounting his horse; and, waving his hand to me, he was soon out of sight.

from JOSEPH ANDREWS
Henry Fielding

The following extract details the sexual adventures of a capricious chambermaid whose good nature, generosity and warmth prove a volatile combination.

Betty, who was the occasion of all this hurry, had some good qualities: she had good-nature, generosity, and compassion; but unfortunately her constitution was composed of those warm ingredients which, though the purity of courts or nunneries might have happily controlled them, were by no means enabled to endure the ticklish situation of a chambermaid at an inn; who is daily liable to the solicitations of lovers of all complexions; to the dangerous addresses of fine gentlemen of the army, who sometimes are obliged to reside with them a whole year together; and, above all, are exposed to the caresses of footmen, stage-coachmen, and drawers: all of whom employ the whole artillery of kissing, flattering, bribing, and every other weapon which is to be found in the whole armoury of love, against them.

Betty, who was but one-and-twenty, had now lived three years in this dangerous situation, during which she had escaped pretty well. An ensign of foot was the first person who made an impression on her heart: he did, indeed, raise a flame in her, which required the care of a surgeon to cool.

While she burned for him, several others burned for her. Officers of the army, young gentlemen travelling the western circuit, inoffensive squires, and some of graver character, were set a-fire by her charms.

At length, having perfectly recovered the effects of her first unhappy passion, she seemed to have vowed a state of perpetual chastity. She was long deaf to all the sufferings of her lovers, till one day, at a neighbouring fair, the rhetoric of John the ostler, with a new straw hat and a pint of wine, made a second conquest over her.

She did not, however, feel any of those flames on this occasion which had been the consequence of her former amour; nor, indeed, those other ill effects which prudent young women very justly apprehend from too absolute an indulgence to the pressing endearments of their lovers. This latter, perhaps, was a little owing to her not being entirely constant to John, with whom she permitted Tom Whipwell, the stage-coachman, and now and then a handsome young traveller, to share her favours.

Mr Tow-wouse had for some time cast the languishing eyes of affection on this young maiden: he had laid hold on every opportunity of saying tender things to her, squeezing her by the hand, and sometimes kissing her lips; for as the violence of his passion had considerably abated to Mrs Tow-wouse, so, like water which is stopped from its usual current in one place, it naturally sought a vent in another. Mrs Tow-wouse is thought to have perceived this abatement, and probably it added very little to the natural sweetness of her temper; for though she was as true to her husband as the dial to the sun, she was rather more desirous of being shone on, as being more capable of feeling his warmth.

Ever since Joseph's arrival, Betty had conceived an extraordinary liking to him, which discovered itself more and more, as he grew better and better, till that fatal evening when, as she was warming his bed, her passion grew to such a height, and so perfectly mastered both her modesty and her reason, that, after many fruitless hints and sly insinuations, she at last threw down the warming-pan, and, embracing him with great eagerness, swore he was the handsomest creature she had ever seen.

Joseph, in great confusion, leaped from her, and told her he was sorry to see a young woman cast off all regard to modesty; but she had gone too far to recede, and grew so very indecent, that Joseph was obliged, contrary to his inclination, to use some violence to her; and, taking her in his arms, he shut her out of the room, and locked the door.

How ought man to rejoice that his chastity is always in his own power; that if he has sufficient strength of mind, he has always a competent strength of body to defend himself: and cannot, like a poor weak woman, be ravished against his will!

Betty was in the most violent agitation at this disappointment. Rage and lust pulled her heart, as with two strings, two different ways. One moment she thought of stabbing Joseph; the next, of taking him in her arms, and devouring him with kisses; but the latter passion was far more prevalent. Then she thought of revenging his refusal on herself; but whilst she was engaged in this meditation, happily death presented himself to her in so many shapes of drowning, hanging, poisoning, &c., that her distracted mind could resolve on none.

In this perturbation of spirit, it accidentally occurred to her memory that her master's bed was not made: she therefore went directly to his room, where he happened at that time to be engaged at his bureau. As soon as she saw him, she attempted to retire; but he called her back, and taking her by the hand, squeezed her so tenderly, at the same time whispering so many soft things into her ears, and then pressed her so closely with his kisses, that the vanquished fair one, whose passions were already raised, and which were not so whimsically capricious that one man only could lay them – though perhaps she would have rather preferred that one – the vanquished fair one quietly submitted, I say, to her master's will, who had just attained the accomplishment of his bliss, when Mrs Tow-wouse unexpectedly entered the room, and caused all that confusion which we have before seen, and which it is not necessary at present to take any farther notice of, since, without the assistance of a single hint from us, every reader of any speculation or experience, though not married himself, may easily conjecture that it concluded with the discharge of Betty, the submission of Mr Tow-wouse, with some things to be performed on his side by way of gratitude for his wife's goodness in being reconciled to him, with many hearty promises never to offend any more in the like manner, and, lastly, his quietly and contentedly bearing to be reminded of his transgressions, as a kind of penance, once or twice a day, during the residue of his life.

DILDOIDES
Samuel Butler

Light-hearted and amusing, here Samuel Butler describes the public burning of a barrel full of dildoes at Stocksmarket, England, in 1672.

Such a sad tale prepare to hear,
As claims from either sex a tear.
Twelve dildoes meant for the support
Of aged lechers of the Court
Were lately burnt by impious hand
Of trading rascals of the land,
Who envying their curious frame,
Expos'd those Priaps to the flame.
Oh! barbarous times! when deities
Are made themselves a sacrifice!
Some were composed of shining horns,
More precious than the unicorn's.
Some were of wax, where ev'ry vein,
And smallest fibre were made plain.

Some were for tender virgins fit,
Some for the large salacious slit
Of a rank lady, tho' so torn,
She hardly feels when child is born.
　　Dildo has nose, but cannot smell,
No stink can his great courage que'l;
Nor faintly ask you what you ail;
E're pintle, damn'd rogue, will do his duty,
And then sometimes he will not stand too,
Whate'er his gallant or mistress can do.
　　But I too long have left my heroes,
Who fell into worse hands than Nero's,
Twelve of them shut up in a box,
Martyrs as true as are in Fox
Were seiz'd upon as goods forbidden,
Deep, under unlawful traffick hidden;
When Council grave, of deepest beard,
Were call'd for, out of city-herd.
But see the fate of cruel treachery,
Those goats in head, but not in lechery,
Forgetting each his wife and daughter,
Condemn'd these dildoes to the slaughter;
Cuckolds with rage were blinded so,
They did not their preservers know.
One less fanatic than the rest,
Stood up, and thus himself address'd:
　　These dildoes may do harm, I know;
But pray what is it may not so;
Plenty has often made men proud,
And above Law advanc'd the crowd:
Religion's self has ruin'd nations,
And caused vast depopulations;
Yet no wise people e'er refus'd it,
'Cause knaves and fools sometimes abus'd it.
Are you afraid, lest merry griggs
Will wear false pricks like periwigs;
And being but to small ones born,
Will great ones have of wax and horn;
Since even that promotes our gain,
Methinks unjustly we complain,

If ladies rather chuse to handle
Our wax in dildo than in candle,
Much good may't do 'em, so they pay for it,
And that the merchants never stay for't.
For, neighbours, is't not all one, whether
In dildoes or shoes they wear our leather?
Whether of horn they make a comb,
Or instrument to chafe the womb,
Like you, I Monsieur Dildo hate;
But the invention let's translate.
You treat 'em may like Turks or Jews,
But I'll have two for my own use,
Priapus was a Roman deity,
And much has been the world's variety,
I am resolv'd I'll none provoke,
From the humble garlic to the oak.
He paus'd, another straight steps in,
With limber prick and grisly chin,
And thus did his harangue begin:
      For soldiers, maim'd by chance of war,
We artificial limbs prepare;
Why then should we bear so much spite
To lechers maim'd in am'rous fight?
That what the French send for relief,
We thus condemn as witch or thief?
By dildoe, Monsieur there intends
For his French pox to make amends;
Dildoe, without the least disgrace,
May well supply the lover's place,
And make our elder girls ne'er care for't,
Though 'twere their fortune to dance bare-foot.
Lechers, whom clap or drink disable,
Might here have dildoes to the navel.
Did not a lady of great honour
Marry a footman waiting on her?
When one of these, timely apply'd,
Had eas'd her lust, and sav'd her pride,
Safely her ladyship might have spent,
While such gallants in pocket went.
Honour itself might use the trade,

While dildo goes in masquerade.
Which of us able to prevent is
His girl from lying with his 'prentice,
Unless we other means provide
For nature to be satisfy'd?
And what more proper than his engine,
Which would outdo 'em, should three men join.
I therefore hold it very foolish,
Things so convenient to abolish;
Which should we burn men justly may
To that one act the ruin lay,
Of all that thrown themselves away.
    At this, all parents' hearts began
To melt apace, and not a man
In all the assembly, but found
These reasons solid were and sound.
Poor widows then with voices shrill,
And shouts of joy the hall did fill;
For wicked pricks have no mind to her,
Who has no money, nor no jointure.
    Then one in haste broke thro' the throng,
And cry'd aloud, are we among
Heathens or devils, to let 'scape us
The image of the God Priapus?
Green-sickness girls will strait adore him,
And wickedly fall down before him.
From him each superstitious hussy
Will temples make of tussy mussy.
Idolatry will fill the land,
And all true pricks forget to stand.
Curst be the wretch, who found these arts
Of losing us to women's hearts;
For will they not henceforth refuse one
When they have all that they had use on?
Or how shall I make one to pity me,
Who enjoys Man in his epitome?
Besides, what greater deviation
From sacred rights of propagation,
Than turning th'action of the pool
Whence we all come to ridicule?

The man that would have thunder made,
With brazen road, for courser made,
In my mind did not half so ill do.
As he that found this wicked dildo.
Then let's with common indignation,
Now cause a sudden conflagration
Of all these instruments of lewdness;
And, ladies, take it not for rudeness;
For never was so base a treachery
Contriv'd by mortals against lechery,
Men would kind husbands seem, and able,
With feign'd lust, and borrow'd bawble.
Lovers themselves would dress their passion
In this fantastic new French fashion;
And with false heart and member too,
Rich widows for convenience woo.
But the wise City will take care,
That men shall vend no such false ware.
See now th'unstable vulgar mind
Shook like a leaf with ev'ry wind;
No sooner has he spoke, but all
With a great rage for faggots call:
The reasons which before seem'd good,
Were now no longer understood.
This last speech had the fatal power
To bring the dildoes' latest hour.

Priapus thus, in box opprest,
Burnt like a phoenix in her nest;
But with this fatal difference dies,
No dildoes from the ashes rise.

TO THE VIRGINS, TO MAKE MUCH OF TIME

Robert Herrick

Gather ye rose-buds while ye may,
    Old Time is still a-flying,
And this same flower that smiles to-day,
    To-morrow will be dying.

The glorious lamp of heaven, the sun,
    The higher he's a-getting
The sooner will his race be run,
    And nearer he's to setting.

That age is best which is the first,
    When youth and blood are warmer;
But being spent, the worse, and worst
    Times still succeed the former.

Then be not coy, but use your time;
    And while ye may, go marry:
For having lost but once your prime,
    You may for ever tarry.

TO AMANDA, DESIROUS
TO GO TO BED

Nicholas Hookes

Sleepy, my dear? yes, yes, I see
Morpheus is fallen in love with thee;
Morpheus, my worst of rivals, tries
To draw the curtains of thine eyes,
And fans them with his wing asleep;
Makes drowsy love to play bopeep.
How prettily his feathers blow
Those fleshy shuttings to and fro!
O how he makes me Tantalise
With those fair apples of thine eyes!
Equivocates and cheats me still,
Opening and shutting at his will,
Now both, now one! the doting god
Plays with thine eyes at even or odd.
My stammering tongue doubts which it might
Bid thee, goodmorrow or goodnight.
So thy eyes twinkle brighter far
Than the bright trembling evening star;
So a wax taper burnt within
The socket, plays at out and in.
      Thus did Morpheus court thine eye,
Meaning there all night to lie:
Cupid and he play Whoop, All-Hid!
The eye, their bed and coverlid.
      Fairest, let me thy nightclothes air;
Come, I'll unlace thy stomacher.

Make me thy maiden chamberman,
Or let me be thy warming-pan.
O that I might but lay my head
At thy bed's feet i' th' trundle-bed.
Then i' th' morning ere I rose,
I'd kiss thy pretty pettitoes,
Those smaller feet with which i' th' day
My love so neatly trips away.
        Since you I must not wait upon,
Most modest lady, I'll be gone;
And though I cannot sleep with thee,
Oh may my dearest dream of me!
All the night long dream that we move
To the main centre of our love;
And if I chance to dream of thee,
Oh may I dream eternally!
Dream that we freely act and play
Those postures which we dream by day;
Spending our thoughts i' th' best delight
Chaste dreams allow of in the night.

TO HIS MISTRIS GOING TO BED

John Donne

Come, Madam, come, all rest my powers defie,
   Until I labour, I in labour lie.
The foe oft-times having the foe in sight,
Is tir'd with standing though he never fight.
Off with that girdle, like heavens Zone glistering,
But a far fairer world incompassing.
Unpin that spangled breastplate which you wear,
That th'eyes of busie fooles may be stopt there.
Unlace your self, for that harmonious chyme,
Tell me from you, that now it is bed time.
Off with that happy busk, which I envie,
That still can be, and still can stand so nigh
Your gown going off, such beautious state reveals,
As when from flowry meads th'hills shadow steales.
Off with that wyerie Coronet and shew
The haiery Diademe which on you doth grow:
Now off with those shooes, and then safely tread
In this loves hallow'd temple, this soft bed.
In such white robes, heaven's Angels us'd to be
Receavd by men; Thou Angel bringst with thee
A heaven like Mahomets Paradice; and though
Ill spirits walk in white, we easly know,
By this these Angels from an evil sprite,
Those set our hairs, but these our flesh upright.
   Licence my roaving hands, and let them go,

170

Before, behind, between, above, below.
O my America! my new-found-land,
My kingdome, safeliest when with one man man'd,
My Myne of precious stones, My Emperie,
How blest am I in this discovering thee!
To enter in these bonds, is to be free;
Then where my hand is set, my seal shall be.
  Full nakedness! All joyes are due to thee,
As souls unbodied, bodies uncloth'd must be,
To taste whole joyes. Gems which you women use
Are like Atlanta's balls, cast in mens views,
That when a fools eye lighteth on a Gem,
His earthly soul may covet theirs, not them.
Like pictures, or like books gay coverings made
For lay-men, are all women thus array'd;
Themselves are mystick books, which only wee
(Whom their imputed grace will dignifie)
Must see reveal'd. Then since that I may know;
As liberally, as to a Midwife, shew
Thy self: cast all, yea, this white lynnen hence,
There is no pennance due to innocence.
  To teach thee, I am naked first; why then
What needst thou have more covering than a man.

from ROXANA
Daniel Defoe

Best remembered for his Robinson Crusoe, we see another side to Daniel Defoe's writings here, where a mistress generously shares her husband with her maid.

Amy was dressing me one morning, for now I had two maids, and Amy was my chambermaid. 'Dear madam,' says Amy, 'what! ain't you with child yet?' 'No, Amy,' says I, 'nor any sign of it.' 'Law, madam,' says Amy, 'what have you been doing? Why, you have been married a year and a half; I warrant you master would have got me with child twice in that time.' 'It may be so, Amy,' says I, 'let him try, can't you?' 'No,' says Amy, 'you'll forbid it now; before, I told you he should with all my heart, but I won't now, now he's all your own.' 'Oh,' says I, 'Amy, I'll freely give you my consent, it will be nothing at all to me; nay, I'll put you to bed to him myself one night or other if you are willing.' 'No, madam, no,' says Amy, 'not now he's yours.'

'Why, you fool you,' says I, 'don't I tell you I'll put you to bed to him myself?'

'Nay, nay,' says Amy, 'if you put me to bed to him, that's another case; I believe I shall not rise again very soon.'

'I'll venture that, Amy,' says I.

After supper that night, and before we were risen from table, I said to him, Amy being by, 'Hark ye, Mr –, do you know that you are to lie with Amy tonight?' 'No, not I,' says he; but turns to Amy, 'Is it so, Amy?' says he. 'No, sir,' says she. 'Nay, don't say no, you fool; did not I promise to put you to bed to him?' But the girl said no still, and it passed off.

At night, when we came to go to bed, Amy came into the chamber to undress me, and her master slipped into bed first. Then I began and told him all that Amy had said about my not being with child, and of her being with child twice in that time. 'Ay, Mrs Amy,' says he, 'I believe so too; come hither and we'll try.' But Amy did not go. 'Go, you fool,' says I, 'can't you; I freely give you both leave.' But Amy would not go. 'Nay, you whore,' says I, 'you said if I would put you to bed you would with all your heart'; and with that I sat her down, pulled off her stockings and shoes, and all her clothes, piece by piece, and led her to the bed to him. 'Here,' says I, 'try what you can do with your maid Amy.' She pulled back a little, would not let me pull off her clothes at first, but it was hot weather and she had not many clothes on, and particularly no stays on; and at last, when she saw I was in earnest, she let me do what I would; so I fairly stripped her, and then I threw open the bed and thrust her in.

I need say no more; this is enough to convince anybody that I did not think him my husband, and that I had cast off all principle and all modesty and had effectually stifled conscience.

Amy, I dare say, began now to repent, and would fain have got out of bed again, but he said to her, 'Nay, Amy,

173

you see your mistress has put you to bed, 'tis all her doing, you must blame her.' So he held her fast, and the wench being naked in bed with him, 'twas too late to look back, so she lay still and let him do what he would with her.

from DON LEON

*In this scandalous poem, a frustrated
father-to-be gratifies himself in a novel way.*

That time it was, as we in parlance wiled
   Away the hours, my wife was big with child.
Her waist, which looked so taper when a maid
Like some swol'n butt its bellying orb displayed,
And Love, chagrined, beheld his favourite cell
From mounds opposing scarce accessible.
'Look, Bell,' I cried; 'yon moon, which just now rose
Will be the ninth; and your parturient throes
May soon Lucina's dainty hand require
To make a nurse of thee, of me a sire.
I burn to press thee, but I fear to try,
Lest like an incubus my weight should lie;
Lest, from the close encounter we should doom
Thy quickening fœtus to an early tomb.
Thy size repels me, whilst thy charms invite;
Then, say, how celebrate the marriage rite?
Learn'd Galen, Celsus, and Hippocrates,
Have held it good, in knotty points like these,
Lest mischief from too rude assaults should come,
To copulate ex more pecudum.

What sayst thou, dearest? Do not cry me nay;
We cannot err where science shows the way.'
She answered not; but silence gave consent,
And by that threshold boldly in I went.

So clever statesmen, who concoct by stealth
Some weighty measures for the commonwealth,
All comers by the usual door refuse,
And let the favoured few the back stairs use.

Who that has seen a woman wavering lie
Betwixt her shame and curiosity,
Knowing her sex's failing, will not deem,
That in the balance shame would kick the beam?
Ah, fatal hour, that saw my prayer succeed,
And my fond bride enact the Ganymede.
Quick from my mouth some bland saliva spread
The ingress smoothed to her new maidenhead,
The Thespian God his rosy pinions beat,
And laughed to see his victory complete.
'Tis true, that from her lips some murmurs fell –
In joy or anger, 'tis too late to tell;
But this I swear, that not a single sign
Proved that her pleasure did not equal mine.
Ah, fatal hour! for thence my sorrows date:
Thence sprung the source of her undying hate.
Fiends from her breast the sacred secret wrung,
Then called me monster; and, with evil tongue,
Mysterious tales of false Satanic art
Devised, and forced us evermore to part.

from 'THE BOUDOIR'

This passage from The Boudoir, *shows why it was a popular erotic magazine of the Victorian age.*

Suddenly, I heard a noise in the passage. I rose with a bound, rushed to the door, and looked through the keyhole. If it was my husband, we were lost. Happily, I was mistaken.

I sighed to F. that there was naught to fear. In this position, with my eye fixed to the lock, my buttocks were exposed, and my shift was all tucked up. In a twinkling, my lover was behind me, and before I had time to collect myself I was penetrated again, filled up by that adorable instrument that seemed to know no rest. Ah! How I helped him by opening and shutting the cheeks of my backside . . . by writhing, twisting, and swooning with joy.

Our time had passed quickly. In haste, I sent away my lover, made the bed afresh, and arranged a neat toilette for the promenade. I was scarcely ready when the carriage drove up, and my husband came to fetch me. He found me flushed and lively, I answered that, overcome by the heat, I had fallen asleep.

We went downstairs, and I was joyfully saluted by the gentlemen, who complimented me on the novelty and good taste of my costume. On the sly, I looked at F., but nothing happily betrayed that anything extraordinary had taken place. We started off.

The forest we were exploring was deliciously cool and picturesque; we went to the lodge of a game-keeper, where a slight rustic repast had been prepared. Our collation was merrily enjoyed, I was forced to drink several glasses of champagne, although I did not require that to stimulate me.

After the meal we set out walking again, my husband gossiped with F. I was with them. The two guests had strolled into another path when we arrived at a wild spot, studded with rocks, and shaded with large trees.

At this moment one of the gentlemen, who were far off, called out to my husband: 'Come, quick, come and see!'

Charles ran away and left us. Directly he had disappeared from view, F. glued his mouth to mine.

'Angel,' said he, 'let us profit by this moment!'

'You are mad!'

'No, I love you, let me do as I will.'

'My God, we shall be discovered! I am lost!'

'Not if you hurry. Stoop!'

'Are you in?'

'Here I am. It's going in!'

'Ah! make haste. I tremble!'

'There, darling . . . spend . . . spend again!'

'Ah! I've come! Now go away.'

'Oh! Go.'

Only just in time. My petticoats, all up behind, were barely readjusted, when I heard the rest of the party returning.

I went to meet them, and we found they had fetched

us to see a swarm of bees captured from the top of a tree.

We got into our carriages and returned to the town. We danced at night at the Pump-rooms, and then said farewell to the gentlemen, who went away early the next morning, but my husband stopped with me.

It is easy to guess my thoughts when at home once more, I began to undress for the night. I was brushing my hair in front of my looking-glass, and my husband, delighted with the day's outing, was very gay and tender.

I was in my shift, that clung tightly to my figure behind, and showed the seductive shape of my backside. I could see in the glass that Charles was looking at it, and that his eyes sparkled.

'Aha!' said I to myself, 'can it be possible that for once in a way he will be able to do it to me twice in the same day?'

I wanted him to make me and coquettishly struck an attitude that threw out into still greater relief what I knew was one of my greatest beauties; then negligently putting one foot on a chair, taking care that my chemise should be more raised than was absolutely necessary, I undid my garter.

This play succeeded. Charles, also in his shirt, got up, and coming nearer me kissed me on the neck, and put his hand between the cheeks of my bottom.

'Oh! oh!' said I, turning round and returning his kiss, 'whatever ails you to-night?'

'My dear wife, I find that you are extremely handsome!'

'Am I not the same every day?'

'Oh, yes; but this evening still more so!'

'Well, what are you driving at? – come!'

So saying, I put my hand on his instrument, that stood a little, although far from being in a proper state of erection.

'You see that you can't do anything!'

'Oh, yes, I can! Prithee caress him a little bit!'

'What makes you so excited?'

'Why, his . . . his . . .'

'Well now – what?'

'Your beautiful bottom!'

'Indeed, sir, Well, you shan't see any more of it!'

As supple as a kitten, I trussed up my linen with one hand, so that my posteriors were naked, while my front parts were reflected in the mirror; at the same time my other hand had not loosened its grasp, and cleverly excited what it held. I soon had the satisfaction to feel it get hard. Wishing to profit by his momentary desire, I made Charles sit and got striding over him, but I soon found that such a position stretched me too much, and, widening the particular part, was quite unsuited for his thin tool.

I got up, and had to begin all over again . . . I was too excited to be baulked, and once more started the caress of my agile hand. I resolved to do my best, and he helped, so that soon I was pleased to see it once more in its most splendid state! Then I drew a chair to the glass, placed one foot upon it and the other on the ground, and put it in from behind.

Charles, led on by me till he was almost beside himself, did it in such a manner that I spent three times.

from MY LIFE AND LOVES
Frank Harris

The irreverent Frank Harris, besides being a magazine editor of genius was also a libertine. Here he recounts his sexual experiences with an enthusiasm and candour which delights, shocks and scandalizes.

One girl alone sang alto and she and I were separated from the other boys and girls; the upright piano was put across the corner of the room and we two sat or stood behind it, almost out of sight of all the other singers, the organist, of course, being seated in front of the piano. The girl E. . . ., who sang alto with me, was about my own age; she was very pretty, or seemed so to me, with golden hair and blue eyes, and I always made up to her as well as I could, in my boyish way. One day while the organist was explaining

181

something, E. . . . stood up on the chair and leant over the back of the piano to hear better or see more. Seated in my chair behind her, I caught sight of her legs, for her dress rucked up behind as she leaned over; at once my breath stuck in my throat. Her legs were lovely, I thought, and the temptation came to touch them; for no one could see.

I got up immediately and stood by the chair she was standing on. Casually I let my hand fall against her left leg. She didn't draw her leg away or seem to feel my hand, so I touched her more boldly. She never moved, though now I knew she must have felt my hand. I began to slide my hand up her leg and suddenly my fingers felt the warm flesh on her thigh where the stocking ended above the knee. The feel of her warm flesh made me literally choke with emotion: my hand went on up, warmer and warmer, when suddenly I touched her sex; there was soft down on it. The heart-pulse throbbed in my throat. I have no words to describe the intensity of my sensations.

Thank God, E. . . . did not move or show any sign of distaste. Curiosity was stronger even than desire in me and I felt her sex all over, and at once the idea came into my head that it was like a fig (the Italians, I learned later, called it familiarly *fica*); it opened at my touches and I inserted my finger gently, as Strangways had told me that Mary had taught him to do; still E. . . . did not move. Gently I rubbed the front part of her sex with my finger. I could have kissed her a thousand times out of gratitude.

Suddenly, as I went on, I felt her move, and then again; plainly she was showing me where my touch gave her most pleasure: I could have died for her in thanks; again she moved and I could feel a little mound or small button of flesh right in the front of her sex, above the junction of her inner lips; of course it was her clitoris. I had forgotten all the old Methodist doctor's books till that moment; this fragment of long forgotten knowledge came back to me: gently I rubbed the clitoris and at once she pressed down on my finger for a moment or two. I tried to insert my finger into the vagina; but she drew away at once and quickly, closing her sex as if hurt, so I went back to caressing her tickler.

Suddenly the miracle ceased. The cursed organist had finished his explanation of the new plain chant, and as he touched the first notes on the piano, E. . . . drew her legs together; I took away my hand and she stepped down from the chair. 'You darling, darling,' I whispered, but she frowned, and then just gave me a smile out of the corner of her eye to show me she was not displeased.

Ah, how lovely, how seductive she seemed to me now, a thousand times lovelier and more desirable than ever before. As we stood up to sing again, I whispered to her: 'I love you, love you, dear, dear!'

I can never express the passion of gratitude I felt to her for her goodness, her sweetness in letting me touch her sex. E. . . . it was who opened the Gates of Paradise to me and let me first taste the hidden mysteries of sexual delight. Still after more than fifty years I feel the thrill of the joy she gave me by her response, and the passionate reverence of my gratitude is still alive in me.

I came back to the Gregorys' for dinner and discussed in my own mind whether I should go to Mrs Mayhew's, as I had promised, or work at Greek. I decided to work and then and there made a vow always to prefer work, a vow more honored in the breach, I fear, than in the observance. But at least I wrote to Mrs Mayhew, excusing myself, and promising her the next afternoon. I set myself to learn by heart the two pages in the *Memorabilia*.

That evening I sat near the end of the table; the head of it was taken by the university professor of physics, a dull pedant!

Every time Kate came near me I was ceremoniously polite: 'Thank you, very much! It is very kind of you!' and not a word more. As soon as I could, I went to my room to work.

Next day at three o'clock I knocked at Mrs Mayhew's: she opened the door herself. I cried, 'How kind of you!' and once in the room drew her to me and kissed her time and time again: she seemed cold and numb.

For some moments she didn't speak, then: 'I feel as if I had passed through fever,' she said, putting her hands through her hair, lifting it in a gesture I was to know well in the days to come. 'Never promise again if you don't come; I thought I should go mad: waiting is a horrible torture! Who kept you – some girl?' and her eyes searched mine.

I excused myself; but her intensity chilled me. At the risk of alienating my girl readers, I must confess this was the effect her passion had on me. When I kissed her, her lips were cold. But by the time we had got upstairs, she had thawed. She shut the door after us gravely and began: 'See how ready I am for you!' and in a moment she had thrown back her robe and stood before me naked. She tossed the garment on a chair; it fell on the floor. She stooped to pick it up with her bottom toward me: I kissed her soft bottom and caught her up by it with my hand on her sex.

She turned her head over her shoulder: 'I've washed and scented myself for you, Sir: how do you like the perfume? and how do you like this bush of hair?' and she touched her mount with a grimace. 'I was so ashamed of it as a girl: I used to shave it off, that's what made it grow so thick, I believe. One day my mother saw it and made me stop shaving. Oh! how ashamed of it I was: it's animal, ugly, – don't you hate it? Oh, tell the truth!' she cried, 'Or rather, don't; tell me you love it.'

'I love it,' I exclaimed, 'because it's yours!'

'Oh, you dear lover,' she smiled, 'you always find the right word, the flattering salve for the sore!'

'Are you ready for me,' I asked, 'ripe-ready, or shall I kiss you first and caress pussy?'

'Whatever you do will be right,' she said. 'You know I am rotten-ripe, soft and wet for you always!'

184

All this while I was taking off my clothes; now I too was naked.

'I want you to draw up your knees,' I said: 'I want to see the Holy of Holies, the shrine of my idolatry.'

At once she did as I asked. Her legs and bottom were well-shaped without being statuesque: but her clitoris was much more than the average button: it stuck out fully half an inch and the inner lips of her vulva hung down a little below the outer lip. I knew I should see prettier pussies. Kate's was better shaped, I felt sure, and the heavy, madder-brown lips put me off a little.

The next moment I began caressing her red clitoris with my hot, stiff organ: Lorna sighed deeply once or twice and her eyes turned up; slowly I pushed my prick in to the full and drew it out again to the lips, then in again, and I felt her warm love-juice gush as she drew up her knees even higher to let me further in. 'Oh, it's divine,' she sighed, 'better even than the first time,' and, when my thrusts grew quick and hard as the orgasm shook me, she writhed down on my prick as I withdrew, as if she would hold it, and as my seed spirted into her, she bit my shoulder and held her legs tight as if to keep my sex in her. We lay a few moments bathed in bliss. Then, as I began to move again to sharpen the sensation, she half rose on her arm. 'Do you know,' she said, 'I dreamed yesterday of getting on you and doing it to you, do you mind if I try?'

'No, indeed!' I cried. 'Go to it, I am your prey!' She got up smiling and straddled kneeling across me, and put my cock in her pussy and sank down on me with a deep sigh. She tried to move up and down on my organ and at once came up too high and had to use her hand to put my Tommy in again; then she sank down on it as far as possible. 'I can sink down all right,' she cried, smiling at the double meaning, 'but I cannot rise so well! What fools we women are, we can't master even the act of love; we are so awkward!'

'Your awkwardness, however, excites me,' I said.

'Does it?' she cried. 'Then I'll do my best,' and for some time she rose and sank rhythmically, but, as her excitement grew, she just let herself lie on me and wiggled her bottom till we both came. She was flushed and hot and I couldn't help asking her a question.

'Does your excitement grow to a spasm of pleasure,' I asked, 'or do you go on getting more and more excited continually?'

'I get more and more excited,' she said, 'till the other day with you, for the first time in my life, the pleasure became unbearably intense and I was hysterical, you wonder-lover!'

Since then I have read lascivious books in half a dozen languages and they all represent women coming to an orgasm in the act, as men do, followed by a period of content; which only shows that the books are all written by men, and ignorant, insensitive men at that. The truth is: hardly one married woman in a thousand is ever brought to her highest pitch of feeling; usually, just when she begins to feel, her husband goes to sleep. If the majority of husbands satisfied their wives occasionally, the woman's revolt would soon move to another purpose: women want above all a lover who lives to excite them to the top of their bent. As a rule, men through economic conditions marry so late that they have already half-exhausted their virile power before they marry. And when they marry young, they are so ignorant and self-centered that they imagine their wives must be satisfied when they are. Mrs Mayhew told me that her husband had never excited her, really. She denied that she had ever had any real acute pleasure from his embraces.

'Shall I make you hysterical again?' I asked, out of boyish vanity. 'I can, you know!'

'You mustn't tire yourself!' she warned. 'My husband taught me long ago that when a woman tires a man, he gets a distaste for her, and I want your love, your desire, dear, a thousand times more even than the delight you give me – '

'Don't be afraid,' I broke in. 'You are sweet; you couldn't tire me; turn sideways and put your left leg up, and I'll just let my sex caress your clitoris back and forth gently: every now and then I'll let it go right in until our hairs meet.' I kept on this game perhaps half an hour until she first sighed and sighed and then made awkward movements with her pussy which I sought to divine and meet as she wished, when suddenly she cried:

'Oh! Oh! Hurt me, please! hurt me, or I'll bite you! Oh God, oh, oh,' panting, breathless till again the tears poured down!

'You darling,' she sobbed. 'How you can love! Could you go on forever?'

I got up and went to the windows; one gave on the porch, but the other directly on the garden. 'What are you looking at?' she asked, coming to me.

'I was just looking for the best way to get out if ever we were surprised,' I said. 'If we leave this window open I can always drop into the garden and get away quickly.'

'You would hurt yourself,' she cried.

'Not a bit of it,' I answered. 'I could drop half as far again without injury; the only thing is, I must have boots on and trousers, or those thorns of yours would gip!'

'You boy,' she exclaimed laughing. 'I think after your strength and passion, it is your boyishness I love best' – and she kissed me again and again.

'I must work,' I warned her; 'Smith has given me a lot to do.'

'Oh, my dear,' she said, her eyes filling with tears, 'that means you won't come tomorrow or,' she added hastily, 'even the day after?'

'I can't possibly,' I declared. 'I have a good week's work in front of me; but you know I'll come the first afternoon I can make myself free and I'll let you know the day before, sweet!'

She looked at me with tearful eyes and quivering lips.

'Love is its own torment!' she sighed, while I dressed and got away quickly.

The truth was I was already satiated. Her passion held nothing new in it: she had taught me all she could and had nothing more in her, I thought; while Kate was prettier and much younger and a virgin. Why shouldn't I confess it? It was Kate's virginity that attracted me irresistibly: I pictured her legs to myself, her hips and thighs . . .

The next few days passed in reading the books Smith had lent me, especially *Das Kapital*, the second book of which, with its frank exposure of the English factory system, was simply enthralling. I read some of Tacitus, too, and Xenophon with a crib, and learned a page of Greek every day by heart, and whenever I felt tired of work I laid siege to Kate. That is, I continued my plan of campaign. One day I called her brother into my room and told him true stories of buffalo hunting and of fighting with Indians; another day I talked theology with the father or drew the dear mother out to tell of her girlish days in Cornwall. 'I never thought I'd come to work like this in my old age, but then children take all and give little; I was no better as a girl, I remember,' – and I got a scene of her brief courtship!

I had won the whole household long before I said a word to Kate beyond the merest courtesies. A week or so passed like this till one day I held them all after dinner while I told the story of our raid into Mexico. I took care, of course, that Kate was out of the room. Towards the end of my tale, Kate came in: at once I hastened to end abruptly, and after excusing myself, went into the garden.

Half an hour later I saw she was in my room tidying up; I took thought and then went up the outside steps. As soon as I saw her I pretended surprise. 'I beg your pardon,' I said. 'I'll just get a book and go at once; please don't let me disturb you!' and I pretended to look for the book.

She turned sharply and looked at me fixedly. 'Why do you treat me like this!' she burst out, shaking with indignation.

'Like what?' I repeated, pretending surprise.

'You know quite well,' she went on angrily, hastily. 'At first I thought it was chance, unintentional; now I know you mean it. Whenever you are talking or telling a story, as soon as I come into the room you stop and hurry away as if you hated me. Why? Why?' she cried with quivering lips. 'What have I done to make you dislike me so?' and the tears gathered in her lovely eyes.

I felt the moment had come: I put my hands on her shoulders and looked with my whole soul into her eyes. 'Did you never guess, Kate, that it might be love, not hate?' I asked.

'No, no!' she cried, the tears falling. 'Love does not act like that!'

'Fear to miss love does, I can assure you,' I cried. 'I thought at first that you disliked me and already I had begun to care for you' (my arms went around her waist and I drew her to me), 'to love you and want you. Kiss me, dear,' and at once she gave me her lips, while my hand got busy on her breasts and then went down of itself to her sex.

Suddenly she looked at me gaily, brightly, while heaving a big sigh of relief. 'I'm glad, glad!' she said. 'If you only knew how hurt I was and how I tortured myself; one moment I was angry, then I was sad. Yesterday I made up my mind to speak, but today I said to myself, I'll just be obstinate and cold as he is and now – ' and of her own accord she put her arms around my neck and kissed me – 'you are a dear, dear! Anyway, I love you.'

'You mustn't give me those bird-pecks!' I exclaimed. 'Those are not kisses: I want your lips to open and cling to mine,' and I kissed her while my tongue darted into her mouth and I stroked her sex gently. She flushed, but at first didn't understand; then suddenly she blushed rosy red as her lips grew hot and she fairly ran from the room.

I exulted: I knew I had won: I must be very quiet and

reserved and the bird would come to the lure; I felt exultingly certain!

Meanwhile I spent nearly every morning with Smith: golden hours! Always, always before we parted, he showed me some new beauty or revealed some new truth: he seemed to me the most wonderful creature in this strange, sunlit world. I used to hang entranced on his eloquent lips! (Strange! I was sixty-five before I found such a hero-worshiper as I was to Smith, who was only four or five and twenty!) He made me know all the Greek dramatists: Aeschylus, Sophocles and Euripides and put them for me in a truer light than English or German scholars have set them yet. He knew that Sophocles was the greatest, and from his lips I learned every chorus in the *Oedipus Rex* and *Colonnus* before I had completely mastered the Greek grammar; indeed, it was the supreme beauty of the literature that forced me to learn the language. In teaching me the choruses, he was careful to point out that it was possible to keep the measure and yet mark the accent too: in fact, he made classic Greek a living language to me, as living as English. And he would not let me neglect Latin: in the first year with him I knew poems of Catullus by heart, almost as well as I knew Swinburne. Thanks to Professor Smith, I had no difficulty in entering the junior class at the university; in fact, after my first three or four months' work [I] was easily the first in the class, which included Ned Stephens, the brother of Smith's inamorata. I soon discovered that Smith was heels over head in love with Kate Stephens, shot through the heart, as Mercutio would say, with a fair girl's blue eye!

And small wonder, for Kate was lovely; a little above middle height with slight, rounded figure and most attractive face: the oval, a thought long, rather than round, with dainty, perfect features, lit up by a pair of superlative grey-blue eyes, eyes by turns delightful and reflective and appealing, that mirrored a really extraordinary intelligence.

She was in the senior class and afterwards for years held the position of Professor of Greek in the university. I shall have something to say of her in a later volume of this history, for I met her again in New York nearly fifty years later. But in 1872 or '73, her brother Ned, a handsome lad of eighteen who was in my class, interested me more. The only other member of the senior class of this time was a fine fellow, Ned Bancroft, who later came to France with me to study.

At this time, curiously enough, Kate Stephens was by way of being engaged to Ned Bancroft; but already it was plain that she was in love with Smith, and my outspoken admiration of Smith helped her, I hope, as I am sure it helped him, to a better mutual understanding. Bancroft accepted the situation with extraordinary self-sacrifice, losing neither Smith's nor Kate's friendship: I have seldom seen nobler self-abnegation; indeed, his high-mindedness in this crisis was what first won my admiration and showed me his other fine qualities.

Almost in the beginning I had serious disquietude: every little while Smith was ill and had to keep [to] his bed for a day or two. There was no explanation of this illness, which puzzled me and caused me a certain anxiety.

One day in midwinter there was a new development. Smith was in doubt how to act and confided in me. He had found Professor Kellogg, in whose house he lived, trying to kiss the pretty help, Rose, entirely against her will. Smith was emphatic on this point: the girl was struggling angrily to free herself, when by chance he interrupted them.

I relieved Smith's solemn gravity a little by roaring with laughter. The idea of an old professor and clergyman trying to win a girl by force filled me with amusement: 'What a fool the man must be!' was my English judgment; Smith took the American high moral tone at first.

'Think of his disloyalty to his wife in the same house,' he cried, 'and then the scandal if the girl talked, and she is sure to talk!'

'Sure not to talk,' I corrected. 'Girls are afraid of the effect of such revelations; besides a word from you asking her to shield Mrs Kellogg will ensure her silence.'

'Oh, I cannot advise her,' cried Smith. 'I will not be mixed up in it: I told Kellogg at the time, I must leave the house, yet I don't know where to go! It's too disgraceful of him! His wife is really a dear woman!'

For the first time I became conscious of a rooted difference between Smith and myself: his high moral condemnation on very insufficient data seemed to me childish, but no doubt many of my readers will think my tolerance a proof of my shameless libertinism! However, I jumped at the opportunity of talking to Rose on such a scabrous matter and at the same time solved Smith's difficulty by proposing that he should come and take room and board with the Gregorys – a great stroke of practical diplomacy on my part, or so it appeared to me, for thereby I did the Gregorys, Smith and myself an immense, an incalculable service. Smith jumped at the idea, asked me to see about it at once and let him know, and then rang for Rose.

She came half-scared, half-angry, on the defensive, I could see; so I spoke first, smiling. 'Oh Rose,' I said, 'Professor Smith has been telling me of your trouble; but you ought not to be angry: for you are so pretty that no wonder a man wants to kiss you; you must blame your lovely eyes and mouth.'

Rose laughed outright: she had come expecting reproof and found sweet flattery.

'There's only one thing, Rose,' I went on. 'The story would hurt Mrs Kellogg if it got out and she's not very strong, so you must say nothing about it, for her sake. That's what Professor Smith wanted to say to you,' I added.

'I'm not likely to tell,' cried Rose. 'I'll soon forget all about it, but I guess I'd better get another job: he's liable to try again, though I gave him a good, hard slap,' and she laughed merrily.

'I'm so glad for Mrs Kellogg's sake,' said Smith gravely, 'and if I can help you get another place, please call upon me.'

'I guess I'll have no difficulty,' answered Rose flippantly, with a shade of dislike of the professor's solemnity. 'Mrs Kellogg will give me a good character,' and the healthy young minx grinned, 'besides I'm not sure but I'll go stay home a spell. I'm fed up with working and would like a holiday, and mother wants me – '

'Where do you live, Rose?' I asked with a keen eye for future opportunities.

'On the other side of the river,' she replied, 'next door to Elder Conklin's, where your brother boards,' she added smiling.

When Rose went I begged Smith to pack his boxes, for I would get him the best room at the Gregorys' and assured him it was really large and comfortable and would hold all his books, etc.; and off I went to make my promise good. On the way, I set myself to think how I could turn the kindness I was doing the Gregorys to the advantage of my love. I decided to make Kate a partner in the good deed, or at least a herald of the good news. So when I got home I rang the bell in my room, and as I had hoped Kate answered it. When I heard her footsteps I was shaking, hot with desire, and now I wish to describe a feeling I then began to notice in myself. I longed to take possession of the girl, so to speak, abruptly, ravish her in fact, or at least thrust both hands up her dress at once and feel her bottom and sex altogether; but already I knew enough to realize certainly that girls prefer gentle and courteous approaches. Why? Of the fact I am sure. So I said, 'Come in, Kate,' gravely. 'I want to ask you whether the best bedroom is still free, and if you'd like Professor Smith to have it, if I could get him to come here?'

'I'm sure, Mother would be delighted,' she exclaimed.

'You see,' I went on, 'I'm trying to serve you all I can, yet you don't even kiss me of your own accord.' She smiled,

193

and so I drew her to the bed and lifted her up on it. I saw her glance and answered it: 'The door is shut, dear,' and half lying on her, I began kissing her passionately, while my hands went up her clothes to her sex. To my delight she wore no drawers, but at first she kept her legs tight together frowning. 'Love denies nothing, Kate,' I said gravely; slowly she drew her legs apart, half-pouting, half-smiling, and let me caress her sex. When her love-juice came, I kissed her and stopped. 'It's dangerous here,' I said, 'that door you came in is open; but I must see your lovely limbs,' and I turned up her dress. I hadn't exaggerated; she had limbs like a Greek statue and her triangle of brown hair lay in little silky curls on her belly and then – the sweetest cunny in the world. I bent down and kissed it.

In a moment Kate was on her feet, smoothing her dress down. 'What a boy you are,' she exclaimed, 'but that's partly why I love you; oh, I hope you'll love me half as much. Say you will, Sir, and I'll do anything you wish!'

'I will,' I replied, 'but oh, I'm glad you want love; can you come to me tonight? I want a couple of hours with you uninterrupted.'

'This afternoon,' she said, 'I'll say I'm going for a walk and I'll come to you, dear! They are all resting then or out and I shan't be missed.'

I could only wait and think. One thing was fixed in me, I must have her, make her mine before Smith came: he was altogether too fascinating, I thought, to be trusted with such a pretty girl; but I was afraid she would bleed and I did not want to hurt her this first time, so I went out and bought a syringe and a pot of cold cream which I put beside my bed.

Oh, how that dinner lagged! Mrs Gregory thanked me warmly for my kindness to them all (which seemed to me pleasantly ironical!) and Mr Gregory followed her lead; but at length everyone had finished and I went to my room to prepare. First I locked the outside door and drew down

194

the blinds: then I studied the bed and turned it back and arranged a towel along the edge; happily the bed was just about the right height! Then I loosened my trousers, unbuttoned the front and pulled up my shirt: a little later Kate put her lovely face in at the door and slipped inside. I shot the bolt and began kissing her; girls are strange mortals; she had taken off her corset, just as I had put a towel handy. I lifted up her clothes and touched her sex, caressing it gently while kissing her: in a moment or two her love-milk came.

I lifted her up on the bed, pushed down my trousers, anointed my prick with the cream and then, parting her legs and getting her to pull her knees up, I drew her bottom to the edge of the bed: she frowned at that, but I explained quickly: 'It may give a little pain, at first, dear: and I want to give you as little as possible,' and I slipped the head of my cock gently, slowly into her. Even greased, her pussy was tight and at the very entrance I felt the obstacle, her maidenhead, in the way; I lay on her and kissed her and let her or Mother Nature help me.

As soon as Kate found that I was leaving it to her, she pushed forward boldly and the obstacle yielded. 'O – O!' she cried, and then pushed forward again roughly and my organ went in her to the hilt and her clitoris must have felt my belly. Resolutely, I refrained from thrusting or withdrawing for a minute or two and then drew out slowly to her lips and, as I pushed Tommy gently in again, she leaned up and kissed me passionately. Slowly, with extremest care, I governed myself and pushed in and out with long slow thrusts, though I longed, longed to plunge it in hard and quicken the strokes as much as possible; but I knew from Mrs Mayhew that the long, gentle thrusts and slow withdrawals were the aptest to excite a woman's passion and I was determined to win Kate.

In two or three minutes, she had again let down a flow of love-juice, or so I believed, and I kept right on with

195

the love-game, knowing that the first experience is never forgotten by a girl and resolved to keep on to dinner-time if necessary to make her first love-joust ever memorable to her. Kate lasted longer than Mrs Mayhew; I came ever so many times, passing ever more slowly from orgasm to orgasm before she began to move to me; but at length her breath began to get shorter and shorter and she held me to her violently, moving her pussy the while up and down harshly against my man-root. Suddenly she relaxed and fell back: there was no hysteria; but plainly I could feel the mouth of her womb fasten on my cock as if to suck it. That excited me fiercely and for the first time I indulged in quick, hard thrusts till a spasm of intensest pleasure shook me and my seed spirted or seemed to spirt for the sixth or seventh time.

Now began for me a most delightful time. Sommerfeld relieved me of nearly all the office work: I had only to get up the speeches, for he prepared the cases for me. My income was so large that I only slept in my office-room for convenience sake, or rather for my lechery's sake.

I kept a buggy and horse at a livery stable and used to drive Lily or Rose out nearly every day. As Rose lived on the other side of the river, it was easy to keep the two separate, and indeed neither of them ever dreamed of the other's existence. I had a very soft spot in my heart for Rose: her beauty of face and form always excited and pleased me and her mind, too, grew quickly through our talks and the books I gave her. I'll never forget her joy when I first bought a small bookcase and sent it to her home one morning, full of books I thought she would like and ought to read.

In the evening she came straight to my office, told me it was the very thing she had most wanted, and she let me study her beauties one by one; but when I turned her round and kissed her bottom, she wanted me to stop. 'You can't possibly like or admire that,' was her verdict.

'Indeed I do,' I cried, but I confessed to myself that she was right, her bottom was adorably dimpled but it was a little too fat, and the line underneath it was not perfect. One of her breasts, too, was prettier than the other, though both were small and stuck out boldly: my critical sense would find no fault with her triangle or her sex; the lips of it were perfect, very small and rose-red and her clitoris was like a tiny, tiny button. I often wished it were half an inch long like Mrs Mayhew's. Only once in our intercourse did I try to bring her to ecstasy and only half succeeded; consequently, I used simply to have her just to enjoy myself, and only now and then went on to a second orgasm so as really to warm her to the love-play; Rose was anything but sensual, though invariably sweet and an excellent companion. How she could be so affectionate though sexually cold was always a puzzle to me.

Lily, as I have said, was totally different: a merry little grig and born child of Venus: now and then she gave me a really poignant sensation. She was always deriding Mrs Mayhew, but curiously enough, she was very much like her in many intimate ways – a sort of understudy of the older and more passionate woman, with a child's mischievous gaiety to boot and a childish joy of living.

But a great and new sensation was now to come into my life. One evening a girl without a hat on and without knocking came into my office. Sommerfeld had gone home for the night and I was just putting my things straight before going out. She took my breath; she was astoundingly good looking, very dark with great, black eyes and slight girlish figure. 'I'm Topsy,' she announced and stood there smiling, as if the mere name told enough.

'Come in,' I said, 'and take a seat: I've heard of you!' And I had.

She was a privileged character in the town: she rode on the street-cars and railroads, too, without paying. Those who challenged her were all 'poor white trash,' she said, and some man was always eager to pay for her. She never hesitated to go up to any man and ask him for a dollar or even five dollars – and invariably got what she wanted: her beauty was as compelling to men as her scornful aloofness. I had often heard of her as 'that d . . . d pretty nigger girl!' but I could see no trace of any Negro characteristic in her pure loveliness. She took the seat and said with a faint southern accent I found pleasing, 'You' name Harris?'

'That's my name,' I replied smiling.

'You here instead of Barker?' she went on. 'He sure deserve to die hicuppin': pore white trash!'

'What's your real name?' I asked.

'They call me "Topsy",' she replied, 'but ma real true name is Sophy, Sophy Beveridge. You was very kind to my mother who lives upstairs. Yes,' she went on defiantly, 'she's my mother and a mighty good mother, too, and don't you fergit it,' she added, tossing her head in contempt of my astonishment.

'Your father must have been white,' I couldn't help remarking, for I couldn't couple Topsy with the old octoroon, do what I would. She nodded, 'He was white all right: that is, his skin was,' and she got up and wandered about the office as if it belonged to her.

'I'll call you "Sophy,"' I said, for I felt a passionate revolt of injured pride in her. She smiled at me with pleasure.

I didn't know what to do. I must not go with a colored girl, though I could see no sign of black blood in Sophy, and certainly she was astonishingly good looking, even in her simple sprigged gown. As she moved about I could not but remark the lithe panther-like grace of her and her little breasts stuck out against the thin cotton garment with a most provocative allurement. My mouth was parching when she swung round on me. 'You ondressing me,' she said smiling, 'and I'se glad, 'cause my mother likes you and I loves her – sure pop!'

There was something childish, direct, innocent, even, about her frankness that fascinated me, and her good looks made sunshine in the darkening room.

'I like you, Sophy,' I said, 'but anyone would have done as much for your mother as I did. She was ill!'

'Hoo!' she snorted indignantly. 'Most white folk would have let her die right there on the stairs. I know them: they'd have been angry with her for groaning. I hate 'em!' And her great eyes glowered.

She came over to me in a flash:

'If you'd been an American, I could never have come to you, never! I'd rather have died, or saved and stole and paid you – ' the scorn in her voice was bitter with hate: evidently the Negro question had a side I had never realized.

'But you're different,' she went on, 'an' I just came – ' and she paused, lifting her great eyes to mine with an unspoken offer in their lingering regard.

'I'm glad,' I said lamely, staving off the temptation, 'and I hope you'll come again soon and we'll be great friends – eh, Sophy?' and I held out my hand smiling; but she pouted and looked at me with reproach or appeal or disappointment in her eyes. I could not resist: I took her hand and drew her to me and kissed her on the lips, slipping my right hand the while up to her left breast. It was as firm as India rubber: at once I felt my sex stand up and throb: resolve and desire fought in me, but I was accustomed to make my will supreme.

'You are the loveliest girl in Lawrence,' I said, 'but I must really go now. I have an appointment and I'm late.'

She smiled enigmatically as I seized my hat and went, not stopping even to shut or lock the office door.

As I walked up the street, my thoughts and feelings were

all in a whirl. 'Did I want her? Should I have her? Would she come again?

'Oh, Hell! women are the very devil and he's not so black as he's painted! Black?'

That night I was awakened by a loud knocking at my office door; I sprang up and opened without thinking and at once Sophy came in laughing.

'What is it?' I cried, half asleep still.

'I'se tired waiting,' she answered cheekily, 'and anyways I just came.' I was about to remonstrate with her when she cried: 'You go right to bed,' and she took my head in her hands and kissed me.

My wish to resist died out of me. 'Come quickly!' I said, getting into bed and watching her as she stripped. In a hand's turn she had undressed to her chemise. 'I reckon this'll do,' she said coquettishly.

'Please take it off,' I cried, and the next moment she was in my arms naked. As I touched her sex, she wound her arms round my neck and kissed me greedily with hot lips. To my astonishment her sex was well formed and very small: I had always heard that Negroes had far larger genitals than white people; but the lips of Sophy's sex were thick and firm. 'Have you ever been had, Sophy?' I asked.

'No, sir!' she replied. 'I liked you because you never came after me and you was so kind and I thot that I'd be sure to do it sometime, so I'd rather let you have me than anyone else. I don't like colored men,' she added, 'and the white men all look down on me and despise me and I – I love you,' she whispered, burying her face on my neck.

'It'll hurt you at first, Sophy, I'm afraid,' but she stilled all scruples with, 'Shucks, I don't care. If I gives you pleasure, I'se satisfied,' and she opened her legs, stretching herself as I got on her. The next moment my sex was caressing her clitoris and of herself she drew up her

200

knees and suddenly with one movement brought my sex into hers and against the maiden barrier. Sophy had no hesitation: she moved her body lithely against me and the next moment I had forced the passage and was in her. I waited a little while and then began the love game. At once Sophy followed my movements, lifting her sex up to me as I pushed in and depressing it to hold me as I withdrew. Even when I quickened, she kept time and so gave me the most intense pleasure, thrill on thrill, and, as I came and my seed spirted into her, the muscle inside her vagina gripped my sex, heightening the sensation to an acute pang; she even kissed me more passionately than any other girl, licking the inside of my lips with her hot tongue. When I went on again with the slow in-and-out movements, she followed in perfect time and her trick of bending her sex down on mine as I withdrew and gripping it at the same time excited me madly; soon, of her own accord, she quickened while gripping and thrilling me till again we both spent together in an ecstasy.

'You're a perfect wonder,' I cried to her then, panting in my turn, 'but how did you learn so quickly?'

'I loves you,' she said, 'so I do whatever I think you'd like then I likes that too, see?' And her lovely face glowed against mine.

I got up to show her the use of the syringe and found we were in a bath of blood. In a moment she had stripped the sheet off. 'I'll wash that in the morning,' she said laughing, while doubling it into a ball and throwing it in the corner. I turned the gas on full: never was there a more seductive figure. Her skin was darkish, it is true, but not darker than that of an ordinary Italian or Spanish girl, and her form had a curious attraction for me: her breasts, small and firm as elastic, stood out provocatively: her hips, however, were narrower than even Lily's, though the cheeks of her bottom were full; her legs, too, were well-rounded, not a trace of the sticks of the negro; her feet even were slender and high arched.

'You are the loveliest girl I've ever seen!' I cried as I helped to put in the syringe and wash her sex.

'You're mah man,' she said proudly, 'an' I want to show you that I can love better than any white trash; they only give themselves airs!'

'You are white,' I cried, 'don't be absurd!'

She shook her little head. 'If you knew,' she said. 'When I was a girl, a child, old white men, the best in town, used to say dirty words to me in the street and try to touch me – the beasts!' I gasped: I had had no idea of such contempt and persecution.

When we were back in bed together: 'Tell me, Sophy dear, how you learned to move with me in time as you do and give me such thrills?'

'Hoo!' she cried, gurgling with pleased joy. 'That's easy to tell. I was scared you didn't like me, so this afternoon I went to wise old niggah woman and ask her how to make man love you really! She told me to go right to bed with you and do that,' and she smiled.

'Nothing more?' I asked.

Her eyes opened brightly. 'Shu!' she cried. 'If you want to do love again, I show you!' The next moment, I was in her and now she kept even better time than at first and somehow or other the thick, firm lips of her sex seemed to excite me more than anyone had ever excited me. Instinctively the lust grew in me and I quickened and as I came to the short, hard strokes, she suddenly slipped her legs together under me and closing them tightly held my sex as in a firm grip and then began 'milking' me – no other word conveys the meaning – with extraordinary skill and speed, so that, in a moment, I was gasping and choking with the intensity of the sensation and my seed came in hot jets while she continued the milking movement, tireless, indefatigable!

'What a marvel you are,' I exclaimed as soon as I got

202

breath enough to speak, 'the best bedfellow I've ever had; wonderful, you dear, you!'

All glowing with my praise, she wound her arms about my neck and mounted me as Lorna Mayhew had done once; but what a difference! Lorna was so intent on gratifying her own lust that she often forgot my feelings altogether and her movements were awkward in the extreme; but Sophy thought only of me and, whereas Lorna was always slipping my sex out of her sheath, Sophy in some way seated herself on me and then began rocking her body back and forth while lifting it a little at each churning movement, so that my sex in the grip of her firm, thick lips had a sort of double movement. When she felt me coming as I soon did, she twirled half round on my organ half a dozen times with a new movement and then began rocking herself again, so that my seed was dragged out of me, so to speak, giving me indescribably acute, almost painful sensations. I was breathless, thrilling with her every movement.

'Had you any pleasure, Sophy?' I asked as soon as we were lying side by side again.

'Shuah!' she said smiling. 'You're very strong, and you,' she asked, 'were you pleased?'

'Great God,' I cried, 'I felt as if all the hairs of my head were traveling down my backbone like an army! You are extraordinary, you dear!'

'Keep me with you, Frank,' she whispered. 'If you want me, I'll do anything, everything for you: I never hoped to have such a lover as you. Oh, this child's real glad her breasties and sex please you. You taught me that word, instead of the nasty word all white folks use. "Sex" is a good word, very good!' and she crowed with delight.

'What do colored people call it?' I asked. 'Coozie,' she replied smiling, 'Coozie. Good word too, very good!'

Long years later I heard an American story which recalled Sophy's performance vividly.

An engineer with a pretty daughter had an assistant who showed extraordinary qualities as a machinist and was quiet and well behaved to boot. The father introduced his helper to his daughter and the match was soon arranged. After the marriage, however, the son-in-law drew away and it was in vain that the father-in-law tried to guess the reason of the estrangement. At length he asked his son-in-law boldly for the reason. 'I meant right, Bill,' he began earnestly, 'but if I've made a mistake I'll be sorry. Warn't the goods accordin' to specification? Warn't she a virgin?'

'It don't matter nothin'!' replied Bill frowning.

'Treat me fair, Bill,' cried the father. 'War she a virgin?'

'How can I tell?' exclaimed Bill. 'All I can say is, I never know'd a virgin before that had that cinder-shifting movement.'

Sophy was the first to show me the 'cinder-shifting' movement, and she surely was a virgin!

As a mistress Sophy was perfection perfected and the long lines and slight curves of her lovely body came to have a special attraction for me as the very highest of the pleasure-giving type.

Lily first and then Rose were astonished and perhaps a little hurt at the sudden cooling off of my passion for them. From time to time I took Rose out or sent her books, and I had Lily anywhere, anywhen; but neither of them could compare with Sophy as a bedfellow, and her talk even fascinated me more the better I knew her. She had learned life from the streets, from the animal side first, but it was astonishing how quickly she grew in understanding: love is the only magical teacher! In a fortnight her speech was better than Lily's; in a month she talked as well as any of the American girls I had had; her desire of knowledge and her sponge-like ease of acquirement were always surprising me. She had a lovelier figure than even Rose and ten times the seduction even of Lily: she never hesitated to take my sex in her hand and caress it; she was a child of nature, bold with an animal's boldness and had besides a thousand endearing familiarities. I had only to hint a wish for her to gratify it. Sophy was the pearl of all the girls I met in this first stage of my development and I only wish I could convey to the reader a suggestion of her quaint, enthralling caresses.

from DAFFODIL
Cecil Barr

Daffodil, *a titillating novel of the 1920s, was part of the erotica which came out of Paris. Here we see the completely natural manner in which the French treat love and sex.*

'**D**affodil!'
　　'*Ma tante*, darling!'
'How old are you?'

With some curiosity I glanced across our frugally laid table at my dear adoptive aunt. Surely she knew my age at least as well as I!

'Nineteen, *ma tante*, nearly twenty.'

'Twenty! Good God, twenty!' For a moment she hesitated, her teeth toying with chop. Then she asked me to pass the salt, fixing me with her round, frozen-blue eyes, her fine chesty figure bent slightly forward; very handsome and active, but not so young as she had been. I passed her the salt. She hummed and ha'd. Evidently she was finding difficulty in telling me whatever was on her mind. What could it be?

'Daffodil!'

'*Ma tante*, darling?'

'What do you – know?'

'What do I know?' I repeated dreamily. 'The Chinese philosopher said: those who know do not tell: those who tell do not know.'

'Stop that!' *ma tante* said smartly. 'Don't show off to me.'

'Show off!' I protested, grief-stricken.

'What I'm asking you is what you know, facts of life – '

'What every young girl ought to know.'

'Now take sex, Daffodil.'

'I'm against it.'

Ma tante pished. She didn't approve of flippancy on that holy subject.

'What do you mean, against it? Wait a minute while the girl brings the cheese.'

'It's too hot for cheese, *ma tante*.'

'I'll have my bit of cheese, hot or not hot.'

I accompanied her with decadent grapes. When the 'girl' had gone *ma tante* resumed:

'Against sex? That's ignorance talking.'

'Not ignorance: innocence. I know all about it, theoretically. You're taught it nowadays. You begin with botany and wonder why the botany mistress doesn't get to the point a little faster. But of course I've had no experiences – and I don't want any, either.'

'It'll come over you all of a sudden', *ma tante* warned me gloomily. 'And what about the young man you're sharing the studio with: is he against sex too?'

'We've never discussed it.'

'Oh, come! It sounds unnatural to me.'

I smiled, to comfort her. I could guess she was making

comparisons with her own youth. She looked so puzzled. Perhaps, I suggested, it was the fact that I was illegitimate, a foundling, that had caused in me so enduring an aversion for the causes that had brought me superfluously into the world. I was less than a month old when *ma tante* had undertaken the charge of me. She was an English-woman who had married a French *chef* called Sanglot, but she had an avid temperament and so was soon left a widow; and she had been glad of the money that was settled on me by my cold-hearted and unidentifiable parents. A French notaire had the care of the money, but a three-monthly cheque was all we could ever elicit from him. I had been expensively educated in Switzerland and England, and I had enjoyed that and profited by it. I knew few girls who had read so widely, so hun-grily as I. And one of the results of my reading was to increase this strange resentment against the stranglehold of sex . . .

More than a year before all this we had come to Paris. Paris was the best town in which to live cheaply and comfortably. We hadn't much money, but I hoped eventually to make more by sculpture. It was my turn: *ma tante* had eked out in the past, by methods of her own. But now she was approaching fifty.

'Well, Daffodil, I'm sure I don't know what I ought to say. I believe you know more than I do. I hope you'll look after yourself. This Paris is a dreadful place. My own life hasn't been spotless -- '

It hadn't. In the past I should guess the average had been about one spot a month; there was nothing leopard-like about *ma tante* and so she had had no trouble about chang-ing her spots. We all have our favourite diversions. Hers was – spots. Mine was art. And thanks to Slutsky . . .

It was Slutsky, the picture dealer, who had first called me Daffodil, on account of my yellow hair. That had been years and years ago, and I had even forgotten how he had come to know *ma tante*. But it was easy to guess. Slutsky must have been an outsize in spots.

When we settled in Paris and I decided upon art as a career, I also decided on Daffodil as a name. After all, being nameless I had at least the right to decide for myself what I should be called. And as a surname implies a family and I had no family, I dispensed with a surname. It was as Daffodil that I dawned upon the gay world beside the Seine.

. . . *Ma tante* was thinking over my remark about my illegitimacy, of which I wasn't, of course, ashamed, although I often felt quite spiteful about it. She definitely refused to admit that it could have any effect on my really deep and important (i.e. sexual) feelings.

'That's not enough to protect you from the wicked world. Be careful, my dear. It may come over you any day. Men are deceitful, selfish creatures, and clever devils at getting their own way. You're the prettiest girl in Paris' – I made a sweeping bow of acknowledgment – 'and they won't let you off easily. Once it's done it can't be undone, and you go on as you begin.'

'I'm an impregnable fortress, *ma tante*; you're wasting your time.'

'Yes. Well, I'm sure I don't like these conversations. They're from a sense of duty, Daffodil, not a dirty mind. When was the last time we talked about such things? When you were thirteen, and you *had* to be told? And if there's anything you want to know now, ask me, and I'll tell you if I can.'

But in theory, anyhow, there was nothing *ma tante* could teach me.

Lunch was over and I began to think of going to my work. But *ma tante* was not yet done with me.

'Next year you'll be twenty-one,' she said with melancholy, 'and you can say adioo to me if you want to; you'll be your own mistress – '

'But, darling!' I cried aghast, 'you don't think I'd ever

for a moment dream of parting from you. We're as one and indivisible as the Siamese twins, for ever and ever, till death us do part. What should I do without you?'

Her round blue eyes unfroze, and I, too, felt for a horrid moment as if all this might end in tears. What was the matter with us? The cheese, the heat? I began to storm. One didn't deliberately try to make oneself unhappy for the mere pleasure of overflowing at the eyes. There were bills for that, and laddered stockings, and what one has to be told when one's thirteen or thereabouts, and God knows how many vexations.

'You might get married, Daffodil.'

'What a masochist you are, darling.'

'Don't you call me names, miss! And that Brian – '

I sighed.

'Your *mind*! You know that we're partners in a studio, we share the expenses of models – '

'What else do you share?'

'Nothing,' I snapped. 'You must really try to believe that nowadays a girl can be on friendly terms with a man and not necessarily be his bedfellow. And as for marriage, even if I wanted to get married, can you see the son of the Bishop of Spinchester marrying me, a penniless foundling?'

I got up and collected my hat. I really must be going.

'Rubbish!' *ma tante* exclaimed. 'With your colouring and your figure you could marry the bishop himself.'

It was terribly hot in our little dining-room, and I saw that *ma tante* was looking tired, worn, almost her age.

'Darling, you're run down; you want a change. Why don't you go away?'

She started, glancing at me curiously.

'Well, I never! Fancy you saying that! As it happened I did get a letter this morning . . .'

Uncanny how often two females living together in close intimacy guess each other's most private thoughts. Perhaps *ma tante* had not herself suspected it, but all this talk had

210

been leading up to the suggestion that she should dash over to England for a week or so, to stay with the sister, Annie, whose husband had the milk round. A *good* boy (aged fifty-eight); he'd never given Annie a moment's anxiety, unlike Sanglot who, worn out by his wife's enthusiasm, had simply gone and died. There was something respectable about them too, that would be soothing after the years on the Continent. *Ma tante* was far from being narrow-minded, but all the same, this Paris life, artists, and so on . . . She didn't want to hinder my career, and if it brought in a bit of money all the better, but a change, say a week or a fortnight in Acton . . .

'But how'll you do alone, Daffodil? And whatever sort of mischief will you be getting into?'

'That's my only trouble about you, darling.' I put my arms around her neck and kissed her suddenly under the ear, where it always made her squeak. 'How do I know you are not going to put *ideas* into Edwin's head, and then what will Annie have to say about it?'

Ma tante purred but protested.

'No, I'm too old, Daffodil. I'm on the shelf. A few years ago, perhaps, – but not with the family. But I don't like leaving you, I really don't.'

'You can go, *ma tante* darling, if you promise to be good.'

But it wasn't settled so easily as that. Suppose I was up to my *tricks*? What tricks? *I* knew well enough what she meant.

'*Ma tante* darling, I've had nearly twenty years' practice at sleeping alone in a bed.'

'Adam and Eve needed no bed in the Garden of Eden. It's a lot easier to get in the family way than out of it, Daffodil, as you ought to be the first to realise.'

I argued that if my one object in life was to go through the motions of becoming *enceinte*, I could achieve it without her crossing the Channel and putting *ideas* into the eager

211

Edwin's head. It was well known to be the work of a moment.

'Yes,' *ma tante* said darkly, 'one minute's pleasure, nine months' – '

'And anyhow, there's Marie Stopes,' I began, but *ma tante* told me not to be rude.

'There's decency in everything. I've kept out of trouble all my life, and I've done it without diagrams. And there's your food.'

'Oh, Ninette will look after me all right.'

'That girl . . .' But at last she allowed herself to be persuaded that she might safely leave me for a week or ten days to my own devices, whatever they might be, and in view of her constitutional disbelief in innocence, they could only be one thing: vices, not devices; the vice that breathed o'er Eden. She exasperated me.

'You know perfectly well I'm a pure girl, and intend to remain so. I can't help it if it sounds eccentric . . .'

'There may be something in it,' *ma tante* mused. 'I daresay it'll come back to fashion sooner or later. Purity, I mean.'

'And that's where I shall score.'

'Well, it's one way of scoring. Going misère, I call it. However, as long as you declare your suit, I suppose you're paid.'

'Chastity's the one original suit left worth playing. I shall play it – to win.'

'How you do talk, I'm sure,' *ma tante* said, with a touch of pettishness. She hated such words as chastity or virgin, preferring to convey them by a meaning silence or a roundabout phrase. 'Very well, then, my dear, I'll go and start packing. But if you'll take my advice, you'll keep your eye on that young man. Parsons' sons are always the worst.'

'He's a bishop's son, *ma tante*. There's a subtle difference.'

212

'Egg-shells!' said *ma tante*, or words to that effect.

II

'Ah, merrrde! I have the feet full of ants!'

Lolette, the model, rolled her eyes and her body trembled impatiently. It was so hot in the studio that I envied her her nakedness, and wondered if Brian, dressed in a shirt, a pair of worn grey trousers and espadrilles, was cooler than I. The wax model I was working on would not come right. Lolette, for all her Academic beauty, was useless to me, and I knew that this figurine would never be cast in bronze and sold in the art departments of the great stores.

'Ah, merrde! – '

'Lolette,' I said severely, 'do you realise that Monsieur is the son of a great church dignitary . . . a bishop?'

To be sure Brian had nothing of the church and nothing of the dignitary about him, – and if possible less of the artist; he looked (what he was) an excellent amateur footballer and had the regular, handsome, god-like features of those heroes of fiction who are continually and heartily exchanging spots of beer with their friends, and outwitting with ease incredibly ferocious and detestable villains. But even at nineteen I had discovered that a man's soul did not necessarily correspond to his physical appearance. Brian did not drink beer.

Lolette held the pose in spite of pins and needles. Such was discipline, and I admired her. Brian painted on, remorselessly.

'A bishop! If he were the son of an ant-eater, it would be more useful,' Lolette muttered between clenched teeth. Darling Brian, he painted so badly, too, and because of his charming personality none of his friends (and I least of all) dared tell him so. As for selling his pictures, that was beside the question; even geniuses starved; to starve is a prerogative of genius.

'Be a good lass, Lolette,' Brian said. 'Hold the pose another couple of minutes, and then I've finished for the day.'

'So have I,' I said. 'This isn't the temperature to deal with wax.'

'Ah, merrde! Two minutes, they can be as long as two hours.'

'Oh, very well.' Regretfully Brian broke away from his work and Lolette got down stiffly from her eminence. 'Any good?' he grinned across at me.

'No good at all.' I didn't want to crab our mutual model, for his sake, but Lolette was wasting my time. Patience. It would be my turn to choose the next.

'I'm sorry, Daffodil. What is it? The heat?'

'Perhaps.'

Lolette was meandering about the studio in her body, unstiffening her joints. Brian had no mercy; the word is unknown to that god-like type of man. Lolette's unstiffening was a long process, she had no qualms about displaying her person. Wasn't she a very clean model indeed? She wouldn't have missed her Saturday bath for nine francs ninety. To be sure to-day was Friday, and certain faint marks I observed were due to disappear on the morrow. She halted in front of Brian's canvas and sniffed. Poor Brian! but he did not seem to mind. And presently having stodged his eyes with his masterpiece he came across to me. My formless lump of wax conveyed nothing to him – there was nothing to convey; and his comments, if comments he made, which I do not believe, were made in silence.

'It's five o'clock,' said Brian. 'What about tea?' Lolette's eyes rolled.

I arose and unlocked a cupboard and got out a bottle of port, a bottle of imitation (but potent) absinthe, a box of biscuits, and glasses. As if a tocsin had been rung steps sounded on the stairs. I got out more glasses. Our studio was very *chic*, it had its own private water-tap. I let the water run long so that we might drink cold. Before I had finished my preparations the door opened, and three representative French artists entered. I breathed a small sigh of relief; after all, it might have been six or seven, and those two bottles had still several days to last out.

Our visitors grouped themselves about the room, Brian washed his hands at the tap, Lolette stretched her naked modesty in our chief ornament, a wicker easy-chair. I served drinks.

Vinel could paint, he was a genius, but was inclined to be unclean. Janigaud occasionally sold a picture which was a good thing for he was married and had two children, and they depended on him for their daily bread. He was quite dependable too. There is so much nonsense talked about artists. Vinel was the most painstaking and hard-working man I have known. Janigaud was disgustingly respectable. His unique vice was luxoriousness. Fanotin was still tied to his mother's apronstrings, elastic though they might be; he was only a few months older than I.

Even Lolette had a husband whose bed she shared more often than not. He was a plumber. Hence perhaps the weekly bath.

Glasses securely in hand, the visitors gathered round Brian's canvas, praising it sedulously, (1) out of gratitude to their host; (2) because if they didn't they could naturally expect no praise from him.

Brian was not deceived by their remarks. He smiled comfortably.

'Never mind. I can always end up as a pavement artist.'

'In Paris,' said Vinel, '"pavement artists wear silk drawers."'

'Or none at all,' said Fanotin, with the kind of wit characteristic of his years. But I blushed. It had been so hot that morning – even when I was dressing, and visibility in the studio was – well, high. I pulled down my shirt as far as it would go.

After the picture, its original became the centre of attraction. References were made to our Lolette's past, and prophecies were hazarded about her future. Lolette began to enjoy herself. This was the language she understood and she ably occupied their attention. Except Fanotin's. He came and sat on the floor beside the very ancient rocking-chair upon which I had draped myself. He was a beautiful youth, the despair of his parents who idolised and spoiled their only child, and he grossly profited by their love. He was slight and effeminate in appearance, but he had iron wrists and bought his clothes from a London tailor. He wore a silk shirt and pale beige trousers and brown Bond Street shoes, and he was so clean and comely to behold that I was ashamed of our dusty floor. He took my hand and brushed it with his lips.

'Dear Daffodil, how beautiful you are to-day. The heat suits you; it gives you an appearance of languor, and your eyes are larger than ever. You have no right to such brown eyes with that daffodil hair – what is the word? gossamer, as if each hair had been separately dipped in golden nectar. Do you know, Daffodil, do you know that you are the loveliest thing in Paris?'

'Dear Fanotin, it gives me such pleasure to listen to you.'

'And when I hold your hand and look into your eyes as I am doing now, I cannot help dreaming, however painful it is for me, of a fairy's bedroom in some Mediterranean castle, and a balcony overlooking the sea. Moonlight, of course, one must have moonlight as nothing better has been invented. And you in my arms, you in your silver body and my naked arms about you. Oh, my adored Daffodil, I would kiss your lips and then your sweet breast and then – '

'You would awake from your delicious dream.'

'– and then your lips again, and from being cold they

216

would grow warmer and warmer and burning hot, and your teeth would part and – '

'You would awake from your delicious dream.'

But I am afraid I may have been blushing again, he said it all so nicely, and he clasped my hand with urgent pressure, and moved round so that his head leaned against my knee.

'Daffodil, Daffodil darling, I have something to say to you, my sweet, something quite particular . . .'

'Does it concern a bed, a fairy's bed?'

'Intimately.'

'Then, dear Fanotin, I'm afraid – '

'But you are so hard, Daffodil, so cruel. It isn't flower-like to be so cruel. And I who want to offer you the first fruits – '

'Oh, oh, first fruits! But who doesn't know that you were very nearly a father when you were sixteen, and it was only thanks to some clever friends that you weren't? Darling Fanotin, be probable.' He frowned delightfully, a Sheik painted on ivory.

'You're a dreadful creature, Daffodil, and no flower at all. Flowers permit one to finish one's sentences. I was about to say the first fruits of my soul.'

'But there's nothing I would more happily accept than the first fruits of your *soul*.'

'Translated, of course – '

'No, Fanotin, I don't like translations. The original or – nothing.'

'Transmitted – ' he appealed, and I have no doubt at all that he was not easy to refuse. Nevertheless I refused, gently and with suitable flattery, as I am sure he expected I would. And he was not averse from a meed of flattery – I have still to come across the young man who is. Moreover, if he hadn't achieved the end he desired it was excellent practice. He sighed profoundly and in an access of defeatism (assumed or otherwise) released my hand which I let fall gently, languorously, upon his head. His hair waved as it listed, and was most pleasant to the caress. Yes, he was the prettiest boy . . .

'Daffodil,' he whispered, 'I want to paint your portrait.'

My laughter shattered the tenuous web that he had spun about our talk.

'Fanotin, Fanotin, that's not worthy of you. At least you must first learn to paint. Why, at present I wouldn't allow you to paint my front door. You must think of a more tempting and a likelier lure.'

'I can paint twenty times as well as that lump Brian,' he sulked, 'and what's more, I can give him a stroke a hole. Daffodil, why do you treat me so abominably? What is the matter with me? I'm young, I know, but so are you, and I'm sure you are not the sort of girl who stipulates grey hair in her lover. Look at Brian.'

'Brian isn't my lover,' I reminded him serenely. 'I have no lovers, neither grey-haired or dark-haired nor fair-haired; and I want no lovers.'

'Narcissism,' he fumed. 'You are telling me that you are sufficient unto yourself.'

'Fanotin, I'm not sure that you're not making an indecent accusation.'

He shrugged his shoulders in a way that was hopelessly out of harmony with his brown Bond Street shoes, and presently Lolette, tiring of the conversation which was now dealing with the subject of tennis, decided to dress and leave us. Thoughtlessly I returned the bottles to the cupboard. The disgusting cuckoo-clock left by a previous tenant cuckooed seven times. Lolette went. Vinel borrowed a last cigarette. Janigaud shuddered slightly as his eyes once more fell on Brian's canvas. Fanotin leaned disconsolately against the door-post. Brian looked hungry. I yawned.

In a few moments we were alone.

'They're decent fellows,' Brian offered handsomely, 'if they *are* Frenchmen, and if they *do* think my painting's muck. What do you think of it, Daffodil?'

'I like it, you know, Brian dear. Of course we're all only learning – '

Brian grinned delightfully.

'Nothing further is necessary. I say, I'm most frightfully hungry. Come and split a steak with me somewhere.'

But I explained that was impossible, I couldn't leave *ma tante* alone the last evening. As far as that was concerned, Brian countered, there was no reason I should put myself out for a silly old dowager of her kind.

'But, Brian, she's a darling. I adore her.'

'Oh, I say, Daffodil, don't tell me – '

'But I do. She's the only person I love in the world.'

'And Fanotin?' He glanced round at me impudently, and I chided him as he deserved. Fanotin indeed! I proposed that he should join *ma tante* and me; but he was doubtful.

'I don't think the old lady likes me so much.'

'She won't if you treat her as an old lady. Yes, you had better come, Brian, if only to reassure her about us.'

'About us? What about us? Oh, the silly old creature she must be! I see what you mean.'

'She finds it hard to believe in a relationship so pure as ours.'

'You're a damned pretty girl, of course,' Brian admitted. 'But we'll convince her easily enough, if that's all that's the matter. Leave it to me, Daffodil. Now if I were a fellow like Fanotin – '

'Can he really give you a stroke a hole?'

Brian looked deeply disgusted. 'Is that what he said? He's certainly pretty hot; some of these Latins . . . I suppose he was making love to you all the time he was camping out on the floor by your rocking-chair?'

'Well, really, Brian dear, I suppose he was.'
'He would be,' said Brian. I put on my hat and sighed, but inaudibly.
'He does it remarkably well,' I said.

from LADY CHATTERLEY'S LOVER

D. H. Lawrence

An infinite tenderness and quiet passion underlines this magical passage from Lawrence's famous work, Lady Chatterley's Lover.

Connie crouched in front of the last coop. The three chicks had run in. But still their cheeky heads came poking sharply through the yellow feathers, then withdrawing, then only one beady little head eyeing forth from the vast mother-body.

'I'd love to touch them.' she said, putting her fingers gingerly through the bars of the coop. But the mother-hen pecked at her hand fiercely, and Connie drew back startled and frightened.

'How she peeks at me! She hates me!' she said in a wondering voice. 'But I wouldn't hurt them!'

The man standing above her laughed, and crouched down beside her, knees apart, and put his hand with quiet confidence slowly into the coop. The old hen peeked at him, but not so savagely. And slowly, softly, with sure gentle fingers, he felt among the old bird's feathers and drew out a faintly-peeping chick in his closed hand.

'There!' he said, holding out his hand to her. She took the little drab thing between her hands, and there it stood, on its impossible little stalks of legs, its atom of balancing life trembling through its almost weightless feet into Connie's hands. But it lifted its handsome, clean-shaped little head boldly, and looked sharply round, and gave a little 'peep'. 'So adorable! So cheeky!' she said softly.

The keeper, squatting beside her, was also watching with an amused face the bold little bird in her hands. Suddenly he saw a tear fall on to her wrist.

And he stood up, and stood away, moving to the other coop. For suddenly he was aware of the old flame shooting and leaping up in his loins, that he had hoped was quiescent for ever. He fought against it, turning his back to her. But it leapt, and leapt downwards, circling in his knees.

He turned again to look at her. She, was kneeling and holding her two hands slowly forward, blindly, so that the chicken should run in to the mother-hen again. And there was something so mute and forlorn in her, compassion flamed in his bowels for her.

Without knowing, he came quickly towards her and crouched beside her again, taking the chick from her hands, because she was afraid of the hen, and putting it back in the coop. At the back of his loins the fire suddenly darted stronger.

He glanced apprehensively at her. Her face was averted, and she was crying blindly, in all the anguish of her generation's forlornness. His heart melted suddenly, like a drop of fire, and he put out his hand and laid his fingers on her knee.

'You shouldn't cry,' he said softly.

But then she put her hands over her face and felt that really her heart was broken and nothing mattered any more.

He laid his hand on her shoulder, and softly, gently, it

began to travel down the curve of her back, blindly, with a blind stroking motion, to the curve of her crouching loins. And there his hand softly, softly, stroked the curve of her flank, in the blind instinctive caress.

She had found her scrap of handkerchief and was blindly trying to dry her face.

'Shall you come to the hut?' he said, in a quiet, neutral voice.

And closing his hand softly on her upper arm, he drew her up and led her slowly to the hut, not letting go of her till she was inside. Then he cleared aside the chair and table, and took a brown soldier's blanket from the tool chest, spreading it slowly. She glanced at his face, as she stood motionless.

His face was pale and without expression, like that of a man submitting to fate.

'You lie there,' he said softly, and he shut the door, so that it was dark, quite dark.

With a queer obedience, she lay down on the blanket. Then she felt the soft, groping, helplessly desirous hand touching her body, feeling for her face. The hand stroked her face softly, softly, with infinite soothing and assurance, and at last there was the soft touch of a kiss on her cheek.

She lay quite still, in a sort of sleep, in a sort of dream. Then she quivered as she felt his hand groping softly, yet with queer thwarted clumsiness, among her clothing. Yet the hand knew, too, how to unclothe her where it wanted. He drew down the thin silk sheath, slowly, carefully, right down and over her feet. Then with a quiver of exquisite pleasure he touched the warm soft body, and touched her navel for a moment in a kiss. And he had to come in to her at once, to enter the peace on earth of her soft, quiescent body. It was the moment of pure peace for him, the entry into the body of the woman.

She lay still, in a kind of sleep, always in a kind of sleep. The activity, the orgasm was his, all his; she could strive for herself no more. Even the tightness of his arms round her, even the intense movement of his body, and the springing of his seed in her, was a kind of sleep, from which she did not begin to rouse till he had finished and lay softly panting against her breast.

Then she wondered, just dimly wondered, why? Why was this necessary? Why had it lifted a great cloud from her and given her peace? Was it real? Was it real?

Her tormented modern-woman's brain still had no rest. Was it real? And she knew, if she gave herself to the man, it was real. But if she kept herself for herself, it was nothing. She was old; millions of years old, she felt. And at last, she could bear the burden of herself no more. She was to be had for the taking. To be had for the taking.

The man lay in a mysterious stillness. What was he feeling? What was he thinking? She did not know. He was a strange man to her, she did not know him. She must only wait, for she did not dare to break his mysterious stillness. He lay there with his arms round her, his body on hers, his wet body touching hers, so close. And completely unknown. Yet not unpeaceful. His very stillness was peaceful.

She knew that, when at last he roused and drew away from her. It was like an abandonment. He drew her dress in the darkness down over her knees and stood a few moments apparently adjusting his own clothing. Then he quietly opened the door and went out.

She saw a very brilliant little moon shining above the afterglow over the oaks. Quickly she got up and arranged herself; she was tidy. Then she went to the door of the hut.

All the lower wood was in shadow, almost darkness. Yet the sky overhead was crystal. But it shed hardly any light. He came through the lower shadow towards her, his face lifted like a pale blotch.

'Shall we go then?' he said.

'Where?'

'I'll go with you to the gate.'

224

He arranged things his own way. He locked the door of the hut and came after her.

'You aren't sorry, are you?' he asked, as he went at her side.

'No! No! Are you?' she said.

'For that! No!' he said. Then after a while he added: 'But there's the rest of things.'

'What rest of things?' she said.

'Sir Clifford. Other folks. All the complications.'

'Why complications?' she said, disappointed.

'It's always so. For you as well as for me. There's always complications.' He walked on steadily in the dark.

'And are you sorry?' she said.

'In a way!' he replied, looking up at the sky. 'I thought I'd done with it all. Now I've begun again.'

'Begun what?'

'Life.'

'Life!' she re-echoed, with a queer thrill.

ESKIMO NELL

When a man grows old and his balls grow cold,
  And the end of his knob turns blue,
When it's bent in the middle like a one-string fiddle,
He can tell you a yarn or two:
So find me a seat and stand me a beer,
And a tale to you I'll tell,
Of Deadeye Dick and Mexico Pete,
And the harlot named Eskimo Nell.
Now when Deadeye Dick and Mexico Pete
Go forth in search of fun,
It's usually Dick who wields the prick,
And Mexico Pete the gun;
And when Deadeye Dick and Mexico Pete
Are sore, depressed and sad,
It's usually a cunt that bears the brunt,
Though the shootin' ain't too bad.
Well, Deadeye Dick and Mexico Pete
Had been hunting in Dead Man's Creek,
And they'd had no luck in the way of a fuck
For nigh on half a week;
Just a moose or two, or a caribou,
Or a reindeer or a doe,
And for Deadeye Dick with his kingly prick,
Fuckin' was mighty slow.
So do or die, he adjusted his fly,

And set out for the Rio Grande,
Deadeye Dick with his muscular prick,
And Pete with his gun in his hand.
And so they blazed a randy trail,
No man their path withstood,
And many a bride who was hubby's pride
Knew pregnant widowhood.
They made the strand of the Rio Grande
At the height of a blazing noon,
And to slake their thirst and to do their worst,
They went into Black Mike's saloon.
And as the door swung open wide,
Both prick and gun flashed free;
'According to sex, you bleeding wrecks,
You drinks or fucks with me.'
Now they'd heard of the prick called Deadeye Dick,
From the Horn to Panama,
And with nothing worse than a muttered curse
Those dagoes sought the bar;
The women too knew his playful ways,
Down on the Rio Grande,
And forty whores took down their drawers
At Deadeye Dick's command.
They saw the finger of Mexico Pete
Twitch on the trigger grip;
They dared not wait; at a fearful rate,
Those whores began to strip.
Now Deadeye Dick was breathing quick,
With lecherous snorts and grunts.
As forty arses were bared to view,
To say nothing of forty cunts.
Now forty arses and forty cunts,
You'll agree if you use your wits,
With a little bit of arithmetic,
Make exactly eighty tits;
And eighty tits make a gladsome sight
For a man with a raging stand,
It may be rare in Berkeley Square,
But not on the Rio Grande.
Our Deadeye Dick, he fucks 'em quick,

So he backed up and took his run,
And made a dart at the nearest tart,
And scores a hole in one.
He threw the whore to the sawdust floor,
And fucked her deep and fine,
And though she grinned it put the wind
Up the other thirty-nine.
Our Deadeye Dick, he fucks 'em quick,
And flinging the first aside,
He was making a pass at the second arse
When the swing doors opened wide,
And entered in, to that hall of sin
Into that harlot-hell,
All unafraid, strode a gentle maid
Whose name was Eskimo Nell.
Our Deadeye Dick, who fucks 'em quick,
Was well into number two,
When Eskimo Nell lets out a yell
And says to him, 'Hey, you!'
That hefty lout, he turned about,
Both nob and face were red,
And with a single flick of his muscular prick
The whore flew over his head.
But Eskimo Nell she took it well,
And looked him straight in the eyes,
With the utmost scorn she sneered at his horn
As it rose from his hairy thighs.
She blew a drag from her smouldering fag
Over his steaming nob,
And so utterly beat was Mexico Pete
He forgot to do his job.
It was Eskimo Nell who broke the spell
In accents calm and cool,
'You cunt-struck shrimp of a Yankee pimp,
D'you call that thing a tool?
If this here town can't wear that down,'
She sneered to the squirming whores,
'There's one little cunt that will do the stunt,
That's Eskimo Nell's, not yours.'
She shed her garments one by one

With an air of conscious pride;
Till at last she stood in her womanhood,
And they saw the Great Divide.
She lay down there on the table bare,
Where someone had left a glass,
And with a twitch of her tits, she crushed it to bits
Between the cheeks of her arse.
She bent her knees with supple ease,
And opened her legs apart,
And with a final nod at the waiting sod,
She gave him his cue to start.
But Deadeye Dick with his kingly prick
Prepared to take his time,
For a girl like this was fucking bliss,
So he staged a pantomime.
He winked his arsehole in and out,
And made his balls inflate,
Until they rose like granite globes
On top of a garden gate.
He rubbed his foreskin up and down,
His knob increased its size;
His mighty prick grew twice as thick,
Till it almost reached his eyes;
He polished the nob with rum and gob
To make it steaming hot,
And to finish the job he sprinkled the nob
With a cayenne pepper pot.
He didn't back up to take a run,
Nor yet a flying leap,
But bent right down and came alongside
With a steady forward creep.
Then he took a sight as a gunman might
Along his mighty tool,
And shoved in his lust with a dexterous thrust,
Firm, calculating and cool.
Have you ever seen the pistons on the giant CPR?
With the driving force of a thousand horse?
Then you know what pistons are;
Or you think you do, but you've yet to view
The awe-inspiring trick,

Of the work that's done on a non-stop run
By a man like Deadeye Dick.
But Eskimo Nell was an infidel,
She equalled a whole harem,
With the strength of ten in her abdomen,
And her rock-of-ages beam;
Amidships she could stand the rush
Like the flush of a water closet,
And she grasped his cock like a Chatswood lock
On the National Safe Deposit.
She lay for a while with a subtle smile,
While the grip of her cunt grew keener,
Then she gave a sigh and sucked him dry,
With the ease of a vacuum cleaner.
She performed this feat in a way so neat
As to set at complete defiance
The primary cause and the basic law
That govern sexual science:
She calmly rode through the phallic code,
Which for years had stood the test,
And the ancient rules of the Classic Schools
In a moment or two went west.
And now, my friend, we draw to the end
Of this copulatory epic –
The effect on Dick was sudden and quick,
Akin to an anaesthetic;
He slipped to the floor and he knew no more,
His passion extinct and dead,
Nor did he shout as his tool came out,
It was stripped right down to a thread.
Mexico Pete he sprang to his feet
To avenge his pal's affront,
With a fearful jolt, for he drew his Colt,
And rammed it up into her cunt;
He shoved it up to the trigger grip
And fired three times three,
But to his surprise she rolled her eyes
And squeaked in ecstasy.
She leaped to her feet with a smile so sweet,
'Bully,' she said, 'for you!

Though I might have guessed it's about the best
You flogged-out sods could do.
When next your friend and you intend
To sally forth for fun,
Buy Deadeye Dick a sugar-stick
And get yourself a bun.
And now I'm off to the frozen North
To the land where spunk is spunk,
Not a trickly stream of lukewarm cream,
But a solid frozen chunk.
Back to the land where they understand
What it means to copulate,
Where even the dead lie two in a bed,
And the infants masturbate.
Back to the land of the mighty stand,
Where the nights are six months long,
Where the polar bear wanks off in his lair,
That's where they'll sing this song.
They'll tell this tale on the Arctic trail,
Where the nights are sixty below,
Where it's so damn cold french letters are sold
Wrapped in a ball of snow;
In the Valley of Death with bated breath,
It's there they'll sing it too,
Where the skeletons rattle in sexual battle,
And the mouldy corpses screw!'

from WEB OF DESIRE
Sophie Danson

The frenzied pace of the Web of Desire *starts with a 'bang'. Stunning in its voluptuousness and sensuality, it leaves one gasping and dazed.*

The early summer sunshine caressed Marcie's naked skin like a lover's fingertips, and she rolled over, catlike and luxurious, searching for Richard's animal warmth.

He grunted as her fingers playfully traced the long curve of his spine, her sharp little nails just brushing the tiny hairs, on his golden-bronze skin.

'Wake up, Richard,' she breathed into the nape of his neck as she bent over and kissed it. 'Wake up and fuck with me.'

A little smile played over Richard's face, and the corners of his mouth twitched, betraying his wakefulness. Just as Marcie thought he was going to play dead forever, his eyelids flickered open, and his blue eyes blinked in the morning light. Rolling onto his back, he seized her arm and pulled her on top of him, crushing her against his burgeoning erection.

It felt good to be there on top of him, her thighs straddling his muscular body, her pubis crushed against the throbbing hardness that lay across his flat belly like a sleeping serpent. She would very soon waken it.

She began to rub her pubic bone against his erect penis, grinding with all her weight against his manhood, forcing him to acknowledge the strength of her desire.

'Little minx. I shall have to teach you a lesson.'

He reached behind her and, pulling up her flimsy silk nightdress, dealt her a hearty slap on her bare backside. With a little squeal she tried to wriggle out of his grasp, but he had her fast and was determined to make the most of the advantage. The flat of his hand rained blows on her naked buttocks, making the flesh sting and redden. But more than that: with the pain and indignity came a more insidious feeling, a creeping warmth that soon began to spread the most delicious sensations of pleasure into the heart of her intimacy.

Marcie's sex was warming, burning, almost aflame now with desire. Her clitoris had swollen to a hard bud, throbbing with an urgent need. All pain and anger forgotten, she gave up struggling and instead set about communicating her own desire to her husband. He was already panting with arousal, and each loud, driving, quivering slap he landed on her backside communicated more stimulation to his own straining cock.

To help him along Marcie slipped a hand between her body and his, and succeeded in grasping his hot hardness. He gasped at the sudden contact, and immediately stopped slapping her backside. Triumphant, she wriggled free of his grasp and slid down his body until she knelt between his thighs. She bent and took his cock into her mouth, sucking it into even greater hardness. He tasted salty, like some lively sea-creature, fresh from the ocean, and she imagined herself and Richard linked together in the cool water, far beneath the waves; never needing to breathe, only to kiss and suck and fuck.

She knew he would endure the delightful torments of her tongue for a little while, but he would not let her suck him to a climax. Richard was hungry now, hungry to be close, to be inside her. She let him prise her mouth off him, hoping that today he would be more adventurous than usual. Perhaps he would even repeat that wonderful drunken night of not so long ago, when he had flung her down on the living-room floor and eased apart her arse-cheeks, sinking deep into her like a knife into butter. She found herself dripping even now, at the memory of his delicious savagery.

But it was not to be. Richard ignored her backside, though she was sure he had reddened it quite alarmingly, and she winced as he rolled her over onto her back and spread her legs. Now that she had teased him in to wakefulness he wanted her, and he wanted her now. He didn't even take the time to pull her breasts from her nightdress, or excite her clitty with his fingers, as he did so well.

He parted her nether lips quite gently, and placed the tip of his prick against the entrance to her womanhood. With a single stroke, he was inside her. Marcie groaned, and thrust her hips upwards to take him deeper inside her. She scratched and clutched at his naked back with her fingernails, trying to excite him to some display of unbridled passion. She wanted him to take her like an animal, and as he slid in and out of her slipperiness she imagined herself as a forest creature being mounted by some snarling beast whose penis burned as it entered her, thrusting into her without the least pretence of gentleness.

She tried to spur him on with cries and powerful thrusts of her hips; but Richard, always and literally a gentleman, continued to make love to her gently, as though embarrassed by the passion her naked backside had inspired in him.

'Fuck me! Fuck me hard! Ride me, oh ride me!'

If he had wanted to punish her, he could not have done it more effectively. Marcie could not reach a climax, though her clitoris throbbed almost painfully for release. With a sigh, Richard spurted into her, kissed her and rolled back onto the bed, obviously quite unaware that he had failed to satisfy her.

Furious, Marcie grabbed his hand and placed it between her legs, forcing him to scoop up his own semen and rub it into her engorged clitoris.

'I'm sorry, darling. Didn't you come?' Realising his mistake, Richard set about masturbating her in the way he knew she liked: a finger working its way between her labia, and the flat of his thumb skating lightly over her clitoris. Gradually, Marcie sank into pleasure, forgiving him in spite of her anger.

Her orgasm washed over her in warm waves, and she sank onto the bed in release.

They lay together for a little while, drowsy in the early morning sunshine which flooded in through the half-open shutters. Richard was evidently quite contented, and lay with his arms wrapped round Marcie, one hand cradling her breast.

But Marcie was troubled. She was still unsatisfied. She needed more – something more extreme, something beyond the realms of safe, pleasant, companionable sex. What was it: danger, pain, fear? She hardly knew. But her clitty was hard and throbbing once again, demanding attention.

When Richard got up to run a bath, Marcie pulled up the bedcovers and slid her hand under the sheet. Eyes closed, a half-smile about the corners of her mouth, she set about caressing the sinuous curves of her body.

She was an attractive woman, there was no doubt about that. Other women might have misgivings about their bodies, but not Marcie. She had spent her young life being pursued by men, and by one or two women, who were only too convinced of her desirability. It wasn't that she was conventionally beautiful – no, her abundance of red hair tumbled about a face whose lines were strong and vibrant, rather than classical. Her eyes were sea-green mirrors in which her lovers lost themselves, but which seldom betrayed the fluctuations of her own emotions.

As her fingers traced the fullness of her breasts, she fantasised about her perfect lover. It wasn't Richard, though Richard was good to her in his own way. On the whole, she was happy with him, though sometimes his amiable apathy made her so mad she wanted to hit him. Or was it really that she wanted him to strike her?

Her fingers slid silently down her belly and into the dense thicket of her pubic hair, toying with the strands, twisting them about her fingertips. She pulled at them, at first gently, then with greater force, enjoying the delicious pain that warmed her pubis and inflamed her swollen lips.

She let her left hand stray to her nipples, stroking and pinching one and then the other until she felt her insides flooding with warm desire. Then, with the fingers of her right hand, she parted the petals of her secret flower and let her index finger plunge in, like a diver parting the warm waves of some tropical lagoon.

Quickly, she sought out the pulsating bud of her clitoris. It yearned for her knowing touch, the touch that was the certain harbinger of delight. Only Marcie knew the secret passwords to the heights of her own pleasure, and she began to rub at her clitty – at first quite gently, then with greater energy, as she felt her pleasure begin, deep within her belly.

In her mind, she was being fucked by a man whose face she could not see. She was on her hands and knees on a cold, marble floor, and he was behind her. She could see no more of him than a dark shadow on the gleaming tiles. The coolness of the stone felt good against her warm flesh; but better still felt the burning of her backside, throbbing still from the cut and swish of his whip. She writhed in silent pleasure as he entered her from behind, quite roughly, paying no heed to her discomfort unless perhaps he intended to heighten it.

She dared not cry out, though he was shafting her with such force that her backside smarted and his penis rammed insistently against the neck of her womb. She dared not make a sound, for he would punish her severely for any transgression.

As her orgasm filled her, like a clear, sea-green liquid pouring into a crystal bottle, a little moan of pleasure escaped from Marcie's lips. She fell back onto the bed, sated at last.

She opened her eyes to see Richard standing in the doorway, his prick rearing skywards.

Silently he smiled, sliding under the sheets, the bath apparently forgotten, his tongue burrowing deep into her warm bounty, lapping up the fragrant juices of her joyful deceit.

Her sister's unruly kids had gone home after their week-long visit, so there was no-one to disturb their late, lascivious breakfast. But Richard had to go to work, as he often did at the weekend. Before long, Marcie was left to her own devices, with nothing more glamorous than the washing-up to look forward to.

She put on a dressing-gown, finished scrubbing the pots and then sprawled on the sofa for half an hour, watching children's television. She had meant to take a quick bath and then switch on the computer to check the money markets. But she felt lazy, imbued with sunshine and sex.

She must have dozed off, she realised as she woke with a start.

There had been noises; rustling noises.

Someone was in the house!

She scrambled off the sofa, pulling her robe around her, quickly deciding what to do. Picking up an iron doorstop for a weapon and for courage, she crept into the kitchen. She peered round the door.

Nothing. There was nobody there.

Then she felt the hands: touching her, tightening about her shoulders, pulling her backwards. The robe fell open, its silky fabric parting, baring her nakedness, wafting the fragrance of her sex into the warm morning air. She opened her mouth to cry out, but no sound emerged.

The hands took hold of her by the waist, and turned her round.

'Hello, Marcie. Did I give you a shock?'

Marcie stared dumbstruck into Alex Donaldson's face. She didn't know whether to hit him or laugh.

'How the hell did you get in here? I never gave you a key.'

He grinned like a mischievous schoolboy, proud of himself.

'You left the window of the outhouse slightly ajar. It was easy to climb in. Piece of cake.' Noticing Marcie's expression of horror, he added, 'It's OK. Nobody saw me. Our little secret is safe.'

She wanted to shout at him, tell him if this was his idea of a joke, he could bloody well forget it. But he looked so abashed, almost boyish, as he stood there, his strong hands resting lightly on her hips, as though beseeching her to come to him, forgive him, make it all better.

His fingers moved from her waist and began exploring. Marcie looked down and saw how the robe had fallen away, slipping down her shoulders and exposing the firm rosebuds of her nipples, the red-gold triangle between her thighs. Transfixed, she watched as Alex's hands began to move over her waxy-white skin. It felt as though she were inside another woman's body, experiencing all her sensations. And she began to tremble with delight and desire.

Alex Donaldson was a good-looking man by anyone's standards: a solid 35-year-old, all muscle, with a slender waist and broad shoulders. Fit and sexy, with naturally wavy golden hair and a closecropped beard. Hardly what you'd expect in a financier who spent most of his day sitting behind a mahogany desk in the City. Marcie could have spent hours just tracing the smooth, firm curves of his muscles. But they seldom had the luxury of hours. Their relationship consisted of snatched moments of clandestine lust, wherever they could make excuses to be alone. It was easier for Marcie; working from home, at her computer terminal, all she had to do was to connect her answering machine and the world could go hang. But it was different for Alex: every moment of his day was planned in advance. Besides, they couldn't afford to be seen together. Not that Richard would be furious: he'd be very understanding about it, very civilised.

Too bloody civilised by half, thought Marcie, as Alex's strong fingers pulled and pinched at her hardening nipples.

Most of the time, sex with Alex was quickie sex: a raunchy fuck in a spare half-hour. But it was hot sex. The orgasms she had with Alex were much more intense than those she had with her husband – intensified, she was sure, by the spice of danger and the fear of discovery. With Alex, she'd enjoyed sex in hotel rooms, in store-cupboards, in bushes just a few feet away from a society garden party. Without him, her life would be pretty dull. And even with him, there seemed to be something missing.

But she wouldn't dwell on his shortcomings today. Far from it. As she looked down at his hands, she noticed a swelling at the crotch of his hand-sewn suit. Instinctively, she stretched out and touched it, letting its warmth soak into her hand. There was an electricity in his hardness, a pulsating life that made her wet with anticipation.

He nuzzled into her neck.

'You smell delicious, my darling.' He lavished kisses on

239

her neck, her lips, her throat, her breasts. 'The smell of sex.'

She was still caressing his penis, sliding her fingers up and down the line of his zip, feeling his enjoyment swelling, hardening, pressing against the inside of his trousers. But when she made to take hold of the zipper and tug it downwards, he stopped her with a kiss, and to her surprise slid to his knees before her, pressing his face into her pubic curls.

Marcie began to moan softly as Alex's strong hands slid between her thighs, prising them apart, forcing her to slide her feet across the smooth, tiled floor. She felt dizzy, disorientated, as she gazed down at her lover, immaculately dressed in his dark business suit, his diamond cufflinks sparkling on the virginal white cuffs of his Jermyn Street shirt. He seemed so far away, cool, perfect, inhuman.

Almost like being screwed by a robot.

She wondered what it would be like to have a cold steel penis inside her, moving in and out of her soft wetness like some crazy piston. In, out; in, out; feel the steam building up, ready to blow; metal and flesh in unnatural harmony.

His face was pressed hard up against her inner lips, his tongue seeking out the centre of her intimacy. She could smell the strong scent of her sex, the mingled animal odours of Richard's semen and her own sex-juice and sweat; and she knew that he could smell and taste the odours, too, and that they were exciting him to fever-pitch.

Her clitoris burned with a fever of expectation, a fire that could not be assuaged except by a man inside her. She tried to tell Alex, but the only sound that came out of her mouth was the moaning of a bitch on heat, the inarticulate cry of all-consuming lust.

Alex looked up at her. His lips were wet and fragrant with her juices, mingled with Richard's semen. The sight of him, wearing the badge of her own lasciviousness, so excited Marcie that she at last found her voice.

'Fuck me, Alex. Fuck me, please, please.'

She was trembling like a little hind, waiting for a stag to mount her. She craved the rough rutting of beasts, the uncomplicated coupling of savages on the forest floor.

As though he had read her mind, Alex sprang to his feet and seized Marcie by the arm.

'You're hurting me. What are you doing?'

Without answering, Alex dragged her across the kitchen and through the back door, into the garden. Her silky dressing-gown slid from her shoulders and began to trail on the ground. She was utterly naked, utterly vulnerable in the unforgiving sun of an August morning.

Looking up into his face, she understood with a shiver what he intended.

'No, Alex. We can't! Not here.'

But Alex paid no attention. Instead he unfastened the belt which had held the dressing-gown about her waist. He pulled it off, quickly and efficiently, and threw it onto the warm grass under the apple trees.

Richard and Marcie had chosen the cottage because of its orchard: a dozen or more mature fruit trees, their gnarled boughs arching over the tufted lawns, touching in places to form a mottled green canopy. At the bottom of the garden was a stream, on the other side of which were more cottages, and the village shop. And there were also houses on other side: big, prosperous houses where respectable businessmen lived, put up shelves and had comfortable sex with their wives on Saturday nights. Even as she looked towards them, Marcie thought she saw the twitch of a curtain, an imperceptible movement behind the leaded lights.

She put her hands up to cover what remained of her modesty, but Alex was having none of it. He took hold of her wrists and pulled down her hands, exposing her bare breasts to the hot summer sun and to whatever eyes happened to be watching.

Marcie's head was spinning. She was unable to cope with the suddenness of Alex's unaccustomed initiative. The terror of being seen by her straight-laced neighbours made her tremble, but not just with fear. With a secret excitement. She thought of the Colonel and his wife; and old Mr Pearson, who'd most probably not had a woman for twenty years. What would he think if he looked out of his window right now? Would his flaccid old penis twitch into life? She suddenly liked to think of herself as a resurrectionist; liked to think of the old man gazing open-mouthed at her creamy breasts, the fine, smooth curve of her buttocks, the gingery triangle that marked the door to her sex. She imagined his trembling old hand fumbling with his fly-buttons, taking out his cock for the first time in years, and handling it with a half-forgotten skill.

And what about the Jameson-Laceys, over there in their big house? Marcie was pretty sure Andrea Jameson-Lacey hadn't had it in her for years. Her fat, middle-aged husband worked so many hours a day, he couldn't raise a smile. Well, Andrea, this one's for you, Marcie thought as she submitted graciously to her lover's incautious embraces, scarcely veiled by the overarching apple boughs.

He seemed intent on obliging her to display all her charms, bending and shaping her body into obscene postures. It seemed so strange to be naked, to be robbed of her every secret, while her demon lover stood before her fully clothed, directing the course of her humiliation like some Satanic ringmaster.

She was bending backwards now, knees bent and her supple spine arching until at last her hands met the softness of the grass and she was transformed into a shameless four-legged beast, its face upturned to heaven and its sex open to the eyes of the whole world.

242

The wind whispered through the apple trees, and the bees' drowsy hum spoke of secrets no longer hidden, of a soul whose deepest desire was also its most base. Marcie savoured her fall into decadence, welcomed it as she would welcome a new lover; she was beginning to realise that only a new excitement could cut through the weariness that was eating away at her, threatening to seal her forever within the tedium of a perfect existence.

But her guilty, half-realised dream was not to be fulfilled. Alex's mask of stern subjugation cracked into a grin, and he threw back his head and laughed. The spell was broken, the sweetness of degradation gone within the space of a single breath.

In a moment, Alex was upon her, rolling her onto her back on the soft grass as he tugged at the waistband of his trousers. And she was returning the passion of his caresses, at once elated by the novelty of the game and disappointed that it had not been taken to its uttermost extremes.

She felt for his cock. It was hot and smooth in her palm. She slid her fingers over the moist glans and down the silky-smooth shaft, lubricating it with its own slippery sex-fluid. The channel between her legs felt like a river of boiling desire, hot and wet and pulsating with its own secret rhythm. She ached for a finger on her clit, a shaft to stretch her sex, a hot rush of spunk to drown the fires of her lust. The air was full of the heady scent from inside her, the mingled fragrances of semen and desire. Marcie was dizzy with need.

'Fuck me, fuck me, now!'

With a single hard thrust, he slid into her, his eagerness grinding her soft white flesh into the sharp twigs and stones lying on the grass. The discomfort served only to excite Marcie more than ever. As his hardness penetrated her, she gasped and clutched at him, her nails digging into his back through the crisp white fabric of his shirt. Locked together, oblivious now to prying eyes, they rode together towards the summit of pleasure.

Marcie's orgasm was not long in coming; and the convulsive spasms were enough to make Alex flood her with jet after jet of pearly semen.